THE
CONNOISSEUR

AMY HOFF

Erebus Society

First published in Great Britain in 2017
by Erebus Society

First Edition

Editor: Bella Book
Copyright of text © Amy Hoff 2017
Cover & illustration copyright © Constantin Vaughn 2017

ISBN: 978-1-912461-03-5

www.erebussociety.com

To hot guys everywhere. You know who you are. *winks*

TABLE OF CONTENTS

About the Author

Amy Hoff has been on the road for years. She used to drive across the U.S. and live out of cheap motels, collecting stories. Eventually she left the United States to travel the world. She doesn't live anywhere; her home is the road, in whatever form that takes. Sunsets off the bow when she was a sailor, flying into Incheon International in Seoul, driving the lonely American highways, walking across borders in the Americas, in Europe and Asia. The stories of Scotland are her favourite, and she became a Ph.D. researcher, an expert in Scottish monster stories. She still travels, and is now a researcher of monster folklore worldwide. Check out the darker parts of any pub, if you are ever washed up on strange shores. You might see her there, looking for stories to tell and be told.

The Connoisseur

Legend of the Great War

Amala was once a continent.

In its time of glory, under the royal family of Aleyta, Amala had known only wealth and prosperity.

The Sea King, jealous of the power of the Song of Life, wanted to destroy everything those of Amala held dear. Members of the royal family began to die under suspicious circumstances. Every time one of them died, a part of the land fell into the sea, until the islands were all that remained of Amala. Betrayed by their own people, the benevolent royal family escaped to the Citadel of Ona. The warrior tribes, especially the Ulu'u, 'Joy in the Battle', fought back the hordes of merpeople. Those who sided with the Sea King were banished as traitors to the crown. The war robbed the world of ocean fish as well as the safety of travel and trade.

Of course, all that is lost to history.

I

Prologue

There is but one regret I have, in all my long life.

It was but a single choice in my youth.

Do not look so surprised! Yes, I too was young once.

I was no princess or, at that time, even a warrior.

I was a Connoisseur. The very last.

No, you will not recognise the title, for those days are long gone.

This is the tale of Amala, the glittering Kingdom of the Sea.

Aiea

The small girl stood beside the palm tree, rubbing her fingertips over its texture, curiously rough and smooth. Her long, black hair was tied off with a band, and she stood in the spidered shadow of the fronds that swayed above her, although she was indifferent to the heat. She smiled, as she was waiting for her friend.

Olai was late. Olai was always late.

The girl heard the crunching of his sandals in the gravel before she saw him, and her heart beat wildly, hummingbird-fast in her chest.

"Olai!" she called, waving. He ran to greet her, throwing himself into her arms.

"You're late," she chastised him.

"There is news from the city," he said breathlessly.

"You always have an excuse," she said, teasing.

Olai held her shoulders and stepped back. She looked into his brown eyes, multifaceted in the late tropical sunlight, and looked away before she got lost.

"No, Aiea," he said. "Not this time."

Aiea's smile faded. What could it possibly be?

"The Connoisseur is dead."

Later that evening, the Elders of their village spoke in hushed voices. Aiea and Olai sat together, speaking little. The Connoisseur had taken her own life, an event so rare the people of their island didn't have a word for it.

The position of Connoisseur was the most valued in Amala. A woman was selected in childhood and trained her entire life in order to travel and collect rare items for Loka'i, the cultural capital of the world. The trouble was that her position, as Connoisseur, could not easily be filled; the Connoisseur trained her successor, but this one had been young – so young, in fact, that Aiea should have lived her entire life before a new Connoisseur was chosen.

The entirety of Amala was in discussion about what would happen next.

Aiea touched Olai's arm, and indicated they should leave the circle. He followed her to the palm tree grove, away from the sadness and confusion of the evening.

The palm fronds above them whispered in the moonlight as Aiea guided Olai down toward the warm springs at the other end of the grove. She turned to look at him.

"Tonight we have lost so much," she said. "I feel I must confess a secret."

Olai smiled at her, puzzled.

"A secret? We've never had secrets from each other, Aiea," he said.

"And we never will," she replied. "Olai, I am in love with you. I have been ever since I can remember."

Olai stared at her. She looked at the soft grass growing around her feet.

To her shock, he turned and ran back towards the village.

"Olai! Come back!" she shouted, but he did not turn around. Shame and embarrassment flooded through her, and she cursed herself for her foolishness, brought about by the grief and loss of the day. Her instincts could not have been more wrong.

Aiea blinked back tears and walked through the grove alone, back to her mother's hut, gritting her teeth against love, loss, and the treachery of the heart.

Aiea and Olai were five years old.

Saya

The king of Loka'i stepped out onto the terrace, where the early morning sun had already warmed the soft stone tiles under his bare feet. He looked out across the view that greeted him every day, always the same, but now so markedly different.

A servant boy appeared at his elbow and milked the bloodflower in his hand, liquid dripping into his glass from the large red blossom to make the tea he drank every morning.

Just like every morning, the boy then bowed and retired. Saya took a sip of his drink and sighed.

The view that spread out beneath him stretched from the palace to the sea. There was a long path through the jungle, covered in the white skyflowers so loved by the Ulu'u, the tribe of Loka'i. The pride and joy of the Ulu'u was what lay beyond the jungle: the wide rolling green hills that met the white sand crescent of beach and blue sea. White pavilions, including the Connoisseur's, dotted the landscape. The handsome men of the Loka'i harem walked together, sat in groups, or slept in their pavilions, curled around each other for comfort, as this was a day for grieving. They were lost without their Connoisseur, an unimaginable sorrow.

Saya shook his head. He was only glad that he had not been the one to find her. The man who had done so had described it, in a shaking, breathless voice while on his knees before Saya in the throne room.

The morning dawned like any other, the man had said. He was to bring the Connoisseur towels after her bath, and had stood watch facing towards the sea, as was the custom. The breeze blew softly across the white beach as cerulean blue waves caressed the sand. Handsome men lay here and there upon the lush green lawns. The white domes of the pavilions that served as their living quarters gleamed in the tropical sun. Much like any other day, the man had said; much like every other day.

After the appointed time, the Connoisseur did not call for him and so he turned, an apology ready on his lips for taking such liberties. The breeze swept white sand across the red stone floor, settling in tiny snowdrifts against the white marble bath.

He saw her arm, hanging over the edge of the bath, as rivulets of blood dripped from her fingers to the tiles.

The sight before him was so unbelievable that his mind could not completely comprehend it until he looked into her eyes. They were like glass, no longer like the sea.

He had fallen to his knees then, a wild sound tearing its way out of his throat, a wordless nameless cry of grief, echoing so loudly even those in the palace could hear.

Saya sat down in his chair, watching the men walk listlessly between the pavilions. He wondered if they would be marked as the only harem to have experienced this kind of tragedy, and whether they would find husbands and wives upon retirement. He wondered what kind of world he would be leaving to his son, Irya. As the king, Saya could not afford the luxury of grieving over the loss of the Connoisseur. He was responsible for all of Loka'i.

Saya's role was a difficult one. Loka'i had become the cultural capital of Amala and he needed to think of the impact this death had on the rest of the world. The Ulu'u had once been a fierce warrior race. Their name meant 'Joy in the Battle' and they had lived up to it frequently, but those days were in the past. The Ulu'u were also clever and wise, lovers of great beauty and good taste. After the violence of the Great War, the tribe had abandoned their weapons and instead created an empire of beauty.

There was nowhere as beautiful as Loka'i, and no greater pleasures could be had anywhere. It was the responsibility of the Connoisseur to gather and perpetuate this beauty; to lose her, especially in this way, was an international incident. Every year, the graduating class from the Academy, boys from all over Amala who were trained in the hope of cultivating themselves for acceptance into the harem, visited Loka'i to meet the Connoisseur. This year's visit could not have been more poorly timed. The students now sat on benches outside the harem walls, drinking sadly out of coconut milk juice boxes. Everyone was lost, and it was Saya's responsibility to restore order.

He finished his tea, made a sound of frustration, and stood to greet foreign dignitaries who had arrived with far too many questions. He swallowed his own grief until it was a burning coal in his stomach, a smaller fire easily ignored.

Aiea

The warm sun woke the little girl the next morning. She could not believe she had finally told Olai her secret. She did not remember a day in her young life when she had not known of love.

"Good morning, Aiea," said her mother, as Aiea sat down to her breakfast of coconut and mango pieces. "I hope you and Olai had fun last night. Children shouldn't have to deal with these things, I keep telling the Elders. There'll be time enough for grief when you're older."

Aiea sighed and began to eat her fruit.

"Oh, honey, what happened?" her mother asked. Aiea refused to look up from her food.

Voices outside the hut attracted her mother's attention, and she drew aside the curtain. There was a commotion in the yard, and then two long shadows darkened the doorway.

"We'll talk in a minute, Aiea," said her mother. "I'm just going to speak to these men."

Aiea pushed the fruit around her plate, feeling more foolish in the light of day than she had the night before. She wished she could hide under the sand and never come out again.

"Aiea?" her mother said, her voice quavering. Aiea looked up.

Two men walked in, tall and threatening. One was thin and the other large. Each wore cotton pantaloons; their chests were oiled and their shining hair hung long against their backs. An orange strip of cloth circled their necks and terminated above their navels. Aiea stared up at them.

One of them knelt before her.

"Aiea, I am a retainer to the Connoisseur of Loka'i," he said. "Do you know what that means?"

Aiea nodded. She stared at the wicked blade at his hip.

The other man, large and imposing, also knelt before her.

"We are here to ask you to take the tests for Connoisseur training," he said. "Do you accept?"

Aiea stared at him.

"Why?" she asked.

The men exchanged looks.

"We are usually accompanied by the Connoisseur," said the thin man, "but she passed away. So we must test alone. Do you accept?"

"But…why me?" Aiea asked again.

"You have the makings of a Connoisseur," he said, "your village Elder says you have youthful passion."

Olai. Traitor! He must have told them. Well, she'd show him. He would feel terrible if she went to the capital and he never saw her again.

Her mouth set in a firm line.

"I accept," she said, a ball of anger in her heart.

Her mother turned away.

The tests began. They were very strange. They asked her about food, drink, and beauty. She answered as honestly as she could. She was too young to know what qualities they were looking for.

Eventually the men nodded to each other and stepped outside. Aiea's mother rushed forward and swept her up.

"What's wrong?" Aiea asked, confused and frightened again. Her mother didn't respond, only hugged her tighter.

The thin man returned and bowed deeply to them.

"We have decided," he said.

Aiea's mother raised her head and wiped her eyes. She held her close.

"Aiea will be trained as the next Connoisseur," said the man.

Her mother laughed, slumping in relief, and kissed Aiea's cheek. She looked into her daughter's eyes.

"You must go with them alone," she said. "Please understand. I will visit you as often as I can."

Aiea nodded. This opportunity could mean everything. Fame and wealth for her village, and prosperity for her mother, who would be elevated to a higher social class by association. Aiea may have been young, but she understood that much.

The thin man held his hand out to her and for the first time, he smiled.

"Don't worry, Aiea," he said. "It will be all right."

Hesitantly, she put her hand in his and walked out into the tropical sunlight. Her mother stood in the doorway, tears streaming down her face, and waved goodbye. Aiea wept and waved back. A large number of villagers came out of their huts, Olai among them, beaming at her. It was the sight of Olai, standing proud in his doorway that filled her heart with the most regret.

She could not bear to leave him.

As she walked out of the village between the men, she looked back, but could no longer see her friend in the crowd.

The capital of Loka'i was muted, as if the city was foreign to itself. Aiea had never been there, but her mother had spoken of the place with great love. It was, after all, where her parents met, underneath the great banyan tree during a festival. Aiea's mother spoke of the dazzling lights, the technology, and the sumptuous luxury of the place. She had told Aiea of the food and drink available there, things untasted by the villagers in their far outposts.

Like every other child in Amala, Aiea had already learned about sex. She had an intellectual awareness of it, both as a consensual activity and a commodity. Loka'i boasted the greatest university in the world, and the most celebrated of their professors were those who specialised in sexual education. Loka'i encouraged openness and an environment of learning. So as they walked past the doors of the brothels, Aiea knew the men who waved at her from the windows were men who traded upon the fame of the harem for their livelihood. She smiled and waved back. Although Loka'i was in mourning, many people still emerged from their houses to greet or look upon the small girl who might become their next Connoisseur.

The city that Aiea's mother had known would return to itself soon, Aiea was certain of it. She was eager to explore, as she had heard so much about the capital. The ornate architecture, variety of food, wealth, and wine of the city were celebrated throughout Amala. The retainers did not slow down although she pulled at their hands every time she saw various neighbourhoods she had heard of, or restaurants, cafes, and event parlours where she knew people partook of different services. The men resolutely led her on, and as they turned the final corner, Aiea's breath caught in her throat at her first view of the pleasure palace of Loka'i.

Nestled in the jungle, as if a part of the natural landscape, the delicate white structure clung to the side of a cliff. It consisted of ten stories and each floor had a balcony facing outward and a swimming pool at the edge. Each of the swimming pools had a cascading waterfall that dropped into the pool below it. At the very bottom, a stream filled with many kinds of fish led down into the harem proper. Flowers, vines, and ivy poured down the building, following the course of the cascading water until they met with the jungle again.

There was no pool on the uppermost level, where the retainers led Aiea. It was a wide throne room, edged with high ogee arches, with a fountain running silently in the centre. Like the other floors, the room was open to the air and the view looked out over the harem, the bay, and the blue ocean.

On the right hand of the room sat two stately thrones, gold with ornate detailing, and red velvet cushions. As the retainers approached with Aiea, a fat middle-aged man stood to greet them. On the other throne sat a young boy with oiled black hair and bronze skin, who did nothing but look up at the ceiling and sigh in irritation. Aiea disliked him on sight.

"Come forward," the king commanded. The retainers approached the throne and bowed low. Aiea followed suit a moment afterwards. The king was strong, with a friendly face, and his long hair was white. The little boy in the other throne yawned and kicked his feet. Aiea knew her mother would have sternly reprimanded her for such childish behaviour but the king seemed oblivious.

"This is the new Connoisseur hopeful?" asked the king. "Are you quite sure? She looks rather skinny to me."

"Your Highness, she is in love with a boy in her village," said Ilo, the larger of the two retainers.

"At the age of five?" asked the king, rubbing his chin. "Perhaps…who gave you this knowledge?"

"The boy himself told the village Elder, Sire," said Aio, the smaller retainer. Aiea blushed a deep red.

"What is your name?" the king asked. It was a moment before Aiea realised he was addressing her.

"I am Aiea, Your Majesty," she said, "of the noble village of O'a."

The king rumbled with laughter.

"Hm. Not much noble is left from the days of old," he said, for he despised the modern Ulu'u's obsession with their once-warrior past. "You certainly have come a long way to see us. This is my son, Irya."

"Greetings, Prince Irya," said Aiea politely.

Irya looked away, his nose in the air, and extended his hand. She stood confused for a moment before Aio whispered in her ear, "He desires you to kiss his hand."

Doubtful, Aiea approached and kissed the outstretched fingers. Wordlessly, Irya dropped his hand, once again fascinated with the ceiling.

The king laughed again.

"Ah, my boy is more suited to royalty than I," he said. "He is a natural leader and he will make a great king."

Aiea stared at Irya, thinking she had never met anyone more insufferable in her life, but she said nothing.

"I approve this girl to begin Connoisseur training," said the king. "Thank you, Aio and Ilo, for finding her so quickly. Now, I must preside over court. A pleasure to meet you, Aiea. I hope you will be happy here."

"Thank you, Your Majesty," she said, because it seemed like the thing to say. Aio and Ilo bowed in silence and withdrew, taking Aiea with them.

Aio and Ilo

Aio and Ilo led Aiea down the gravel path from the base of the palace through the jungle. The trees were thick and grew close together, walls of foliage on either side, until the gravel path spilled out into the bright sunlight and wide green manicured lawns gently descended towards the sea.

The white buildings Aiea had seen beyond the trees from the throne room were the pavilions of the harem of Loka'i. Crimson curtains were tied to pillars or flowed like pennants in the soft breeze, and each pavilion showed signs of a unique personality, identifying the young man who lived there. Some were filled with paintings, others with scattered musical instruments.

The young men were something to behold.

They were smoking, gambolling in the water, or strolling with each other, deep in conversation. Only Aio and Ilo wore orange fabric and Aiea realised they must be important. She wanted to stop and speak with some of the men of the harem, but the retainers seemed to have a destination in mind.

They led her into an empty pavilion. Aio, the smaller of the two retainers, indicated she should sit down. Aiea did so, and he poured her a liquid as red as a garnet, with a light like life itself flowing through it. She drank it, only to look up and see Aio and Ilo both staring at her intently.

"What do you think of it?" Ilo asked.

"It's wonderful," said Aiea, "it is beautiful and tastes like sweet water."

Ilo nodded, exchanging a glance with Aio, who crossed his arms against his bare chest.

"This was the last discovery of the former Connoisseur," said Ilo. "It is called bloodflower tea. The people of Chaak produce it, based on an ancient recipe. It was quite a boon for Loka'i."

"In our village we drink mango and coconut juice," said Aiea. "We have not had anything like this!"

"It is relatively new to our island," said Aio, "and trade to the outer villages can be slow."

"You are a very clever girl, Aiea," said Ilo. "A Connoisseur's job is to travel the world and collect items of exotic wonder and beauty. Foodstuffs, spices, fabrics, all for the glory of Loka'i. People come from all over the world to enjoy what we have to offer."

"Will I have to fight?" asked Aiea.

Ilo laughed.

"Oh, no," he said, "it is long since we have raised hand in combat, though we remember our brilliant past as warriors. We hold ceremonies throughout the year to honour that history."

"I will be able to see the faraway lands the Elders speak of?" asked Aiea in excitement. "Will I see Chaak? Or even Cloda? Snt, where the scientists live?"

Aio smiled.

"In your position as Connoisseur, you will see them all," he replied. "The most important thing to remember is that everything has a price. Eventually our king will pay what they ask. Your responsibility as Connoisseur is to find a price for the priceless."

Aiea nodded.

"It does not sound difficult," she said.

"Perhaps," said Ilo. "But your other duties might be."

"Other duties?" asked Aiea. "What do you mean?"

"The Connoisseur collects men for the harem," he said. "We are the pride of Loka'i."

Aiea looked out at the lawn where the young men lay in the grass, talking with each other. She wondered what it must have been like for them, the day they discovered their Connoisseur had died. She turned to Aio.

"The Connoisseur…took her own life?" asked Aiea quietly, although she already knew.

"Yes," he replied. "None of us knows why. She was – everything – to us."

Aio breathed deeply, and then shook his head, walking to the edge of the pavilion to look out at the sea.

Ilo smiled and took Aiea gently by the shoulders, looking into her eyes.

"Don't worry about the grief of two old men," he said gently. "Your education must begin."

As they left the pavilion, Aiea looked at the retainers, and then at the other men scattered across the lawn. She saw no beauty in their adulthood, and wondered how they could expect her to judge strange men when her heart belonged to Olai.

Aiea was seated before a large table laden with different food, jewels, fabrics, and spices.

"Look carefully and make your choice from each," Ilo instructed.

Aiea first stood before the fruits. Some were in bunches, some were square-shaped, some were rich in colour. She handled and sniffed all of them, choosing a small red fruit with strange knobs on it and one with several berries, each of which appeared to be covered in hair.

The retainers exchanged a look. Aiea looked up at Aio.

"Next," said Aio.

Aiea stood before the jewels. They were of every colour imaginable, some large, some small, their facets throwing reflections of light under the tropical sun.

Aiea held a small dark blue stone, rolling it in her palm. She set it back in the pile and chose a large one that seemed to hold rainbows within it. This one she set beside her. She pushed her fingers through the pile until she unearthed a tiny stone that matched the sea, alternating turquoise, navy, and purple. She set this beside the jewel she had already chosen. Finally, she chose one that was perfectly round and red, glowing with a fire that was like the bloodflower tea. She dropped it beside the other two with a click.

"Next," said Ilo.

The next test was a pile of different types of fabric.

Aiea ran the palms of her hands across the various pieces, feeling the differences in texture, the variety of colour and hue. She pulled one from the pile, shining blue with tiny geometric shapes imprinted on it, holding it up to the light. She placed it beside her on the table. She looked closely at a dark, heavy woolen fabric, and another that twined back upon itself like a tapestry. She touched a soft fluffy one and removed it from the pile because it reminded her of a family blanket at home. Aiea looked at Ilo, hoping for encouragement or disapproval, but he merely repeated, "Next."

The next pile was before Aiea: meats, cheeses, bread, and some unidentifiable types of what looked like porridge. She smelled and touched each one. She took only one item from the pile: a block of cheese no larger and thicker than her own tiny hand.

"The last test is the spices," said Ilo. He set three small bags before her.

Aiea peered into them. One was brown powder, then red, then yellow. She sniffed each bag. The brown had a dark, strange smell; the yellow and red smelled delicious.

She remembered the men in the village cooking, and words spoken in laughter, discussing favourite recipes, gossiping –

And among the spices, what do we find?

Red is for fire, for passion, for love

Yellow is the colour of the sun, warmth and heat, summer-day spice

Red is rage and anger. Red is death.

Yellow....some days are sunny and biting cold. Yellow lies.

Brown is the drab colour of hidden birds, and hidden beauty. That which is appetising to the eyes is not always appetising to the tongue.

Aiea chose the brown powder.

"Retire to the pavilion," said Aio, inscrutable. "We will discuss these findings with the king."

Aiea made her way back, heart pounding. What if she had chosen wrong?

The king was busy with his subjects, presiding over the court, when the retainers arrived. Upon seeing them, the king dismissed everyone.

"Well?" he asked when they were alone.

"Your Majesty," said Ilo breathlessly, bowing in haste. "This village girl—"

"—we believe she is a natural," Aio finished.

"A natural?" asked the king doubtfully, "but...a natural Connoisseur is so rare. We have not had one in centuries."

"The way she performed the tests!" cried Ilo. "Your Majesty, we are in agreement!"

"How did she do?" asked the king, "And please try to contain yourselves. I will decide if there is cause for excitement."

Ilo bowed again.

"I am sorry, sire," he said, "but you can imagine our feelings."

"Quite," said the king, unconvinced.

"In fruits, she chose the best Connoisseur finds in a century! Other fruits were spoiled inside, some even made of wax, but several were items she would have known and loved from her village."

"So she is clever with fruits," sighed the king. "What else?"

"For fabrics – she chose the first jewel pressed and put into a loom!" said Aio. "And the wool that was your special interest, you recall – you traded a family heirloom to Nona for it."

"Yes, I did," admitted the king, beginning to be interested in spite of himself, "and what of the others?"

"Jewels – rainbow quartz, and blood diamond. Foodstuffs – she chose only Wanderer's cheese of the Wylt, which the Connoisseur won in a roulette game for her own life!"

"Incredible!" mumbled the king into his beard, "and the spices? What choices were given?"

"Allspice from Snt, ginger from Chaak, and…" Ilo faltered.

"Deathspice from Hois," supplied Aio.

The king started.

"*Deathspice*?!" he cried. "You tested a Connoisseur hopeful with *deathspice*?! She would have died on the spot if she had tasted it!"

"She tasted none of them," said Ilo. "She looked and smelled, but did not dip her finger in any."

"I am sorry, Your Majesty," Aio said. "We had to know."

The king sighed, making a mighty effort to control his temper.

"What did she choose?" he asked.

"She chose the ginger," said Ilo triumphantly.

The king sat back, speechless.

"A natural Connoisseur," he said. "You have outdone yourselves."

He stood and smiled.

"You may go with my blessing."

"Thank you, Your Majesty," Ilo said, and bowed deeply.

Aiea paced the pavilion. She missed her mother and her village, not to mention Olai, but she also feared her failure and the dishonour it would bring upon her family.

She heard voices and laughter and rushed out onto the lawn to see Ilo and Aio returning down the gravel path. She was amazed when they approached her and bowed to the ground.

"The king wishes to train you as his next Connoisseur," said Aio. "This means you will answer to Prince Irya, his son. You will not be able to return to your village and your life will be lived out in the harem. The way will be long and difficult. Aiea, do you accept?"

Aiea thought of her village, of her mother, and, with a pang in her heart, of Olai. Then she thought of the foods she had tasted, the colour and noise of the capital city, the honour bestowed upon her village in her absence, and most of all, the travel to faraway lands.

She swallowed and stepped forward.

"I accept," Aiea said.

Aio and Ilo smiled.

The following evening, Aiea was led to the pavilion of the Connoisseur. She was sleepy from the surgery; Connoisseurs, having accepted their appointment, were then sterilised. While the men of the harem would eventually be able to retire and have their own families, the Connoisseur was expected to live out her life in the harem and dedicate herself to Loka'i.

"This is now yours," said Aio. "Your bath is being constructed. We do not wish the spirit of the last Connoisseur to haunt you."

The pavilion was fringed with thick red curtains. The bed was set in the exact centre, and a small couch sat off to the side near one of the pillars. The bathing area was set back from the main living space, towards the jungle.

It was now night; the stars were out, and Aiea was exhausted. She crawled into the soft, warm bed as Aio and Ilo took their places outside, as her new guards and protectors. As she fell asleep, caressed by the warm breezes from the sea, Aiea smiled to think she would bring great honour to her people... but her last thought, as always, was of Olai, and the proud look that would be in his eyes when he discovered that she had become the Connoisseur. She drifted off to sleep, imagining this would somehow win his heart.

The Alyetan

The man set sail alone on dark waters, deathspice packed safely in a water-tight container.

He had heard the legends all his life, as most had in Amala, but had only recently discovered they were more than stories. He was alone in the world and determined to sail to Alyeta to find the elusive land that would one day call him king.

Alyeta was, by this time, a myth.

The royal family of Amala, the benevolent rulers of the long-ago past, were said to originate from an island so far away no sailor alive could find it. Alyeta was often called the Far Lands because of its incredible distance from the rest of the world. Saya and Irya may have been the rulers of Loka'i, and there were other leaders across the various islands, but the Alyetan family that once ruled Amala outranked them all.

Alyeta was rumoured to have been destroyed by a tidal wave after the last king's father perished. The legends went that the royal family had possessed magic unlike that of any other inhabitant of Amala. They could sing the land into being, they could destroy everything with their song. The eventual loss of the Song of Life, as this magic was called, was said to have caused most of the Kingdom of Amala to sink once more beneath the surface of the sea, leaving behind only the islands that existed today.

And what of Alyeta itself? The forgotten customs and joys of that long-lost island? The private whispers and cafe gossip all revolved around whether Alyeta and Amala's powerful rulers had survived, and if they would even want contact with the outside world. It was an exciting question, and one people feared to answer. They were ashamed to acknowledge that they themselves had long ago consigned the island to the stuff of legend.

The man alone in his small boat smiled into the darkness because he knew the world was wrong.

Kholi

Dawn rose as it always had and always would upon the lost island of Alyeta.

Kholi spread his hands, palms up, as he approached the shrine. His skin was brown and shining, his long black hair tied tight behind his head. He was well built but small, with a gleam in his dark eyes.

Posts with pictograms of the gods stood five feet apart all along the pathway. He had to kneel reverently before each one, palms still up, before he could enter the shrine.

The Alyetans told each other about the Lost Lands, of the gods that lived in the sea, of powerful men and beautiful women that lived on the united continent that once was. They mourned the loss of the Song of Life but were a practical people. Things were as they should be.

The Alyetans believed themselves alone in the world.

Inside the shrine were countless books. Literature and education were the religions of Alyeta. The young man, Kholi, was the closest approximation to a priest the Alyetans had. He was the official librarian, as his father had been before him. His people came to him for answers.

It had been a long time since Alyeta had been a celebrated, sophisticated land where wine flowed like a river, a mysterious place of dark and sun-dappled secret caverns where the water was a deep blue, lit from below. Alyeta had once been a destination that adventurers would risk their lives to visit. The Jasmine Palace, once home to the royal family of Alyeta and the Song of Life, had been abandoned for the solid darkness of the castle and the windswept snows of Ona. The white edifice that once stood above the thoroughfares of the great city was now in ruins. Rainforest vines had overtaken it, so that none alive now knew of its existence, or could find it even if they did. The Sea King harried Alyeta no more, and so the island had also forgotten that there were people in the sea.

Every Alyetan retained a rudimentary version of the Song of Life. Only the royal family possessed the pure strain. An army singing together could almost match the power of one of the royal family singing alone. The armies had to be well organised and the harmonies exact for it to work, but the armies of the island hadn't marched in an age. For years long past, Alyeta had been leaderless and silent.

Almost as if they were waiting for something.

Soft fragrant smoke suffused the library with a warm glow. Kholi sat on the pillows in the incense-laden room, studying a book he feared he did not yet know intimately. The role of Student in the tribe was important, and one had to train himself to desire all kinds of knowledge. Any discovery of boredom with subject matter required lashings with the flail hung on the wall, chasing out the boredom with pain, disciplining the mind. Kholi had been a difficult child; it had taken years to bring his mind under control, as it had been filled with legends, travel, and adventure.

There were steps on the sacred stones outside. Kholi looked up. A visitor was approaching.

"Enter," said Kholi. A young man ducked through the door. When Kholi saw his face, he stood up in absolute disbelief.

Kholi was speechless. He had lovingly memorised every line of the ancient portraits of the royal family, read every legend of the Wide Lands that was extant. Here, in strange wild clothing, was the image of the royals in the flesh.

"I was told to come speak with you," the man faltered, "for they say you remember."

"Yes," breathed Kholi, beckoning for him to sit. Kholi reached out and touched the stranger's face.

"I remember."

The man sat against the cushions in the shrine, listening to his host explain the history of the royal family. He was thrilled to simply be there, to feel the power that was his right.

"Memory in Alyeta is not what it once was or ever will be again," Kholi said. "Alyetans know, and remember, nothing. This keeps them relatively calm and happy. I, and those in my position, am Memory itself. I am the memory of Alyeta. I dream of the days of the Jasmine Palace, of the skyflowers that sent messages back and forth, spinning across the water, the magic of kings. I dream of the songs, of the days of peace and battle. I dream of azure skies and fair maidens with flowers in their hair. I dream of cold water in silver jugs, of summer, of dainties and foodstuffs, of beauty. But mostly I dream of who we were, the royalty of the Wide Lands. Once, the royal family of Alyeta ruled all. Now, the people of Amala do not know us, and the Song has died in the hearts and throats of those that would sing it. I dream of a beautiful face, etched upon my memory like stone, a face like yours. Am I still dreaming? Are you but the hope of a memory long-forgotten by the rest of the world?"

The man smiled, and Kholi's heart filled with love and longing.

"I know the others don't believe in the lands beyond this island," Kholi said, "tell me, dream, of your wild country, and how it is you made it home."

"I am no dream, Kholi," he said. "I have come back to find my past, to know my people, and to re-establish my kingdom."

Tears sprang unbidden to Kholi's eyes. He clasped the man's hand.

"To think you have returned to us!" Kholi said. "The Song of Life restored to Alyeta."

"I will return to the Jasmine Palace one day, Kholi," said the stranger, "but I long to know my people, our culture, and our ways, before I return to the kingship."

Kholi beamed.

"I will teach you, Your Majesty," he said, "and one day, perhaps, when you sing the Wide Lands above the water once again, you will come home to stay."

Eld

The sometime inhabitants of Wylt, called the Wyltai, were the pirates of Amala. Darkly beautiful, they grew their jet-black hair long, tied it back with leather thongs and decorated it with bits of feathers, beads, and oddments. They wore vests or went bare-chested, dressed in black pantaloons and high boots with bindings. They were bronze-skinned and hardy, wild and handsome to look upon. The Wyltai women were thin, wide-eyed and catlike, and their men short, black-bearded, and barrel-chested. Their homeland was empty of houses and the land was used mainly as a harbour for their low black ships, unique for the unicorn-horn bowsprits they claimed had been taken from monstrous creatures of the deep. They liked heavy foods and a thin, dark drink they swore kept them awake for as long as they consumed it. They stole most of what they owned, hunted animals on their lands, and made cookfires on the various beaches. Their climate was milder than the other northern islands. It rained often, and the land was always green. The Wyltai were feared and hated the world over. There were no Wyltai in the Loka'i harem, and there never had been.

Their ships were moored around the harbour and all taverns and shops were on the wharf. Beyond lay the wilderness, where the Wyltai hunted. Their ships were lashed together when in port and were of an interlocking build, so the Wyltai could walk between them on the planking. The configuration was always changing as different ships put into port or left again. Each ship carried a clan of its own. A Wyltai man was fortunate to have four wives and pitiful if he had but one. The women wandered off frequently on their own, sometimes never to return. This meant that even if a man had multiple wives in name, he was often a single parent in practice.

The sky was grey and the sea a still mirror as the foreign ships slid into the bay of Wylt, slipping in among the Wyltai vessels. Kholi stood on the deck, his face wrapped in white cloth, and asked his gods' forgiveness.

When the stranger had come to Alyeta, Kholi thought himself educated. His entire life had been devoted to the royal family, and when the lost king had turned up on the steps of the library, asking for an education, Kholi believed himself blessed. Chosen. He would be the one to teach the lost king the ways of Alyeta. Kholi would be remembered throughout history as the one who welcomed the king home.

His face now twisted into an expression of hatred and regret. The legends never mentioned the depravity and abuse of power he had seen at the hands of the king.

Kholi thought of Alyetans, dead or dying, and of the terrible infliction the king had caused. Poison in their wine, their food, the end of his people by the hand of one who should have been their protector, one whose desire for power had destroyed all that Kholi held dear.

Kholi had taken the king's life without thought to what would happen to Amala should the last of the royal line be destroyed and the Song of Life die with him. He thought of the man he had killed, the man who had been his king, and of the dagger piercing his breast. When the king had died but the islands still remained, Kholi knew.

The king had a child.

Kholi wondered if the child had been abandoned and adopted by the Wyltai, who took in the unwanted of the world. He felt a measure of guilt for the task set before him, as the kind of people who would take in a strange child and raise him as their own were a vast improvement on the kind of man his king had been.

Kholi sighed, but there was nothing for it. The child must be destroyed, at any cost. Unfortunately, the Wyltai were descendants of the Alyetans, and so any of the children could have been the king's.

The few Alyetans who remained had joined Kholi on what he knew would be a suicide mission. It was not for the Wyltai they came, but for the children. They must be certain that Alyeta would never see the likes of the king again.

Kholi shook his head. The faith he had was gone. What lies legends were.

Like cats, the last of the Alyetans crept among the sleeping Wyltai; moving silently from ship to ship before anyone could sound the alarm, their knives sharp and true. Most never knew their attackers as death walked among the sleeping tribe.

Kholi stood from the bunk of yet another lifeless body. He saw through the porthole that the purple dawn had woken one of the Wylt, a large man with a long black beard who had stumbled above deck to yawn at the sky. Scratching his beard, he stared at the new ships in the harbour.

Kholi felt his stomach drop as he watched the man realise what was happening, as he registered that the new ships did not have unicorn bowsprits.

Then, the man gave voice to a keening cry that made Kholi's blood run cold. A cry so like the cry of the king in his last moments that Kholi now was certain the Wyltai were lost Alyetans. So long had they thought they were alone in the world. He realised too late that he had gone to war against the very people he had wanted to save.

The element of surprise now absent, Kholi ran above deck to see the Wyltai emerging from their holds, the keening cry met with another, and another, as they discovered the wolves in the fold and the bodies of their loved ones.

Kholi signed to his own people to meet him on the beach, as he ran from ship to ship fending off Wyltai who stood in his way, until he leaped upon the white sand.

He found himself standing in front of the first man who had sounded the alarm and stared the man down. The Wyltai who were assembled on the beach screamed as they met the last of the Alyetans in battle.

Kholi stared into a face, and eyes, so like his own. He was startled and transfixed. The Wyltai were running from the battle or fighting, death all around them, and all Kholi could do was stare at the man before him. He thought he had been hypnotised, but Kholi looked down and saw himself spit upon the man's spear.

Eld, the bearded man who had sounded the first alarm, stared at the stranger he had killed and was surprised to see the terrible fear and utter regret in his eyes. He almost looked Wyltai, but Eld had never seen these ships before, or the stranger's manner of dress. No one ever attacked the Wyltai – they were feared the world over.

Later, after the fighting, smoke poured into the sky in the new silence of the day, punctuated by the quiet sobs of those who had lost their loved ones. A woman approached Eld and gazed at him with hollow eyes.

"They would have destroyed us all," she said. "Thank you for the warning."

"It was too late for many even as it was," he replied. "How many were lost?"

"Almost the whole tribe," she said, "they even killed the little ones. Why did they do this?"

"I don't know, Essa," he said, shaking his head. "Fear, maybe. Perhaps the superstitions of others have gotten the better of us. I know we are hated, but I have never seen anything like this."

"Who will lead us now?" she asked. "Will you? By rights, you should be chieftain, and captain, of our vessel."

Eld nodded. This was no time for false modesty, and action must be taken.

She put a hand on his arm.

"Emydd is not among the children," said Essa.

Eld stared at her. He sighed and rubbed a hand across his face.

"There is nothing I can do," he said, almost to himself rather than Essa.

"Eld," she said, "If you need time – found child or not, he is still your son."

Eld looked down at the ground, and nodded.

"Many have lost sons and daughters this day," he said, "I will grieve later."

He raised his voice.

"Wyltai," he called, "gather to me."

The survivors were very few, many in tears. They circled around him.

"The chieftain is dead," he said, "and we must move far from this place – now. More could be on their way. We are no longer safe."

"We cannot find some of the children," said one of the men, "and several clansmen are missing."

"My Emydd is also gone," said Eld. "Their bodies may be aboard the ships. It is a terrible loss. We must move now before it is complete. Go."

The Wyltai moved off toward their ships. Essa turned to him.

"They could not find the bodies, Eld," she said, "there may be more survivors."

"We cannot wait for them," he said, "we must go now. My responsibility is to the entire clan. They are my main concern. If we wait here, we will be putting everyone in danger. The strength of the clan must go before the concerns of the one."

Essa sighed, then nodded and moved off toward the ships. Eld surveyed the devastation on the beach, holding back anger and tears, then followed her to where the vessels lay waiting in the harbour.

In the trees, where he had run to hide, Emydd of the Wylt stood and watched the ships move slowly against the horizon, carrying the only family he had ever known away from him. The beads and feathers in the little boy's black hair clacked together as he sat down again, burying his face against his knees. He began to cry and wonder who would take care of him now.

Po

The island's name meant Light-on-Leaves, which was strange as Snt no longer had anything resembling foliage.

The people of Snt were as scientifically advanced as those of Loka'i were cultured. Innovation belonged to them. They had jet-black skin, with wide, handsome faces and long limbs. Those born elsewhere who had a scientific bent generally moved to Snt, so there was occasionally a colour variance among the Sntai. They produced machines, advancements in travel, and the weapons used by the Onai navy and army. They also produced a green liquor that brought on sleep and strange dreams. Most of the food and drink on Snt was the result of manipulated chemicals. Their language was entirely comprised of consonants, so when they spoke they sounded as if they were humming. They knew magic existed, but they believed it to be passé; science was the new world.

Snt's architecture was square and low, sleek and new, but without any artistry to it, just endless squat white buildings. It was tropical, but all the trees had been cut down until Snt's metropolis reached the very shores of the island. No real Sntai felt the loss of the beautiful beaches and forests. Past childhood, the Sntai's lives were spent primarily in laboratory darkness.

Ld's laboratory was considered one of the best on the island. He had won several awards for his development of new technology in disease research. Most days, he could be found speaking with his son, Po, as he studied slides underneath a microscope.

"The Sntai are concerned primarily with improving the quality of life," said Ld, whose smooth black skin shone in the dim light of the laboratory. "We now have men in the harem of Loka'i trying to convince the Ulu'u to leave the old ways. The people of Loka'i cling to them, as they cling to magic."

Like the children they are, Po finished his father's implication mechanically. The small boy was a disappointment to his father.

Po was fascinated with magic. What could be accomplished, he thought, if science and magic were united! But the Sntai looked down upon other cultures for being hopelessly primitive and living in the past. Certainly, Snt was not a destination for aesthetes; there was nothing to see, unless laboratories were of interest. All in all, Snt had the appearance of ordered ugliness, the functional empire of a people that spent most of their time in darkened rooms with tiny inexplicable creatures, their pleasures only their mild alcohol and ready-made food. Po had always been different, even as a young child. He had known instinctively from the beginning of his life that there was more to the world than either science or magic. He believed that much more could be accomplished if the stubbornness of the Sntai could be overcome.

Po's father stared at him sternly over the table. His son was a mystery to him. He had educated his child well and shown him all the ways a man could come to glory on Snt. Po did not seem to listen or care. Ld had spent sleepless nights wondering what he may have done wrong, if there had been a flaw in the boy's education. Perhaps it was his own slight derivation from the language by honouring Po with a vowel at the end of his name – giving it a cadence no Sntai found pleasing to the ear. Ld wasn't certain why he had chosen such a rebellious name for his child, but wondered if there was something strange in himself that the child had inherited. His mother had certainly not agreed with the choice, but Ld had liked the idea at the time. He had never expected their son, the child of two of Snt's most respected scientists, to have such dangerous interests.

In the same way that those with scientific skill moved to Snt or were invited to do so if their research was successful, people who had an interest in magic were not welcome on the island. The prejudice against the magical was so severe that it could erupt into violence. Ld feared for his son, and hid the boy's interest from the population. He wanted to keep his son safe, and tried everything he could think to foster a passion for science in the boy, with little success.

Once, he had caught Po looking at a periodical about magic and music, and how the two could be combined. Ld had been horrified. The music, if it could be called that, of Snt was measured and exact, and such entertainment was taken only at prescribed times, like a drug. Po's father had thrown the periodical away, hoping to quash his son's interest in the ways of yesteryear.

"Father," Po said, interrupting his thoughts and bringing him back to the dark reality of the laboratory, "I must speak with you."

The light in Po's eyes was like his father had never seen. His heart was filled with dread at what he might hear.

"I am listening," he said, with a curt nod.

Po sighed.

"I know I disappoint you, sir," he said, "but I wish to learn magic."

Po's father was speechless. He had read so many books about what to do if your child made such an admission, how to understand, and how much life would change. An embarrassment in the streets...

"I believe science and magic can be combined," said Po. "Think of it, Father! The best of the old and the new!"

"How dare you utter such blasphemy at my table!" Ld erupted. "Magic is the old way! Science is the new! Everything we produce, our food, our drink, is better than any other island's!"

"Yes," said Po, "and yet Loka'i ignores it. Perhaps this improvement does not make it better."

Ld shouted, pleaded, tried to reason, but his son was like stone.

"You are against progress more than you know," said Po simply. "You love science as old wizards love magic, and never the twain shall meet."

Ld stared at his son.

"How dare you insult me in my own laboratory," Ld said, his voice low. "Get out. I disown you. Perhaps magic will keep you warm."

Po stared at his father, and tears welled up in his eyes. He nodded and stood from the laboratory table. Then he walked out of the home he had always known, with nowhere else to go.

Po wandered aimlessly through the streets of Snt. No one stopped his progress, as the streets were empty. Everyone was inside, looking for new answers to old questions. He found himself near the last forest of Snt, a carefully constructed wilderness allowed near the seaside as homage to the days before nature was consumed by science.

Po crept up to the edge of the trees and looked through them to the water. He saw the black ship there, riding the waves gently, its unicorn bowsprit pointing out to sea. Po had heard of the pirates that hunted the narwhal across the ocean and decorated their ships with their horns. All thoughts of the fight with his father vanished from his mind. He felt adventure on the wind.

"*Wyltai*," he breathed.

Little fires ranged along the beach, and women, with long and impossibly wild and matted black hair, looked after children running in rags along the edge of the water. Po could not take his eyes off the bronzed, shimmering skin of the women or their bright green haunting eyes. They looked strange and beautiful to him. He had lived a cloistered life in his father's laboratory.

He stepped out onto the beach cautiously. One of the women looked up and fixed him with an icy stare that would burn through his memory for years to come.

A wooden staff sank into the sand inches in front of him and his eyes followed it up to see a wild man. He was huge and bronze-skinned behind a gigantic bristling black beard with long dark hair in many braids, accented with feathers. He was grinning and his muscular arms were each larger than Po's head.

"What have we here?" rumbled the gigantic man. Though he was large and terrifying, he seemed more amused than dangerous and Po found his voice.

"You are Wyltai!" he said.

The man laughed, a mighty sound. "That we are. Do you know your people forbid contact with us?" he asked.

Po nodded.

"Do you know why?" the man continued.

"You're…pirates," whispered Po.

The man threw back his head in laughter and the beads in his hair clicked together.

"Ah! Brigands of the sea!" he shouted.

"Quiet, Eld, they will hear you," said the woman who had looked at Po.

"Let them hear! Those fools! The things they teach their children!" said Eld loudly, then crouched down in front of Po.

"Do I look like a pirate to you?" he demanded.

"Yes," said Po. Eld's great black brows drew together as he grumbled a *hmph* into his beard.

"Well, perhaps I am," he said, "to those who know no better."

He was quiet for a while. Po found his courage in the silence.

"Well, if you aren't pirates, what are you, then?" he asked. "What are the Wyltai?"

"Do you know the legends of Alyeta?" asked Eld. Po nodded.

"We are Alyetans that never found our way home, or so the legend goes," said Eld, sighing. "I've sailed for the Far Lands myself and never found them. Perhaps the Sea King took them, too, when the other lands sank beneath the sea."

"Why are you called pirates?" asked Po.

"Well, we live our lives on the sea," answered Eld.

"Don't be filling the boy's head with lies," the woman cut in. She looked at Po again, and his heart skipped a beat. "How old are you?"

"Ten years and six months," he replied proudly.

"A good age to learn a new legend," she said, and smiled. "During the Great War, we were on the Sea King's side, Alyetans that supported the destruction of the Song. Our own mythology tells a very different story about the royal family of Amala than the one the rest of the world tends to believe. One of greed and violence. No island would have us, and the world named us *wyltai:* traitors. We are not pirates by choice, but as we live on barren rock and the ocean-fish run from all humans, we cannot feed ourselves at sea. We have no choice but piracy, since none will trade with us. We are thieves, dishonoured."

Po stared at her. He had never imagined that any land-dwellers might be on the Sea King's side.

"We were never taught that in school," said Po. "Our lessons tell us that it has always been humans against the sea people."

"They would not bother teaching the truth," said the woman. "They also teach that it was a time of harmony and peace, when the royal family ruled, and that the royals were perfect."

"Careful, Essa," warned Eld.

Po looked out to sea, where the great black ship was waiting.

"Where are you going?" he asked.

"We never know," said Eld.

Po looked at them, and along the beach, at the little fires where the children were playing.

"Take me with you."

A'o

The apartments for the students at the Academy on Chaak were nothing short of luxurious.

A'o and Iana were now both nineteen, and nearing graduation. They lived together in a sprawling white flat, with high ceilings and a spiral staircase. Tall windows overlooked the coastline of Chaak and the room was filled with light. Pride of place was given to a portrait of the Connoisseur that A'o had commissioned. Aiea was only one year older than him, and the portrait had been based upon one of her formal outfits for a dance at the palace. She wore a bright green dress, and was smiling as she looked over her shoulder at the painter, her long dark hair shining. The portrait dominated one wall, and on the other wall was a mirror, so that he could see her from every direction. A'o also had collected miniatures of her portrait, bought memorabilia from whoever he could find selling it, and wrote her letters only Iana was allowed to read. This behaviour was not strange for boys raised with an eye to the Academy, but A'o's passion was remarkable in that he had already devoted his life to her. She was his sun, and his good luck charm; every day, he'd walk in, toss his keys into the dish beneath the portrait, and touch the edge of the painting with reverence.

Iana, A'o's roommate, did not share this passion for the Connoisseur, but rather the mirror across from the painting. Now, alone in the room, Iana watched his eyes in the mirror, always impressed by their clear, limpid blue against the copper of his skin. Like the sand and the ocean, he thought proudly to himself. He examined the way his muscles moved beneath his skin. He should have been satisfied. More than satisfied – chosen.

"Iana, have you seen my brush?" asked a voice as the door opened, and Iana felt the fires of jealousy threaten to consume him. He quietly slipped the knife in his hand into his belt, his fingers still on the handle as he turned.

"No, A'o, I haven't seen it," said Iana, barely swallowing his rage. He watched as A'o completed his ritual, tossing his keys into the ceramic dish, looking up at the painting, touching the frame. He turned to Iana.

"Well, if you do, will you let me know?" he asked.

Oblivious. Aʼo was oblivious. He couldn't feel Iana's seething hatred, and talked to him as though they were still friends.

Iana watched Aʼo lean over the desk and arrange his hair in the mirror. He was an absolute vision, regardless of what he did. His long black hair looked like silk, with never a stray strand. His deep brown eyes were run through with green and gold, and his body was well formed, his muscles perfect, his entire figure more sculpted and defined than Iana's own. The lift of his chin and the slope of his neck would make even the most exacting Connoisseur weep.

And he was brilliant! All this he was born with. Iana felt that it was obvious to everyone that he had to work twice as hard to look half as beautiful. Aʼo had a head start, born with ethereal beauty that would only improve, and an intelligent, creative mind already celebrated by the Academy.

This vitriolic hatred had come swiftly, surprising Iana. He and Aʼo had experienced many of the glories of Chaak together. They'd spent long and drunken nights in one of the puzzle mazes and visited many of the island's secret brothels. Aʼo had accompanied Iana, but always stood aside, refusing to participate.

Aʼo was Iana's best friend. They had grown up together, and lived in the same apartment since they had been accepted into the Academy. One night, things had changed between them, and Aʼo's strict policy against anything sexual before the harem became far more relaxed than it had once been. He still wanted to save himself for the Connoisseur, but now only in the last and final way. He had kept this promise, but it had been close several times, when they had forgotten themselves in the midst of things. Aʼo and Iana had been more than friends for some time.

Until today.

A Chaakai girl whose tiny butterfly lips and slight figure had entirely captivated Iana's heart had told him today she felt the same passion – for Aʼo. She said she could not sleep for thoughts of him. As upsetting as this was, it would not have been Aʼo's fault – but he had kissed her.

"How could you!" Iana finally exploded, "How could you?!"

Aʼo heard the anguish in his friend's voice. He stared at Iana, bewildered.

"How could I what?" he asked.

"You know what!" cried Iana. "You kissed Minai!"

Realisation dawned on A'o's face.

"She kissed me, true," he said, "but I was not interested, Iana. I pushed her away."

"Like hell you did!" cried Iana. "I don't believe you!"

A'o looked at his friend in sadness. He loved Iana deeply, felt a kinship with him that no one else could match. Even his love for the Connoisseur was different. That was a form of worship. He had fallen in love with Iana years before anything had even happened between them. Iana was the most beautiful young man A'o had ever seen. His feelings of unworthiness were unfounded and A'o often worried at how harshly Iana judged himself. Still, A'o loved the other man's fierceness and sense of humour.

"I thought we – you and I," A'o began, and then shook his head. "I was wrong, I see that now. Iana, just because you like someone doesn't mean that everyone does. I have no interest in her at all."

I'm interested in someone else, he thought miserably. *I always have been.*

"What was between you and Minai?" A'o asked out loud. "You never told me."

"And why would I tell *you*?!" cried Iana, "when I wanted *one thing* – just one thing – for myself!"

"What do you mean?" asked A'o, increasingly puzzled.

"You are the most beautiful, the most talented, and the most intelligent at the Academy," said Iana. "Nobody notices me. Except Minai – and now you have her too!"

A'o looked at him sadly.

"You have me," he murmured. "You've always had me, Iana."

"What good is that?" Iana fumed. "In everything, I am second place! This was my chance – and still, I come in second!"

"Never with me," said A'o. "I didn't know you felt this way, Iana. I've always thought we were…best friends."

And more than that, he added silently.

"Were," said Iana, crossing his arms. His words went through A'o's heart.

"How serious was it between you and Minai?" asked A'o.

"She was to be my wife, you fool!" snarled Iana.

This news was more than A'o could bear. His heart was breaking and Iana did not seem to realise his friend's world was crumbling around him.

"Wife? But a harem hopeful can't marry." Aʼo said.

He couldn't even speak for his shock, nor breathe for his grief.

"I thought," he said, "I thought we were going to enter the harem together, you and I. Together, always, like we have been since we were children, Iana."

Iana glared at him.

"And how could I ever enter the harem with you as my competition?" he snapped.

"You're not competition, Iana," said Aʼo, "You're – "

"Couldn't you have left me *one thing*, Aʼo?" said Iana, "Just let me believe that Minai was mine alone?"

"I wouldn't be able to rest if I knew someone was deceiving you," said Aʼo. "Certainly she's not worth your time if she tried to kiss me."

The knife in Iana's hand was hidden until it was almost too late. Aʼo barely deflected it only to have Iana scratching at his face, his eyes, pulling at his hair, doing anything to damage Aʼo's unbelievable beauty. Aʼo eventually pushed him away, and Iana fell backwards, the knife clattering to the floor.

Aʼo kicked the knife away, turning to look at Iana with hurt and betrayal, breathing hard. Iana was pleased to see that the knife had cut into Aʼo's cheek just below his right eye. His heart sank when he realised that the curve of the scar would only illuminate Aʼo's ethereal beauty. He saw that he had only succeeded in making his rival more attractive, and that even in integrity, his friend was the better man. While Iana had hated and wished to deface him, Aʼo had only thought of their friendship.

"Iana—" Aʼo began, reaching a hand towards his friend. Iana struggled as Aʼo pulled him close, kissing him, blood from the wound spreading across Iana's cheeks as Aʼo desperately tried to reclaim with his mouth and hands what his heart had lost.

Iana shoved him away violently. He wiped at the smeared blood on his cheek.

"Don't touch me," said Iana, miserable. "I wanted you to die."

Aʼo fell back against the wall in agony as he watched the young man who held all of his heart leave their flat, slamming the door as he went.

The entire Academy was assembled in the school's dining hall. Iana sat as far away from A'o as possible. Everyone fidgeted in their seats as Aya, the director of the Academy, walked up to the front of the room and stood before them. Her dark hair was pulled away from her face in an intricate configuration, and she wore a matching jacket and skirt. She was not exactly beautiful, but dressed so well that it was difficult to make the distinction.

"You are now all nineteen years old," she said, "and as such are approaching graduation, after which you will be ready for harem candidacy. As part of the education of all our young men, we will be visiting the two cultural capitals – Naia and Loka'i."

A cheer went up. All the young men in the Academy had looked forward to this trip for several years. Aya held up a hand for silence.

"We leave this afternoon," she said. "The ship is in the harbour as we speak. Your roommate will be your partner for this excursion – do not lose each other!"

Iana scowled at this and ignored A'o's pleading look.

"Be careful on Naia," Aya said. "On no condition should you go to Naia Lightside – it is very dangerous. Be respectful to the Nightside Naienes – they are different from us, but much can be learned from them. On Loka'i, we will be greeted by the king, and then you will be allowed to meet the Connoisseur and visit the harem."

Excited conversations broke out around the room and Aya spoke over the noise.

"Now go and pack your things. We will all meet at the pier in two hours' time."

The young men tripped over each other in their hurry to get through the door, thrilled at the prospect of this new adventure. Iana pointedly avoided A'o's attempts to get his attention, as he stolidly walked away with the others.

Days had passed aboard the ship, and the young men of the Academy were restless. The adventure of sea travel had worn off for many of them and they were now impatient to arrive on the islands they had studied for so many years.

"Land!" someone cried, and everyone rushed on deck to see a wall of night approaching even as they stood beneath a clear blue sky. As the darkness enveloped them, a sombre silence followed, and they saw a crowd of pale and strange people awaiting them on the dock.

Naia was a curious island. One side was eternal night, the other eternal day. Each half of the island was populated by creatures that could not survive on the other side. The Nightside Naienes were the blood-drinking dead, and the Lightside Naienes were winged men that were far more dangerous. The boys at the Academy had been taught about Naia Nightside, mostly the virtues of patience, hard work, and slow approaches to beauty, passion, and in particular, food. There was nowhere in Amala, apart from Loka'i, with better cuisine than Naia Nightside.

As the ship pulled in and the lines were cast, A'o approached Iana.

"My friend," he said, "let us put this terrible quarrel behind us. We must be together for this journey, let us experience it as we would once have – as friends."

Iana ignored A'o and continued to watch the docking procedure.

A'o sighed.

"I miss you, Iana," he said, "you are my closest friend, and I love nothing in the world as I love you."

Iana's heart was softened by his friend's words. He turned to A'o.

"I miss you, too," he said.

The agony in A'o's heart lessened, soothed by hope. He touched his friend's hand.

"Let's go down into the city together," said A'o, "and I will share a drink with you."

Naia Nightside was a study in black, white, and silver. The colourlessness of the place was unnerving, as were its inhabitants. Nightsiders could not bear the sunlight, and depended on blood to live. The most famous export from Naia Nightside was the Nightsiders' own blood; it worked like a drug, and was popular in Loka'i. Naia Nightside was also a honeymoon and vacation destination, so the blood was popular worldwide with romantics and those who dreamed of travel.

After a brief orientation, the young men were allowed free time to experience the city. Intoxicated with their rekindled friendship, A'o and Iana ran through the streets laughing, a strange counterpoint to the curiously inanimate Naienes.

They stood in front of a store selling blood in various gift-wrapped packages and giggled at each other's disgust.

"Maybe they bathe in it," said Iana.

"Disgusting!" cried A'o. The storeowner emerged then, in the eerily slow manner of the Naienes, and gave them a disapproving glare. They laughed and ran down the street, away from the shopkeeper, as fast as they could.

They rounded a corner and were blinded by sunlight. The curtain of Nightside darkness ended just in front of them, and there was a small cafe beside it. Several Naeienes were seated there, pretending to eat and drink. As the Naeienes had once been human, they enjoyed mimicking human behaviour. They moved as if they were under water, in a strange and slow dance. They appeared to enjoy the reflected sunlight from Naia Lightside; it was the only way they were ever able to experience the light and warmth of day.

"The Sunrise Club," said Iana, reading the sign. "Let's share that drink you promised me."

"All right," said A'o, and they chose a table nearest the sunlight. Naia Lightside seemed to be an empty desert of rolling hills, bleached white trees, and sand. It was strangely unsettling.

A'o reached across the table and touched his friend's hand.

"Iana, I am so sorry," said A'o. "I really had no idea."

Iana smiled.

"I'm sorry too," he said, "I overreacted. You're right, she wasn't worth our time. So let's not spend any more on her."

"Sounds good to me," A'o replied. He picked up the menu.

"So, what do you want to drink?" he asked.

"Look!" Iana exclaimed quietly. "Naiene blood. Let's get that!"

"Iana, are you crazy?" hissed A'o. "We're not old enough to drink that!"

"Like anyone here will care," Iana hissed back. "Let's do it!"

The waiter glided up to them, his pad at the ready.

"What shall it be, my good sirs?" he asked.

"We'd like—" Iana began, only to be interrupted.

"Ah, my friend, here in Naia we choose beauty over age," he said. "Your friend speaks first."

Iana's mouth dropped open. A'o rolled his eyes.

"I'd like a glass of Naiene blood," he said, his voice quaking a bit. He was not accustomed to breaking rules.

"I'd like the same," said Iana, who had never cared.

"Very well," said the waiter, and he turned to go.

Iana could not contain himself.

"But I'm younger than he is!" he burst out. The waiter revolved toward him slowly.

"If that is so, you are not of age for blood," said the waiter, "I shall bring you a substitute." He turned away from them once again, leaving Iana red in the face and furious.

"Oh, don't listen to him, Iana," said A'o, "he doesn't know what he's talking about."

But he does, Iana thought, *and everyone sees it. How am I going to impress the Connoisseur if even the Naienes laugh at me?*

"Iana, are you really going to listen to some rude Naiene?" A'o asked, "and a *waiter*, for goodness sake."

Iana made a mighty effort to control his emotions and forced a smile.

"No, of course not," he said. "I'm already over it."

"I'll share my blood with you," said A'o in a low voice.

"Okay. Thanks," said Iana. "I'm just going to run to the bathroom. Be right back."

He pushed his chair away from the table and walked into the restaurant, pretending not to notice the way A'o stared after him. Jealousy flooded him, followed by frustration and unhappiness. How was he to compete? He was already showing signs of aging, his beauty was not up to par, and his studies were suffering because his perceived inadequacy was all he could think about.

As he entered the bathroom thinking vicious thoughts about the waiter, an idea began to occur to him. The incredible, stately beauty of the Naienes. Their eternal youth, their effortless culture. He could have that. Making a decision then, and steeling himself, he left the bathroom. He made sure A'o did not see him as he crept around the corner to the back door. He found himself in an alley outside, and walked into the street.

There were several Naienes there, standing still. He walked casually past them until he found one almost hidden in a doorway. He took a deep breath and approached.

"I want to be turned," he announced.

The Naiene suddenly animated and he moved *fast*. Iana blanched, nearly losing his nerve, and he almost ran into the street.

"Are you certain?" the Naiene asked, now moving and speaking like a regular person. This was terrifying in itself.

Iana struggled with his conviction for a moment.

"Yes," he said. "Do it."

"This is a serious decision, not to be based on vanity," the Naiene said. "It is your life and death that hangs in the balance."

"I know," said Iana, and then insisted, "Turn me."

He hadn't even seen the creature move. The penetration deep into his neck electrified his entire body. He gripped the thing tightly, an unknown desire coursing through him, and soon he knew nothing other than the hunger that flowed through him like a current.

The sensation abruptly stopped, and the Naiene was in front of him again.

"Consider, before you do something so foolish again, young man," it said, and then it was gone.

Iana lifted his hand to the wound, which had already healed, and pulled his cloak over it. He was disappointed and also, suddenly, crazed with the desire for *more, more, more* as though it had poisoned his heartbeat. He stumbled back to the restaurant and through the door. As he returned to their table, A'o was startled at the sight of his friend.

"You look terrible!" he cried. Iana looked at him, annoyed.

"Thanks," he said.

"Oh, I didn't mean—! You just look – were you sick?" he asked.

Iana realised that he must be very pale.

"Yes," he said. "I guess sea travel and insults for dessert don't sit well with me."

"Well, we can go—" he said.

"No, it's all right," Iana replied, "we can stay."

"Well, I saved you some, just like I promised," said A'o. He held out the glass of blood.

Iana stared at it, his heart beating in his ears. He realised he could accomplish what the Naiene had only intended as a warning. With a moment's thought, he took the glass in his hand and drank.

Life, desire, and passion flowed through him, and his body sang out a fierce joy. He opened his eyes and saw A'o grinning at him expectantly.

"Isn't it amazing?!" he asked. "It makes you feel…almost immortal."

Iana smiled back.

"Yes," he said. "Yes, it does."

He looked up and his expression changed. A'o turned around and shouted in fear.

Just beyond the curtain of sunlight stood naked men with strange wings of skin and bone, grinning with maws of huge teeth, slavering and staring at them.

Throwing money on the table, A'o grabbed Iana's hand and the two of them ran down the streets, laughing. Iana's triumphant conquering shout gave voice to the joy of replacing his inadequacy with something that would finally overcome all competition forever. For his vanity, the ultimate sacrifice was the ultimate reward.

"Let's go back to our room," said A'o, and kissed Iana hard. Iana's heart leapt in recognition and thirst, tasting his friend's heartbeat through the softness of his lips, blood coursing through his veins to heat his skin. He found in that current a desire unlike any he had ever known.

"Yes," said Iana breathlessly, and A'o led them back through the winding streets. He pulled Iana up the staircase and fumbled with the keys, falling backwards into the room as Iana pushed his shirt up, kissing him.

The room was usual Naiene fare, a large white bed with a silver branching headboard, delicately beautiful and practical. Iana pushed his friend onto the bed, and climbed over A'o, pulling and tearing at his clothes, a wild light in his eyes. A'o was overjoyed. His lover had returned to him, his heart was not lost, and A'o struggled to remove his clothing, exposing his bare skin to the chill night air. Iana kissed down his chest, his mouth greedy, but within his mind, hunger was mixed with something darker, something more.

Iana pressed his fingers against A'o, crazed with desire, and his friend whispered, *I want to, but we can't, not like that, not until the harem.* Iana nodded and took them both in his hand instead, as A'o surrendered to him, breathless and panting. A'o's innocence, his trust and total submission, was intoxicating. Iana tasted the soft, yielding skin of A'o's neck with his tongue, dreaming of sinking down to bite. The dream suddenly changed, becoming a sharp stab of insane hunger as he saw the blood flowing into his mouth as A'o gave himself to Iana in every way, completely. A'o's eternal, ethereal beauty belonging to Iana alone, no longer a threat. Amid these visions, Iana thrust mindlessly against his friend, and cried out as he came, his mind wild with violence. A'o followed soon afterward with a soft noise of surrender, his eyes wide and trusting, his own mind filled only with love and abandon.

Gasping, Iana pushed away from him in horror as the visions of blood and death faded away. A'o blinked up at him through the heat-haze of the after-glow, confused. Reaching for his shirt, he wiped them both clean, and gently pulled Iana towards him.

"Iana," he said softly. "What's wrong?"

Even the question seemed to upset Iana. He couldn't possibly tell A'o the truth of what had happened. He made a great effort to control his features and shook his head, reaching out for A'o, who was only too happy to comply.

"It's all right," murmured Iana into A'o's hair, holding him close. "It's been a while, is all."

And because A'o wanted desperately to believe him, and for everything to have returned to normal, he left it at that, falling asleep content in Iana's arms while his friend stared fixedly out the window for the rest of the night, listen-ing to a heartbeat that had become strange to him in its humanity.

A'o paced the deck, impatient for their arrival on Loka'i. He had enjoyed his time on Naia but felt that he was only seeing the precursor to real culture and beauty. He sighed in contentment; Iana was his again, and he smiled, think-ing of waking up that morning with his head upon his friend's chest. Other students were also on deck, trying to look nonchalant about their excitement to see Loka'i, but they were as impatient as A'o to see the incredible capital they had been studying their entire lives.

"There! There it is!" cried A'o, proud to have been the first to spot the tall silhouette of Lokai's fabled jungle isle that stood against the horizon like a sentinel. The young men rushed to the side of the ship and others came to join them upon hearing the commotion.

As the ship glided through the sapphire sea and into the harbour, the mountainous island towered above them. The green jungle glowed in the afternoon sunlight, accented by the white pavilions and the stretch of beach that heralded the Connoisseur and her harem. Upon sighting the pavilions, a cheer went up from all the boys on board.

Amidst all the chatter, A'o looked for Iana in the crowd, hoping to share this momentous occasion with his best friend and lover.

"Iana?" he called. "Has anyone seen Iana?"

A band on board struck up a lively tune composed by a man from the Lo-ka'i harem. A'o then spotted his friend standing in the sunlight. He looked ill and pale.

"Iana! Loka'i! We have waited our whole lives for this day!" A'o said, his exuberance blinding him to his friend's condition.

"It's beautiful, my friend," Iana said, "but…I am not feeling very well. I can't…"

He backed away from the sunlight and went below deck. Confused, A'o followed him.

"I know that you may not feel well, but we have waited so long to see Lo-ka'i!" said A'o.

"Leave me, A'o," said Iana. "I am certain I will feel better by this evening."

"Iana?" said A'o, and touched his friend's shoulder. Iana turned and looked at him, his skin pale, his hands trembling.

Under A'o's touch, his friend's skin was ice cold, and the veins in his once-beautiful eyes were red. He saw himself offering a glass full of blood to a weak looking Iana the night before, when he thought everything had gone back to normal. Realisation flooded him, along with intense guilt, as he thought of Iana putting his lips to the glass and drinking the Naiene blood.

"Iana. How could you?" he murmured, afraid to speak too loudly. "You will be disqualified and exiled. How could you choose this?"

How could you leave me, he didn't say.

"You're just jealous now that I will be more beautiful than you!" snapped Iana. "Now *I* will be the one that people notice! And I will never age or die. I will be beautiful long after you are gone."

A'o shrank back from the monster he now saw in his friend.

"Iana," he said, "I only wanted to share my life with you – my greatest hope was that we would enter the harem together."

"I will be the one entering the harem, not you," said Iana, his envy of A'o dripping from his words. "I am the beautiful one now."

A'o took a step back.

"You are a monster," said A'o bitterly. "You were beautiful, and I *loved* you, Iana. Why could you never understand that? Why was I never good enough for you? Your unfounded jealousy caused you to lose everything you had –

and everything we might have had together. Your many years on Naia will give you much time to think about that."

"You *would* tell on me, wouldn't you?" said Iana. "How does it feel to be jealous of *me*?"

"I don't plan on telling," said A'o, "but if you can't be outside during the day, how long do you think it will be before they figure it out?"

There was movement behind them. Aya emerged into a shaft of sunlight filtering through from the upper deck. She looked at Iana as if she had never seen him before.

"You are no longer allowed access to Loka'i," said Aya, "and you are hereby expelled from the Academy. Find your own way – only on Naia will they accept your kind. I certainly hope that your choice was worth it. Come, A'o, we are disembarking."

Iana ran forward.

"What?!" he cried. "No! I am more beautiful than A'o! I belong in the harem! I am youth eternal!"

Aya looked at him with a withering glare.

"You are not," she said, "and your outer beauty was never the most important. It's who you are that makes you more or less beautiful. And I call you monster."

Aya called for guards, and Iana sobbed in horror at what he had done, at this decision he could never take back. A'o begged to be allowed to stay at his friend's side as he made the full transition, but Aya refused, claiming it was unhealthy as well as dangerous. She shepherded A'o off the ship with the rest of the young men, leaving Iana shattered and broken, unable to follow his friend. A'o struggled against Aya as he was led away. He kept his eyes on Iana until he could no longer see his lover in the shadows.

Po

Po had been watching the green island wreathed in mist for quite some time. He was enjoying his travels with the Wyltai immensely. Only occasionally did a pang from the loss of his father enter his heart.

Po was now eighteen, and had been travelling with Eld for almost nine years. The old pirate had become like a father to him, and Po was more Wyltai than he had ever been a child of Snt. His own hair had grown long, and formed tight braids, decorated with the customary feathers and beads of the Wylt.

"You don't want to land here, my son," Eld said to Po, who had never seen the Ghost Island of Cloda before and was intrigued.

"Why's that, Captain?" asked Po.

Eld scratched at his whiskers, now gone somewhat grey.

"Haunted," he said. "Evil things befall people who are foolish enough to land there. Also, it's illegal."

Although Po was interested in magic, his Sntai mind was first sceptical. He smiled and shook his head.

"Rumours are often foolish," Po said. "Let us land there and discover firsthand whether the stories are true. I thought the Wyltai feared nothing... especially the law."

The Wyltai chief guffawed into his beard.

"I fear neither men nor magic," said the chief, "for I can fight both. I fear what I cannot fight."

Po smiled. "Most things are only inexplicable at first," he said, "but a way to fight anything can be found. Just think of how the people will sing of your bravery – the first Wyltai to venture onto the Island of Ghosts! Think of the songs the women will sing."

The chief ruminated on this, chewing his beard.

"The women," he muttered thoughtfully. "All right, Po. We will make landfall on Cloda. But I cannot guarantee your safety. If you become lost and there is danger, the ship will leave without you."

Po nodded, though the thought of being abandoned on the Island of Ghosts chilled him.

"Understood," he said, and the ship changed course towards Cloda.

The silence that greeted them as they stepped off the ship began to unnerve Po. He was on the brink of telling the Wyltai chieftain that he had made a mistake but Eld had already vanished into the mist and Po had no choice but to follow him.

Mist curled around them, so thick that Po would have thought himself alone if he couldn't hear the beads in Eld's hair clicking together somewhere in front of him. Po was about to speak when the Wyltai murmured *shhh*. As Po came up beside Eld, he saw that something stood in their path, blocking the way. Eld reached over his shoulder for his spear when the figure spoke.

"Who are you, and why have you come to Cloda?"

The Wyltai chief bowed deeply, but his hands were shaking.

"I beg your forgiveness, spirit," Eld said, "but the boy was curious."

Po stepped forward bravely.

"I am a scientist from Snt interested in magic and the supernatural," said Po. "Much can be learned from your incorporeal state. I wish to learn what you might teach me."

"Call us spirits now, do they?" asked the figure and laughed. He stepped out of the mist. Despite themselves, both Po and Eld gasped.

It appeared to be a man, but every part of his body was covered with hair. It wore a cloak with sapphire brooches and a golden crown.

"Are you...are you Nonai?" asked the Wyltai chief.

"No," said the figure. "I am Ulu'u by birth. Human, as you are. The Ulu'u's obsession with beauty caused us to be exiled here. A pity, since we remember many things the Ulu'u should not have forgotten. Yet they favour beauty over brains, despite what they may tell you. Spirits! What a thing to say."

"Are your people...as you are?" asked Po.

"As for people, I have none," replied the creature. "The Ulu'u were my people. We are the rejects of several islands, and are of all colours, shapes, and sizes. I am as close to a ruler here as one can get. My name is Olo."

"I am chief of the Wyltai, Eld," said the chief, and bowed again, "and this is Po, a Sntai in my charge."

Olo studied them for a moment.

"As you are the first to venture to Cloda without the command of exile, I will allow you entry," said Olo, "but you may never tell what you have seen here nor can you ever return. Curious as the rumour that we are spirits may be, it has protected us from prying eyes that may be less friendly than yours. If you are willing to submit to those requirements, you may come with me. If not, go hither at once, and if you try to return know that we will kill you."

Po bowed.

"May I ask why you would offer us such a favour?" he asked.

"Because there are things you may be able to learn here…things your people should know," said Olo.

"Then we agree to your terms," said Po. Eld nodded his agreement.

Olo nodded to them and indicated that they should follow him down the trail.

When the forest canopy finally broke, they found themselves in what looked like an ordinary, prosperous town. The citizens, however, were like nothing they'd ever seen. They saw a man with three heads arguing in front of a tavern with a woman whose bone structure made her look like a rooster. There were several people who looked quite normal except they were less than three feet tall. There was a group of beautiful women covered in feathers, with chicken feet, and a man taller than the houses and shops.

"These they call spirits," said Olo, "but I assure you we are all quite human. Refugees from beauty. Many of us are no stranger than the Nonai you spoke of, or the fairy men of the Barrens. The obsession with beauty made us exiles on this land forever. At least we can find comfort in our own company."

A shriek came from the crowd. One of the citizens had spotted Po and the Wyltai chieftain. Several of citizens ran into buildings, some hid their faces.

"Fear not, my people!" called Olo, "These visitors are in my charge, and sworn to secrecy. They are here to learn from us what we may teach them. They will then depart. While they are here, be kind to them, as you wished your people had been kind to you. Perhaps then they will look upon their memory of us with fondness. If they can use what we teach them, one day perhaps, when things have changed, they will return to free us and send us home."

Slowly, the people peeked out from behind their hands. Smiles appeared on some faces, although some of these smiles had a few more and sharper teeth than usual.

"But, Eld, how could we ever free them?" Po whispered.

"Let them believe for the moment. Hope is the one kindness we can offer."

Po and Eld therefore smiled at the people and tried to contain their wonder as best they could.

There were two young men standing near the corner of the street, and when they turned to look at the newcomers, Po flinched. Their faces were horrifying; pale skin stretched taut across triangular jaws. They hurriedly stepped into the shadows, their eyes downcast, hands hiding their faces.

"What happened to them?" asked Po. Eld looked away, because he already knew.

Olo sighed.

"Unlike the rest of us, they were not born that way," he said. "They are what is known as *laboratory monsters*. They were promised beauty and so allowed the scientists to carve into their faces; the pain is excruciating but some do benefit. These are the unfortunate ones, the result of botched experiments on Snt. Before their operations, they looked more or less like everyone else, and would not have found a home here on Cloda. As it is, we are the only ones who will have them."

"I am Sntai by birth," said Po, "and I have heard nothing of these experiments. The beautifying surgeries performed on Snt, while disapproved of by the Ulu'u and Loka'i, are second to none. The doctors and scientists are the best in Amala."

"Yes, you may have been told this," said Olo, "but these are not the only refugees from your island. Most of them were born normal, even beautiful, but it was not enough. They break their jaws, shave down the jawbone. Sometimes, the surgery does not come out right."

Po was silent. He could think of nothing to say, and wondered why he hadn't heard of this secret as a child. He supposed his father, and the other scientists, had a vested interest in hiding the truth from him as well as the outside world.

They were following Olo down a quiet side street when he stopped at a little hut, the doors hung with heavy tapestry. The scent of smoke, heavy and spiced, emanated from the darkness. Olo lifted the tapestry and indicated that Po should step inside.

Po looked into the hut and felt a wave of fear. He shot Eld a look that asked if they could trust this strange man they had just met. The chief shrugged his shoulders as if to say, you wished to come here.

"What lies beyond this door?" asked Po nervously.

Olo looked at him, a stern expression on his face.

"That which you need to learn," he said. "Enter now."

Eld moved to join him, but his way was barred. Olo shook his head.

"You are a soldier of fortune," said Olo, "the young man is a scientist. The learning is for him alone."

Po took one last look at the Wyltai chief, and walked into the hut as the tapestries fell closed behind him.

Po walked steadily forward in the darkness. He heard the scratch of tinder, and a hand appeared below the flame, lighting a candle.

"What have you come for, boy from outside?" demanded a strange, scratching voice.

"For education," said Po, frightened.

"It is good for you to be afraid," said the voice, "for your people have not sought our knowledge in ages."

As his eyes became accustomed to the candlelit darkness, he saw what appeared to be a wizened old woman. She was wrapped in colourful scarves, and he saw as he drew closer that it appeared she was sitting on an impossibly large snake. Then he realised that this was the lower half of her body. The massive tail curled beneath her. She sat before a ruby sphere.

"What learning did you come for?" she asked. "You are as strange to me as I seem to you."

"Anything you have to teach me," stammered Po.

"I see forward and backward in time at once," said the woman, "and I have information your people need. I know the one thing that will end this war forever. Not all wars – only this."

Po sat down before her.

"What war?" he asked. "The Great War has been over for centuries."

She stared at him as if he had said something very foolish.

"This has always been the greatest error of your people," she said. "You do not remember, and so you will fail."

Po nodded.

"I am prepared to learn," he said.

"Are you also prepared to sacrifice?" asked the woman.

"Sacrifice what?" asked Po.

"The one thing in your life that is most important to you," said the old woman. "Do you care for learning that much?"

"What is that?" asked Po, searching his mind.

"You will not know until you agree to the sacrifice," said the old woman, "but by then it will be too late."

Po thought of all the things close to his heart, his own research into magic and science, the small box aboard the ship where he had collected interesting things over the years. He could think of nothing he cared for so much that he wouldn't be willing to sacrifice it in the name of education. After all, it was what his father would do.

"I agree," said Po, "as long as the learning is worthwhile."

"He has spoken," said the old woman.

Po sat silently for some time and felt no different. The old woman beckoned him toward the ruby globe.

"Witness your sacrifice," she said.

Po looked into the glass and was surprised to see his father working at a laboratory table. He was much aged, and had lines in his face Po had never known. Po smiled to see his father again, still in pursuit of research. As Po watched, enchanted, Ld gave a sudden start and clawed at his throat, struggling against an unseen foe.

"Father!" cried Po. He watched as Ld fell to the floor in his death throes and then moved no more.

Po glared hatred at the old woman. She nodded sagely.

"True loss is always difficult," she said. "Are you now prepared to learn?"

Po stared at her, deaf with grief.

"What could possibly be worth my father's death?" he demanded.

"I feel your grief as the sting of an arrow," said the old woman, "but someday you will understand the importance of this learning. Your decision was not in vain."

Po was mute. He was frozen with sadness and could do nothing but listen.

"The lives of many depend upon this knowledge," continued the old woman. "Your father had already sacrificed his life to science. He would have required the same of you. Isn't that what was in your mind when you arrived?"

Po remembered his thoughts and knew well that she spoke the truth. Ld had disowned him in the name of science, and as much as Po hated to admit it, he had always been his father's son. He nodded curtly to the old woman.

"I will now tell you the secret of the *iwa* wine."

Aiea

The sound of the boy crushing the soft, firm bulb of the bloodflower, the tea dripping into the glass, woke Aiea as it had every morning for the past several years. Jade-green eyes opened to a day like any other, the tropical sun casting warm shadows onto the red stone floor of her pavilion, the columns a brilliant white flanked by crimson curtains that were tied off or undulating softly in the breeze.

She sat up in bed, the soft red covers pooling around her body, pristine white sheets shoring up the blankets. She accepted the glass from the servant and the boy bowed, retiring.

Aiea's black hair fell curling over her shoulders, and her bright green eyes stood out against her dark skin. She was dressed in only the shapeless, many-layered soft white shift of the Connoisseur's Apprentice, which she was obligated to wear until she graduated.

Today would be the final test.

"Good morning, Aiea," said Ilo, as she walked up to his pavilion. There were crow's feet when he smiled now, and his body showed his age. Yet he was still handsome. Aio entered the pavilion a few moments later.

They had become her friends and confidants over the years. It had been fifteen years since she started her training. Aiea had forgotten her young life and only knew the harem of Loka'i as her home. Her mother had visited once, a few years before, and Aiea was surprised to see her wearing jewels and fine cloth. The village had prospered in her absence because of her title and her mother had wed one of the Elders. Aiea was surprised to see how her mother had aged; her hair had gone prematurely white and her hands were wrinkled now. She had told Aiea how proud they all were of her, and marvelled at what a woman her daughter had become. Aiea had forgiven her for not visiting more often, since she herself had to focus so much on her training. They were from different worlds now, but Aiea still held her mother's memory in her heart.

"Are you ready?" Ilo asked.

Aiea nodded, her heart in her throat. She did not truly know. For this final test, they had given her no training or preparation; a Connoisseur was supposed to simply know at a glance whether a young man was beautiful. She had mastered the tests that she must administer, and had the two retainers for the rest. Aiea wondered how they would be able to judge whether she had chosen well.

She followed the retainers across the lawn to the beach. A line of men awaited her, each looking as nervous as she felt.

"These young men are the hopefuls of all the islands," said Aio. "It is up to you to judge which are worthy to be of the harem of Loka'i. If you pass this test, the former men of the harem will retire. Afterwards, the entire harem, the pride of Loka'i, will belong to you. Now we begin. Choose wisely."

Aiea stared at the men.

There were three Soans, taller than the others, with long white hair and bodies covered in fine white fur. They were the most stoic; one could not read the expressions in their pale blue eyes, shining like ice crystals. There were two from Chaak, small and lithe, with pale skin, black hair, and eyes so brown they appeared black. There were four dark young men from the villages of Loka'i, intelligence beaming from their faces and their soft, round bodies strange beside the muscular and lean figures of the Soans and the Chaakai. A small man, black as onyx, represented the brilliant scientific community of Snt. Several other men awaited her judgement, the most beautiful and talented men from all corners of Amala.

From these men she would choose the first members of the new harem.

She stepped forward, examining each man closely. There was no set rule regarding beauty and each was judged based upon the quality expected from the aesthetic tastes of his homeland.

Aiea petted the fur of the Soan men, and examined the teeth of the candidates from Tika. She caressed the black skin of the Sntai and felt the wiry muscles of the men from Chaak. She approached the Loka'i men and sharply drew in a breath. The young man in front of her smiled.

"Olai?" she whispered, hardly daring to believe it. The men were not given leave to speak until after the trial, so he only smiled wider.

Aiea stepped back, wondering how the boy she had loved and still dreamed about had ended up here, so many years later. Was it a trap? Surely they knew she would choose him, if only from nostalgia!

She took a deep breath and began to examine him as a man. His body was round, soft, and incredibly powerful. It was the type of body a man had when he was destined to be a labourer. He had dark eyes in an open, friendly face. He was, in short, the perfect specimen of a man from Loka'i. Still, how could she take him from his family, as she had been taken? She felt convinced he had only come here to see her again. She was glad he was the last man she had examined, for she had already made her choices with the others. Her mind was spinning as she heard herself speak.

"Those I touch, step forward," she said.

She walked along the line as if she were in a dream, touching one of the Soans, the Sntai, both of the men from Chaak, and the young man from Snt. She hesitated for a moment before the Loka'i men, and then touched two of them. One was Olai.

They stepped forward, looking visibly relieved. The other men who had not been chosen were expressionless.

"Now the tests," said Aio.

Aiea had been trained in this, so she felt more prepared. Each of the men was subjected to tests of intelligence and talent. If they were judged *iao*, beauty-without-mind, they could not belong to the harem of Loka'i.

As she helped administer the tests, she was amazed that those judged *iao* were the men she had not touched. When they had finished, she understood the tests at last: it was not beauty she was meant to distinguish, as all the men before her were perfect physical specimens according to their ways and culture. She was supposed to divine at a glance the spark of intelligence or talent shining out from behind the eyes. She realised this was no easy task. Many are so taken with beauty that they fail to see foolishness or the black heart hidden beneath the façade. It was the job of the Connoisseur to penetrate this veil and choose men who were beautiful both within and without. Could there be a man whose beauty was so great that he could fool even a Connoisseur? She didn't know. She only hoped the retainers agreed that these men were the proper choices. Once she had finished testing the men, Aio and Ilo would also give her their opinions about the test results. For now, however, she was expected to do it on her own, as the Connoisseur's key responsibility.

There was silence as Aiea finished her decree and stepped back to face the two lines of men. Ilo stepped forward.

"The Connoisseur," he announced. "Bow before her, men."

All the men knelt with their foreheads to the sand. Aiea, flattered, beamed proudly at them, and at this new harem of her own choosing. From the corner of her eye, she saw Aio step forward. In the flash of his blade, he took the head from the first man she had pronounced *iao*.

Aiea began to scream in horror; it sounded like it was coming from far away. She felt rooted to the spot, unable to do more than shriek as the retainer efficiently beheaded each man in the back row. She could not understand why the men in the front kept their foreheads pressed to the sand. Why did they not stand to help their brothers? The bodies were taken away, and Aiea remained frozen, silent, uncomprehending, tears streaking her face. As the other men from the harem began the silent work of washing away the bloodied sugar-white sand with seawater, Ilo spoke to her directly for the first time.

"This is how it always ends for those judged *iao*," he said, "for as a Connoisseur you will hear tales of beauty from foreign lands. The king will not waste time and money searching for new men for his menagerie, only to have the Connoisseur find a man already judged *iao* at the end of the journey. If you did not judge seriously today, let this be a lesson to you in future judgment of those named *iao*."

"Why did you not tell me this is how it would end?" whispered Aiea, horrified.

"We could not risk you failing the tests because you wished to save them from death," said Ilo, "and so you would not turn away. A Connoisseur must become accustomed to this sight."

Aiea's mind was reeling. She was unable to believe what she had just seen; the shock had been so pure. She did not think she could ever become used to it.

"Why must it be this way?" Aiea whispered.

"The king has decreed it so," said Ilo. "It has been thus since time out of mind."

Aiea was silent with horror. Finally, she spoke.

"Why did the other men not help them?" she asked, miserable.

"All harem candidates are forewarned of this possible outcome," said Ilo, "and each of us commits himself to harem training voluntarily. For those who win, the rewards are beyond our wildest dreams. We are assured of health, a rich future, and a life of well-fed idleness. We become famous in our home countries, and our families reap great benefits. Our homelands gain respect, and trade booms because one of their men is a part of the harem of Loka'i."

Aiea thought of the long blade she had noticed Aio carrying when he had come to take her from the village.

"And I? I was given no such warning," she asked. "What would have happened if I had refused the training?"

Ilo smiled without humour.

"You have escaped death many times, Aiea," he said. "Consider yourself fortunate. You are the Connoisseur now, and your life is assured."

He paused.

"Remember, Aiea," he said, "I, too, watched my fellow candidates die, and helped to wash the blood from the sand that first day. As retainers, Aio and I have both been responsible for the deaths of many men."

He walked away toward her pavilion and Aiea remembered the men kneeling in the sand.

"Rise," she said weakly, and the men stood before her, filled with pride.

Aio led them off to the pavilions that would be their new homes. Aiea walked back to her own pavilion amid the wild songs of the men of the former harem as they headed off to their new futures and the laughter of the new arrivals upon whom she had conferred the greatest honour of their time. She caught Olai looking at her, before disappearing up a path as he followed the man to his new pavilion. She barely noticed. Her soul was a tumult of emotion and she could not burn out the horrific sight she had just witnessed. It only grew brighter when she closed her eyes.

Irya

The first light of the sun in the capital city chased the shadows into their corners. Prince Irya, soon to be king, pushed the door of his litter open and jumped down onto the flagstones of the street.

Irya was, as he kept telling everyone, as handsome as any of the men in the harem. He was now twenty-six years old and could have been a candidate himself. The people of Loka'i often said that Irya was so proud of this fact that he dressed himself in traditional harem clothing. He also oiled his upper body, and his long black hair shone with the fat he rubbed into it. His hair fell in one perfect, silken curtain, which he tucked along the right side of his head. He was as arrogant as he was beautiful. Given his position, this surprised no one.

He often liked to go into the capital this way, startling the business owners and men of ill repute. Irya, unlike his father, had never thought himself a man of the people. To Irya, the wealth of Loka'i deserved the kind of king who could take full advantage of it.

The owner of the jewellery store waved him away in annoyance; there was still a half hour until opening time and he was enjoying a leisurely blood-flower tea. After meeting Irya's imperious stare, however, the man realised who he was dealing with and leapt up with such a start he spilled his drink over himself. Irya laughed.

"Good morning, Your Majesty," spluttered the man. "I'm sorry, I didn't realise it was you."

"You should be honouring all your customers with this kind of attention," said Irya. "I may receive preferential treatment for my station, but remember a sale is always a sale, Jokjo. And…?"

Jokjo sighed.

"And every sale made is a sale for the continued greatness of Loka'i," he muttered with the air of one who had been made to repeat it countless times.

"I detect an air of disinterest in your voice," said Irya. "Are you not in favour of Loka'i and its prosperity?"

"Of course I am, Your Majesty," Jokjo said. "What can I do for you this morning?"

"I will be honouring a special guest tonight," he said, "and would like to choose something appropriate as a gift."

Jokjo nodded. He went to his cabinet and took out a velvet box.

"I think this will be just the thing," he said, opening the box.

Irya looked inside. A grin spread across his face.

"You've outdone yourself this time, Jokjo," he said. "This will be perfect."

Irya stood waiting in the throne room for the first time. He had never in his life risen from the throne to greet anyone, but he felt it was appropriate given the circumstances.

Aiea stepped into the throne room and looked around, confused at the emptiness.

"Good evening, Aiea," said Irya.

She clenched her teeth against an insult. If she was to be the Connoisseur to this king, she needed to at least feign politeness.

"Good evening, Irya," she said. "What do you want?"

"You were sent here by the retainers?" he asked. She nodded.

He approached her, and bowed deeply. He extended his arms toward her, a red velvet box held out in his hands. She stared at him, puzzled. She'd never seen Irya look directly at her, let alone bow in her presence.

She stepped forward and opened the box. There was a necklace inside, nestled against black velvet, a golden chain hung with a gemstone the colour of bloodflower tea. She looked up at Irya.

"It's a gift," he said, straightening up. She did not move to take it.

Irya indicated the floor near the edge of the throne room, overlooking the harem pavilions and the sea.

"Will you sit with me a while?" he asked. "I have something I would like to suggest. Afterwards, you can choose to accept or deny my offering."

This behaviour was so wildly unlike Irya that Aiea nodded curtly and followed him to the edge of the throne room, where they sat down together. They both looked out over the jungle and the bay in the moonlight. Irya sat in silence for a while, staring out at the sea, while she wondered what was on his mind.

"Choice," he said suddenly, startling her.

"What?" she asked.

"Choice," he repeated. "It is offered to my subjects. Why not to me? Or you?"

Aiea stared hard at the side of his face. He looked out to the sea as if it held answers.

"This was the night you were to be given to me," Irya said softly.

Aiea turned to look at him, startled.

"What?" she demanded. Irya nodded. He seemed sad, or disappointed, by this fact.

"There are too many secrets," said Irya, "and that ends with my rule. My father is old and infirm. I will be king soon, and I will not begin my rule like a thief in the night."

Aiea was silent for a while.

"They did not tell me they would kill the men I did not choose for the harem," she finally said.

Irya nodded.

"There is far too much violence," he said, "and for a place as peaceful and wealthy as Loka'i, there is no call for this anymore."

Irya turned to look at her and in his expression she saw a very different person than the haughty boy she had grown up hating.

"I am asking you to join me in a rebellion, Aiea," he said quietly. "I no more believe I have a right to you than any of my subjects have a right to anyone else. I want to change Loka'i, end the tradition of violence, and build a council to discuss how best to rule. Even the monarchy is outdated. I hope to be the last king. The great and learned at the university teach us that choice is the most hallowed truth for all our people, and the only reason I can see it not applying to royalty is due to some ancient tradition best left in the past where it belongs."

In his eyes, Aiea saw both a frightened child and the determination of a young man aware that he would soon be king of the most culturally important place in the world. She also saw her own worries and fears reflected.

"Will you join me?" he asked again. "We will make a pact, this night, instead of what was meant to happen. We will work together as the new king and Connoisseur to build a different and better world than the one that came before it. No one will know and we must do our best to keep up appearances until the older generation has withered away and no one remembers anything but the world we have built together. We must always have this goal at the front of our minds, in every choice we make, as we slowly put away the barbaric traditions of our ancestors. Knowing all this, will you accept this gift? Will you help me?"

Aiea thought of the horror she had seen earlier that day, and of this night, when she had been sent, trusting, to the palace with no idea what was expected. She thought of the young men and their bright futures, the beautiful lives cut short only that afternoon. Loka'i was in all other aspects extraordinarily consent-oriented. It was diverse and accepting of others. Only the royalty and the harem seemed to be subject to draconian and outdated laws. This was a time of new beginnings and this was her opportunity not only to make a difference in the world but one that was lasting and positive.

She held out her hand for the box. Irya handed it to her, and she put the necklace around her neck, the bloodflower gem nestling in the dip of her collarbone.

"Yes," she said. "I will help you. I do not want to cause further suffering."

"Then it's agreed," said Irya. "However, we cannot let anyone know what we are planning to do. We are still young, and the Elders, the advisers, other well-meaning people will try to stop us. It must look as if everything has gone as they planned."

"Will we meet again like this?" Aiea asked.

"No," he said. "Tonight, they have given me privacy, but the life of the king is never a private one. We will have to sustain ourselves with the knowledge and memory of this night."

Aiea nodded, thinking how she too lacked privacy, although it had not bothered her until now.

"I will bring you messages when and if I can," she promised.

"I too," he said, "but we must be careful."

They sat together and looked out at the sea.

"You are a kinder man than I expected," said Aiea.

"You are not meant to expect kindness from me," said Irya. "I knew, as a child, I wanted to do things differently. I also knew that if the world only saw insufferable, arrogant Irya, they'd never expect such a spoiled little brat

68

to have anything between his ears or any interest in shaking the very foundations of royal society. You learn quickly, when you are young, which way the wind is blowing. I think you know that very well, Aiea. It is, after all, why you were chosen."

Irya smiled at her.

"Let's change the world."

The next morning, amid trumpets and fanfare, Aiea stood in the throne room of the palace of Loka'i. She had not seen Irya's father since her childhood and was surprised at how much the king had aged.

Irya stood beside his father. Although he was laden with jewellery, dripping with gemstones meant to set off the tone of his skin, he wore the outfit of the harem men and his body was oiled like theirs. He did this as a gesture of solidarity with them, not because he believed himself beautiful, as his subjects thought. He wore nothing else that spoke of his royalty, and from the wearied look his father gave him, Aiea surmised that this had been a bone of contention for years. Irya smiled at her, and she smiled back, until she remembered they weren't meant to be friends, and scowled.

"Aiea of the village of O'a," said the king ceremoniously, "I hereby decree that you are the new Connoisseur of Loka'i. It is a title that demands the utmost sacrifice. The fame, the culture, the treasures of Loka'i are now in your hands alone. Serve and protect the men whom it is your duty to watch over. Care for our cultural treasures as you would your own family."

The retainers slowly stripped her of the white shift she always wore and she stood, naked, in the liquid light of the throne room.

"Your old life has fallen away," the king was saying, "and naked, you enter your new life as you entered the old."

Aio and Ilo came up with the skirt, belt, and crown made for Aiea over the weeks leading up to her coronation. The costume consisted of a brassiere, belt, and skirt dripping with white iridescent pearls and other jewels she had chosen in her youth, looping in strings around her. The jewels wrapped around her arms to end in rings around her fingers. Aio and Ilo beamed with pride.

"Now go forth and procure for us those treasures that will be your legacy, like the Connoisseur before you," said the king, as Aio placed the jewelled crown upon her brow.

Irya stepped forward at this point. Aiea touched the gemstone at her throat, and he replied by way of a curt nod. The crowd, aware of tradition, saw this gesture and interpreted it as *remember the gift I gave to you last night.* For Aiea and Irya, it meant *remember our promise. Remember that we are going to change the world.*

"Now you have been given to my son, as the former Connoisseur was given to me," said the king, placing her hand in Irya's.

Irya's gloating, smirking face filled Aiea's vision, and she fought against a smile that threatened, knowing it was all an act for the benefit of the others. She glared at him instead. She, too, had a part to play.

The king gently turned the two of them towards the waiting crowd.

"The Connoisseur," the king announced. The trumpets blew, the people cheered, and Aiea snatched her hand away from Irya's.

Aiea never truly realised Loka'i's wealth until that night. The tables groaned beneath the weight of the food piled upon them; people drank from diamond goblets and dipped their hands in silver bowls. Aio and Ilo were dressed in ceremonial robes, and Aiea was introduced to so many dukes and ladies she could not remember any of their names. To them, she was the Connoisseur – her name no longer accompanied her title.

Irya took her hand, drawing her towards the dance floor, the room glowing gold, the two of them shining like stars. The thousands of flowers, the rich, delectable food, the beautiful music, art, and architecture surrounded them so that everyone present was stunned by the awesome beauty and luxury of Loka'i. For everything beautiful – men and women, animals, flowers, jewels, food, buildings, music, and art – had a home here. Truly, Loka'i was the most breathtaking place the world had ever known. No tribe was wealthier than the Ulu'u, none were happier with their lives. The recent violence Aiea had witnessed faded into memory in the soft light of the ballroom.

That night, dark skies warmly enfolded the white palace and the stars stood as the moon's courtiers, looking down upon the grand people in the ballroom, as Aiea whirled in triumph across the dance floor. The moon shone through the fronds of the palms that fringed the beach, speaking of mystery and romance. The philosophers of the time, and the poets, wrote odes to that evening:

Loka'i, my adopted home
of the hidden river valleys

and waterfalls
the waves of your shore caress my skin
Loka'i the brilliant, Loka'i the sweet
hold me in your arms like a lover.
Paradise
is not worthy of sharing with you
its name.
O, Loka'i, wealth of days
envy of the world
what use have I of heaven
after knowing you?

When Aiea returned to her pavilion the next morning, she was alone. The last of the former Connoisseur's men were leaving that day and a few stopped to wish her well in her new life. The younger men, those she had chosen, were settling into their pavilions.

The last of the former harem to speak with her were the retainers. Aio and Ilo approached her pavilion together as she sipped a glass of bloodflower tea.

Ilo bowed deeply to her.

"Greetings, Connoisseur," he said. Aio nodded.

"Fortune to you in your new lives," Aiea replied formally.

They stood together, silent until Aio spoke.

"We cannot leave until you have chosen new retainers," said Aio. "The first must be from among the men you have already selected. The second must be from another land; the first acquisition from your travels. When your second retainer has been chosen, you will return to Loka'i. From that point onward, you will be on your own."

Aiea nodded.

"Call the men to me," she said. She was prepared to take on the mantle of her new title. She had grown a decade of maturity in a single night, armed with the immunity of her new title and the knowledge of what she and Irya planned to achieve together.

The First Retainer

The men stood before her, expressionless. The position of retainer was not a coveted one, though it brought respect to those who carried it because the position was that of a glorified killer. The harem, however, had been trained to do as the Connoisseur directed, so they awaited her decision in silence.

"Your choice in this matter is important," said Ilo, "you must choose a man you feel will be attractive to all those who see him, for the Connoisseur and her retainers are the symbol of the wealth and beauty of Loka'i across the world. He must be intelligent and charming. He must also have a predilection for other men, as this will help you in your search. Remember these things as you make your choice."

Aiea looked at the men of the harem.

"Those of you who only have interest in women, step back," she said. Several of the men did so, leaving only three before her. One was Soan, one from Loka'i, and one from Chaak.

"State your name, origin, and specialty," said Aio.

"Tla, Soa," said the tall, blue-eyed man with soft white fur. "Song."

"O'ala of Loka'i," said the dark, round man, whose brown eyes shone in the light. "Culinary arts."

"A'o of Chaak," said the thin, muscular man with a long fall of straight black hair like Irya's. "My speciality is history."

Aiea considered the three men for a moment. Given the love of song throughout Amala, the Soan might be useful. However, culinary arts were considered some of the most important, since Naia was considered second only to Loka'i in cultural value, and having another Loka'i citizen as the first retainer would make for fewer cultural misunderstandings.

However, she had never seen any man who looked like A'o. His brown eyes were flecked with green and gold, and his high cheekbones gave him an im-perious beauty Irya would be jealous of. His smooth skin, accented only by a mysterious scar, made him outshine the other men by a very long way.

She had made her decision.

"A'o is chosen," she said, "for the task of testing is not an easy one, and his knowledge will be the most useful. His beauty is classic, and therefore he will display the pride of Loka'i to the best advantage."

The other men bowed deeply, leaving A'o in Aiea's pavilion with Aio and Ilo.

"It is my place to retire first, as I was first chosen," said Ilo. "I wish you all fortune on your first voyage together."

Ilo bowed his farewell, and Aiea held back her emotion, saying goodbye to one of the men who had raised her from childhood, never to see him again.

The First Night

The Connoisseur's pavilion was lit by hundreds of candles, the smoke of the incense floating out into the midnight black of the night where it dispersed towards the white caps of the waves in the darkness. The moon was so bright it was like silver daylight, reflecting white off the palm fronds.

Aiea waited, holding her breath.

A'o stepped inside. He looked at the floor, demure, his hands clasped in front of himself.

"I bring myself as a gift," he said, so quietly she did not hear him at first.

"And I offer you a choice," she whispered back.

A'o's eyes sought hers. The script he had learned for a lifetime had been broken.

"Connoisseur?" he asked.

"A'o," she said, "first chosen, my retainer. I offer you a choice. There will be no consequences, no matter your answer. You may participate, or not."

A'o stared at her, wordless, for many minutes, trying to puzzle out the mystery.

"Is this a test?" he asked.

"No, A'o," said Aiea. "Truly, it is your choice. I am a new Connoisseur. I want to try a new way. But you cannot say anything, not for many years. Some will not understand. Can I trust you to do this?"

A'o nodded firmly; this he knew. He would do anything for her.

"So. Your choice," she said, and sat down on the bed in front of him.

Hesitantly, A'o approached her. He knelt in front of the bed.

"Yes," he said, "I wish to participate. This gift was always meant for you."

Aiea looked at him.

"You do not need to do this in order to prove your loyalty," she repeated. "It is not a test."

"I believe you, my Connoisseur," he said, "but all my life, I have loved you. I had a portrait commissioned of you that still hangs in my flat at the Academy. I have collected items, miniatures, photographs – all my life, Aiea, you were there, watching over me. This is what I have always wanted. This is the culmination of that dream."

Aiea smiled, taken aback by the devotion of the young man she had chosen as retainer. Her instincts here, too, had been impeccable, it seemed. Her confidence in her abilities grew every day, and her memory of the promise she and Irya made echoed in every action.

"Then join me," she said, and he stood, unsure of himself, as he had been taught that the Connoisseur would initiate. A'o climbed onto the bed, trembling in every limb. Here he was, before the goddess of his youth, and she would touch him.

Aiea traced her fingertip down the scar along the side of the young man's face. She felt him resisting the urge to flinch away, and she brought her brilliant jade eyes in line with his.

"What happened?" she murmured.

He swallowed.

"My best friend," he said softly. "We were supposed to test for the harem together."

"And he is not here?" asked Aiea.

The young man shook his head. She nodded. He looked at her, mournful and devastated, thinking that he would be rejected by the woman to whom he had hoped to offer all of himself. The damage to his once-renowned beauty, it seemed, would be eternal.

"Welcome, A'o," she said, smiling. She held out her hand.

A'o took it cautiously.

"Do you understand what we are going to do?" she asked. "This is only done with your consent *at all times*. If there is anything wrong, you need to tell me, but I will also ask."

A'o nodded.

"Please feel free to speak," said Aiea.

"Yes, Connoisseur," he said.

"Do you want to do this?" she asked.

"Yes," said A'o.

"Lay down on the bed."

A'o lay down and disrobed. His Connoisseur stood and stared at him, her eyes taking in every line and curve. A blush rose in his cheeks, spreading across his skin.

"You are breathtaking," Aiea murmured as she knelt above him, touching kisses to his fevered skin, "You are beautiful."

She traced the scar, and brushed her lips across it. A'o sighed, a low keening noise he hadn't expected to make.

"Is this all right?" she whispered.

"Yes, Connoisseur," he said.

"The most important part of this relationship," Aiea said, as she ran the flat of her palms down his chest, to the planes of his hips, "is *trust.*"

A'o's breath was harsh, as she avoided touching him. He was aching, his cock a hard curve against the muscles of his stomach. He stared up into her brilliant eyes. She smiled, and kissed him deeply. She kissed down his stomach and touched her lips to the head of his cock, her tongue darting out, tasting him. A'o clenched his fingers into the sheets and groaned in the back of his throat.

She took his hand, and guided his fingers to where she was wet and swollen.

"Always know your partner is ready," she sighed, "and learn what they like. Every person will be different, but the lesson remains the same."

She then lowered herself onto him, and he felt himself enter that tight, wet heat. A shout caught in his throat; it was too much and not enough all at once. He had never felt anything like this, never dreamed of it, and she was moving, slowly at first but then so quickly he could do nothing but clutch at her thighs and watch her come apart beautifully above him, those lips falling open because of *him*, because he was beautiful, because he *mattered,* and there were tears in his eyes as he finally gave way to the shout, to her, to his Connoisseur, who believed in him and in the trust they would always share together. It was intended as a gift from every new harem member to the Connoisseur, their first time, but for A'o, it had been an exchange, powerful and pure, and it bound him to her heart and soul.

Aiea smiled down at him, then lay down and folded him into her arms. She called for bloodflower tea mixed with sugar water and some fruit.

"Thank you, A'o," she said. "I want you to drink something, and have a little food. Then we can bathe together."

A'o, pillowed on her chest, could only nod and hold her tight. He was hers, now and always, and he made a promise to himself that he would be the most dedicated, celebrated member of the harem. This he would do, for her.

The following night, Aiea welcomed Olai into her pavilion. He stood motionless in the doorway, and she offered him the same choice.

The relief that flooded his features confused her, and he took her hands, thanking her profusely.

"I understand that it will not be the same with everyone," said Aiea, "but given our past history, I am at a loss as to why you are so overjoyed not to be with me?"

"Oh, Aiea," said Olai, "it has nothing to do with you! I love you, heart and soul, as I did as a child, as I do now. I doubt that will ever change."

"Then why?" she asked.

"I," he began, and faltered, "I have no interest in sex. I would have performed as required, I knew this going into training for the harem, but it is something I have no interest in."

"I understand," she said, "and this is exactly the reason that I wanted everyone to have a choice."

"Would you – could we just sit and talk instead, for a while?" asked Olai. "About home, the village? Old times?"

"I'd love to," Aiea smiled, and they moved to the small couch. They held each other's hands, two old friends, and talked throughout the night together about the village they had left behind.

The Second Retainer

"There have been reports the world over of exceptional men," said Aio. "You have your choice of places to visit, Aiea. In each place there are new products to discover. On your first excursion, you are to procure your second retainer. Which island suits you for your first voyage?"

Aiea thought about the things she had heard of each island. Thla or Nona, neither of which had ever had a man in the harem? Cold Soa, the land of eternal silence and the strange *kact* fish? The Forgotten Lands of Soka, where no advances had been made since prehistoric times?

There was one island she had often heard about, where it was said music could be heard a mile offshore. Here the philosophers argued in the cafes and the sculptors fell in love with the painters and writers. It was an island of the arts, its weather eternally temperate.

"I wish to see the island of music, Tika," said Aiea, "what is offered there?"

"A young man named Kane," said Aio. "He has never been trained and is unaware of his society's nomination. However, the island has been asking us to test him in the last year."

"Can he not refuse?" asked Aiea.

"If an island thinks a man is sufficiently talented, it is the law that he must be tested," said Aio, "to prevent the king from spending unnecessary money to investigate a new hopeful, only to find the same man who had earlier refused."

"One would think it better to hide his talents then," A'o spoke up.

"It tends to be impossible," said Aio, "for a natural talent to hide itself. A writer must write. A painter must paint. Passion cannot be hidden forever."

"When can we begin?" asked Aiea.

"A vessel awaits us in the harbour as we speak," said Aio. "We leave whenever you are ready."

"I am ready," Aiea said.

When a ship sailed to Tika, the passengers could hear strains of beautiful music drifting on the sea. The island, in a temperate climate, existed in an eternal summer. No one knew why. Most of the citizens of Tika were very poor. Writers tended to live in huge old apartments with wrought-iron balconies, now grown over with weeds. The problem with a culture entirely devoted to the arts was that much of the practicalities of life were not addressed. They were not an unhappy people, however, and enjoyed the time they spent together in the cafes arguing about philosophy until the early hours of the morning. The men and women in the brothels were the richest among the people of Tika, having chosen an art that paid well. The lonely lakes and glades filled with willow trees and flowers were often the subject of weekend trips with bottles of wine, misremembered later, but all involved spoke fondly of the places beyond the city. Tika, on the whole, was tragic, romantic, and gorgeous. Stories, *real stories*, happened here, so it only made sense that most of its inhabitants were constantly engaged in the activity of writing them down.

The Summerlands were a great mystery to everyone in Amala. There was not a palm tree in sight, but the weather was consistently warm and beautiful. The lands were like their name – a place that should see winter, based on its foliage and location, but winter always failed to arrive.

Kane sat at a café on a boulevard lined with oak trees, listening to the leaves whisper in the endless summer breeze. He was awaiting his friend, Ryg, who was visiting from the rough port island of Thla. Ryg had friends far and wide, and was a red-faced, portly sailor covered in bristles. He imbibed far too much of the Thlai liquor, which was of more use as paint thinner than a drink to the rest of the world. Ryg was gruffly affectionate and full of the kind of wisdom that a man acquires after spending a life on seas fair and foul and in exotic lands among strange people. Kane loved his stories, and his poet's heart awoke and came to life with each transporting tale Ryg told him. Kane himself was a bit of an oddity, a scientist in the Summerlands whose talent for both poetry and logic was well known. This combination, coupled with his handsome looks, had attracted the notice of the council Elders, but they had not thought to notify him, as it was assumed that every man wanted to be in the harem of Loka'i. Such was the bureaucracy of the Summerlands, said to be as esoteric and mysterious as an ancient scroll that no one could decipher. Some said that even the Elders only pretended to know how it worked.

"Having a look at the boys again, *mikka*?" a voice said into his ear, a heavy hand cuffing him on the shoulder. Kane grinned as Ryg threw himself into a chair on the other side of the table. He took out his flask and drank from it, grinning and squinting in the sunlight. He used the term of endearment for fellow-sailors, *mikka*. From a Thlai, who typically used it for Thla-born friends, spouses, or children, this was a gesture of great respect.

"Haven't seen any yet," Kane grinned. "I'm working on a poem."

"Ah!" Ryg said, "I almost forgot––I brought ye somethin'."

He reached into his coat, rummaged around, and pulled out a box that had originally held Onai firespice. His dirty fingers fumbled with the lid. When he finally got it open, Kane saw what looked like a small wooden bird. Ryg lifted his finger – wait – and placed the toy bird in his hand. He stroked its back. Suddenly feathers exploded from the toy and it seemed to come to life, chirping and looking at Kane with bright black eyes.

"Whaddaya think o' that?" Ryg shook his head, "Got it from Snt, last I were there. Beauty, ain't it? Anyways, thought it'd help with the writin'."

Kane grinned down at his gift, amazed at how lifelike it was. A commotion in the street made him turn. A beautiful woman approached, led by the president of the Summerlands. She looked important, the late afternoon sunlight reflecting off the jewels of her costume. The smile faded from Kane's face.

"Will ye look at that fine thing?" Ryg said, leering. "I'd like to—"

A bright knife at his throat, sudden and sharp, silenced him.

"You will show the Connoisseur respect," breathed A'o, who had approached from the other end of the street.

Kane stared at the woman.

"Looks like your salvation approaches," Ryg said. "If the Connoisseur chooses ye, ye'll be set for life."

Kane shook his head gravely.

"Death stands before us, Ryg," he said. "She is Death, surely as she is Life for many."

End

The pale light in the corner of the room served more to accentuate the shadows than to provide illumination. Bottles of *iwa* wine, empty, lined the table, and ashtrays overflowed with the remnants of Onai firespice. There was a large arched opening with a balcony overlooking the busy Plaza of Song and tiny twinkling lights were visible in the trees above the bustling crowd and the cafes.

A hunched figure sat in a corner near the open arch and the balcony, leaning his head against his hand. He was thin, with a rough goatee and a head of black curly hair. He leaned over scribbled pages, his pen occasionally scratching across the paper. He was lonely and believed no one understood him, not an uncommon thought in a land of philosophers and poets. A bottle of half-drunk *iwa* wine kept him company. He liked living on this island of music, with its eternal summer, never too hot or too cold, all the women beautiful and fashionable, but it wasn't enough. He had a horrible secret that would one day cause him to be exiled: he was not a writer, or a musician, or a singer. He felt that pretending to be a novelist was the easiest way to hide this, as musicians always had someone eventually ask them to sing or play their instrument. Nobody had the attention span to read novels, particularly when there were so many other things to hear, read, or experience.

His name was End, and he knew he was *iao*, though he wouldn't recognise the word.

End looked down at the paper in front of him:

Milk

Lettuce

Butter

He shook his head. He didn't even have the inspiration to compose a grocery list.

Everyone assumed that End was a reclusive genius. All he had to do was not produce anything and for some reason people got the idea that he was talented. He knew he'd be found out eventually and the thought of exile no longer worried him as much as it once had. He knew there were other places where he could be mediocre in peace.

A knock came at the door.

"Come in," he called, carefully covering his work.

Kane entered from the shadowy hallway with a bottle in his hand.

"He brought it, End!" Kane said, showing him the bottle. "Ryg brought it from Thla today!"

Whatever artistic talent End may have lacked, he had great abilities in the field of drinking.

"The Thlai are the only ones that will drink this stuff!" End said excitedly, taking the bottle of clear liquid from his friend.

"Well, maybe it tastes awful," Kane offered, sitting down in a broken chair.

"We'll soon find out," End replied. Kane watched his friend pour out the liquor into two glasses.

"Did you hear that the Connoisseur is on the island?" asked Kane.

End almost dropped the precious bottle.

"Who is she here for?" he asked, his hand shaking as he poured. Exile was one thing – losing his life entirely another.

"I thought she might be here for you," said Kane, "but she's here for me."

Relief flooded through End. At least Kane had a real chance.

"When are the tests?" he asked, handing Kane a glass.

"Tomorrow," he said, "so I thought this would be a good time to come by. Either way, I don't know if I will see you again."

End raised his glass.

"Here's to tomorrow, then," he said.

They both took a cautious sip of the drink and made identical faces of disgust.

"Ugh, no wonder nobody drinks this," End said, setting his glass down. The two men laughed, dumping out the contents of their glasses, and spent the rest of the night sharing the last of the *iwa* wine, talking about old times.

Kane

Kane had passed all the tests admirably. Aiea felt that he would be a good choice for her second retainer, as he was well-travelled. He had become their advisor on the long journey from island to island. Aio had taken his leave with grace, giving them his blessing and good hopes for the future. He had returned to Loka'i on another ship while they continued their voyage.

Aiea lay between Kane and A'o on the ship's deck, looking up at the night sky. The creaking of the vessel as it moved through the waves was hypnotic, and the warm winds played with the loose fabric of their robes.

"That one's the Lost Dog," said Kane, pointing up at a collection of stars.

A'o burst out laughing.

"There's no such constellation!" he said.

"I beg to differ," said Kane, trying to keep a straight face. "I am the scientist here, storyteller."

A'o made a noise of mock disgust, throwing a piece of fruit at him. *Storyteller* was a pejorative term used by scientists for experts in any non-scientific field.

"Now, that one is Cat That Has Fallen Off Something And Tries Not To Look Embarrassed," said Kane, pointing at another random group of stars. Aiea laughed, and stopped them before an all-out food fight started.

"A'o," she said, after they were quiet for a while, "tell me a story."

"Oh, I see how it is," said Kane, and Aiea shushed him.

"What kind of a story?" he asked.

"Alyeta," she said, "the lost king."

Kane groaned.

"You'd rather listen to *fairy* tales than scientific fact?" he asked, "Not only that, but the most *traditional* fairy tales we've all heard millions of times?"

"Your constellations weren't exactly in the realm of scientific fact," said A'o, "and there may be some truth behind these stories."

"Historians are all the same," said Kane, "show them a shattered piece of pottery and they faint. Millions of interpretations, millions of possibilities. Science isn't an opinion, it's fact you can't argue with."

"Come on, Kane, you don't even have a *little* magic in you?" asked Aiea, "Honestly, how are you from the poet's island? If I didn't know any better, I'd swear you were Sntai!"

"I'm only interested in proven facts," said Kane. "Math is always there, it's solid. Everything else is slippery, you can't trust it."

"What about poetry?" asked Aiea, "That's not very logical."

"Poetry is like math," said Kane. "It is metered, it has rules."

"And yet people have always told stories," said A'o. "Now quiet down and let me tell the Connoisseur a story."

Kane grumbled, but was silent.

"Long, long ago," A'o began, and Aiea's eyes sparkled as she smiled up at the stars, losing herself in the tale, "The Wide Lands were ruled by the wonderful royal family, greater than our princes and kings today. They were more beautiful than we can imagine and held the power of the Song of Life. They sang the lands into being. We know the Sea King and the merfolk hunted every member of the royal family and killed them, because he was jealous."

"What did he have to be jealous of?" Kane interrupted, "He lives underneath the sea."

"Shh," said Aiea, nudging him.

"Thank you, Connoisseur," said A'o, and continued, "So we lost the Wide Lands, and only the islands remain. The memory of peace, of prosperity, of the perfection that came before, is evident even in tribes like the Hoisdean, the half-human, half merpeople of Hois. This shows that we once lived amicably with the merpeople until their treachery. These stories are well-known, so much so that every child in Amala knows them, and the details, from early childhood onward. Despite appearances, we are still at war. Our oceans are still empty of fish. We do not know what the Sea King's intentions are, or what he and his people are planning, but the continued silence from beneath the waves has been speculated upon for years. The final outpost of the war, Ona, still stands guard.

"Although this story is not new, and is told to children at bedtime nightly around the world, partly to explain Amala's history to them and prepare them for a possible return to war, what I am about to recount is far less known, and may be unfamiliar to you."

At this, even Kane perked up. Both his companions looked over at A'o, but he was caught in the story now, and his eyes stared up into the heavens as if reading it there.

"It is whispered, in some places," said A'o, "that if the royal family had truly been destroyed, there would be no islands at all, but a wide and endless sea. So, some historians and myth-trackers believe that someone has survived."

Aiea sat up at this.

"Are you serious, A'o?" she asked. He nodded.

"Yes," he said, "For a scientist like Kane, it actually makes far more sense than the usual sad lost kingdom we always talk about. If the lands were some-how tied to the royal family, then it stands to reason that once they are all gone, there would be no more land."

"That's true," said Kane. "The story always seemed ridiculous – a fairy tale. Constant chatter about the perfection of the kingdom that existed before this one, but how can we ever know? People have a tendency to romanticise, and that's when their worst mistakes often happen. Scientifically speaking, there may be survivors out there."

"If there are, there's probably only one left, since islands are all that remain of the Wide Lands," said A'o, "and of course, there is the matter of what hap-pens if this survivor is killed or dies in some other way."

"The land will be gone?" asked Aiea.

"Yes," he said, "And so will we."

"This is the reason we want to find a way to undo magic," said Kane, "and replace it with science. Imagine: all of our existences based upon the survival of a single person or family? If they truly possessed the power of the Song of Life, as the old stories say, they would be so immensely powerful that I would hesitate to trust any of them. You can get drunk on that kind of power. I won-der how benevolent they really were, despite what the stories say."

"We'll make a historian of you yet," said A'o, smiling, and Kane lay back down onto the weathered wooden deck.

"Now that storytime is over," said Kane, "may I draw your attention to this constellation, which is called Dead Fish on the Sand."

"Very scientific," A'o said, laughing.

Aiea wasn't paying attention. She was dreaming, of childhood fairytales, the noble royal family, and the possibility that an Alyetan remained in Ama-la, somewhere.

The most captivating aspect of the legend was the rumour that no humans had ever been, or would ever be, as beautiful as the Alyetans. They no longer existed, but were spoken of reverently by everyone on Loka'i, in bakeries and coffee shops, brothels, the harem, even the palace itself. Many of the harem attributes and clothing were based upon old paintings of the Alyetans, but they were so ancient and cracked, paint peeling, that no one could see their faces. Modern artists had taken to painting them without faces because there was no way they could approximate the beauty they saw in their minds when thinking of the Alyetan people and the sad royal family that was relentlessly pursued by an enemy it ultimately could never escape.

The thought turning over and over again in Aiea's mind was this: if there was a survivor, what if he was male? The combined talent and beauty of an Alyetan, the first and rarest specimen in the harem, would make her the most famous and revered Connoisseur of all time. Her village would become the most prosperous on Loka'i, her place in history would be assured, and the harem she chose would be used as the ultimate example for centuries after she had gone.

Aiea wanted to be a legend, just like the royal family, and here she saw her chance.

Aiea

The darkness of Soa was once again complete. Allian wondered if he was the only one who was sick to death of his homeland. "Ice on the branches!" people would say, if they spoke, "The blue light of the snow! The purple dawn over the waves of the chill sea!" But they never spoke. Not to Allian, and not to anybody.

Soa, the Winterlands, where Allian lived, did not see spring. Ice hung from dead branches even in midsummer. He and his fellow Soans shared a uniform look; skin parchment-white, strange ice-blue eyes, and bodies covered with a thin, soft white fur except for the face and the palms of the hands. They were a stately, beautiful people. All Soans had long, white, straight hair. The men were tall and straight-backed, the women big-boned and curvy. They did not do well in the heat. Nevertheless, more than one Soan belonged to the great harem of the Ulu'u. Their primary export was ice to the southerly isles, and the freshwater *kact* fish, which was invisible except for its skeleton, and provided the most delicate meat of any creature known. The Sea King did not control freshwater fish, so the *kact* was in high demand. Ice sculpture was the highest form of art on Soa.

The Soans believed heaven could only be obtained by speaking very little during one's lifetime, so if communication was absolutely necessary it was done by signs or writing. Any form of talk counted. They were reclusive, excessively strict, and some would say both sad and noble, but as they barely communicated no one knew for certain. They did not eat the *kact-fish* themselves; they ate a vegetable mashed with milkfat. Poets sang of the misery of a Soan's life on an island of trees covered in ice and piles of snow. No Soan had ever expressed satisfaction or its opposite; they were a complete mystery.

Allian had spent an entire life on this island, knowing himself to be loquacious, but trapped in silence. His pastor advised him against this temptation, but it was very difficult for him. He did not believe in the religion or the habits of his own people, and felt himself very lonely.

He knew other Soans had travelled, and he hoped to be numbered among them. One of them was even a sailor. They called him Hush, because so far in his life he had not uttered a single syllable. Among Soans, this was tantamount to sainthood.

Allian had never known a time in his life that he hadn't despised Soa. He wanted to leave, but knew he could not follow in Hush's footsteps. Allian felt that he did not have the temperament for such a career, and so he decided that his only way out was to try for the Loka'i harem. He was handsome enough, and intelligent.

He left his small house in the purple twilight, his breath like fog on the air. His feet crunched in the snow as he walked beneath cold pinpoint stars to the island's great gathering place.

He opened the door and warm air escaped, enfolding him as he went to sit by the fire. The room was full and silent. He nodded to a few others he knew, and accepted the beverage handed to him by the wordless serving maid. He wondered what purpose the gathering place served, since there was no conversation. He likewise wondered how people found enough in common to wed.

"Why?" he said, shattering the silence. The others turned and stared, some in surprise, others in horror, depending upon their piety.

There was no answer.

The King of Soa greeted Aiea gravely as she stepped onto the wharf, where a shipment of *kact* was awaiting transport to the various isles. A'o and Kane stood at either side of her, their white cloaks billowing in the snowy wind. All three were freezing, but they made no mention of it. Soans looked with disdain upon those from the fragrant isles, considering fortitude in hardship a mark of nobility. The old Soan king was handsome, his fur a blinding white and his long hair gleaming. His attendants stood behind him, unsmiling.

The old king bowed deeply, gesturing toward a small house on the shore. Aiea and her retainers followed without speaking. Soans valued reticence above all things.

They arrived at the door and knocked. It was opened immediately by a young Soan man, who was obviously waiting impatiently for the Connoisseur's arrival. It was as if the door had opened upon a tropic isle there in that small hamlet, poor and bleak though it was. The boy was exceedingly beautiful, it was true, but the pure joy in his demeanour, sparkling from his eyes, was what made it seem as though sunlight suffused the room.

The boy pointed to a placard – Allian – this was his name. Soans believed that the man who uttered the fewest words during life would become king of heaven. Allian was prepared to sacrifice this hope for a chance to belong to the Ulu'u harem; no doubt his elders looked upon this desire as a lack of strength, and yet they would grudgingly allow him to pursue this dream. Soans knew the value of allegiance, and the prized status of any member of the harem. It would facilitate trade, and possibly allow them to charge a marginally higher price for their *kact*.

A'o and Kane sat Allian down and alternated questions between them. Allian stared hopefully at Aiea, her strange bare skin and her curvaceous body. He, like so many others, hoped she might love him – that he could gain this prize that had eluded so many.

Beautiful as the boy was, he was not bright, or talented enough to qualify. Kane heaved a sigh; he was quite particular about Soan boys, and muttered his pronouncement under his breath.

"*Iao*, Connoisseur," Kane said, sorrow in his voice.

"Do you concur, Honourable A'o?" asked Aiea.

A'o, looking desperate, racked his brains for some other skill the boy could possibly have. The tests were complete; it had been hours. He had no choice.

"*Iao*, Connoisseur," said A'o heavily. "I concur."

Aiea's eyes were shining with tears as she pronounced *iao* on the boy as well. Allian knew what this meant, and hung his head, silent again as was the custom of his people.

Aiea stepped outside to where the old king was waiting.

"*Iao*, Your Majesty," she said softly, apologetically.

The old king's face softened somewhat: the Soan mark of deep sadness. He bowed to her, and held out his hand towards the door. She went back inside and nodded to A'o.

The thin young man unsheathed a long bladed weapon with a curved blade and hook. Allian continued to stare in silence at the floor as A'o, his expression unchanged, cut his head from his body. The three of them bowed as was custom.

A'o wiped the blood from his blade, and stared. He motioned to Aiea. She and Kane went to him and he pointed.

Upon the Soan's writing board, printed in block letters, were the words: ANYTHING WAS PREFERABLE TO THIS.

They exchanged a look of horror.

"He knew he was *iao*," breathed Kane, "he knew, and preferred such an end."

"I'm not certain," said Aiea sadly, "but either answer was an escape. The last Connoisseur..."

The words hung in the air like a sword poised to strike. No one moved. Finally, A'o lay down his blade.

"This is the last life I shall take," he said. "Do as you will with me, my Connoisseur."

Aiea's bright eyes filled with tears.

"Take up your blade, A'o," she said, thinking of the promise she had made to Irya, "and I tell you this now. Life is no longer ours to take. So much has been wasted, in war and in arrogance. Today the traditions are broken."

Kane stared at her, but she held his gaze. She opened the door and walked out into the frozen air as they followed her to where the King of Soa and his retinue were waiting.

The old king accompanied them to the docks. As Aiea was about to board, she grasped the king's hand warmly.

"I am sorry, Your Highness," she said. He bowed deeply, though she thought she saw the glint of tears in the old king's eyes.

Strangely empty, Aiea stood on the deck of the ship, the cold wind stinging her eyes, as she and the cargo of *kact* were carried on silent seas to faraway isles.

Kalu

The slight wind ruffled the cobalt surface of the sea. The palm trees rustled slightly, sharing secrets. Kalu closed his eyes against the breeze and was content.

He walked along the beach to an outcropping of rocks in the shallows, careful not to let his shadow touch the water. The true religion of his island was fish…and fishing. Although the seas were empty, the people of Soka were the last able to coax the fish away from the Sea King. This talent brought great interest from those around the world who could afford it.

Kalu had once known nothing of the fish's value to the rest of the world. He lived on the island of Soka, also called the Forgotten Lands by most of Amala, an isolated fishing society in the south. He longed to one day visit Soa, the land of snow and silence, to try his hand at catching *kact*. He firmly believed in his tribe's fishing superstitions and thought if there could be communication between his island and Soa, he could help increase their catch tenfold. However, the chieftains would start with horror if they discovered one of their own knew anything of the rest of Amala. They did participate in some trade, conducted with rudimentary signs, because the only people allowed to communicate with outsiders had to submit to having their tongues cut out in order to prevent them from telling others about the outside world and so destroy their ancient customs.

Trade was the reason Kalu knew of other lands, for one day he had met a Thlai sailor fishing near this very beach.

Kalu tied his line to his pole, biting off the remainder. He threaded bait onto the hook as he thought of the places the Thlai sailor had told him about. He remembered the day they had met.

Kalu had been surprised to find anyone at the beach – this place was his secret, these particular fishing grounds his own. He was about to challenge the usurper to a fight but stopped short when he saw the man he proposed to duel.

He certainly was not from the island. Kalu had never seen anything like him in his life. Short, rotund, a face bristling with whiskers that were going grey, merry eyes and red cheeks.

He had crept cautiously up to the man, who startled him by turning and giving him a cheery wave.

"What are you?" Kalu asked, clutching his fishing rod tightly.

"A man, like yourself," said the strange hairy creature, startling him by speaking in Kalu's own tongue instead of the common language of Amala, which Kalu himself had never needed to learn.

"No," replied Kalu, cautious, "a man does not have strange…grasses… growing from his face, nor a body like that of a woman with child."

The creature guffawed into its beard.

"Ain't you a smart one," said the creature. "I'd have had ye on the ground with yer eye blacked for sayin' so back home, but ye meant no harm in it, I'm sure. Asides, ye're right: I am a fat old dog, I am."

He laughed again. Kalu stared at him, puzzled by his manner of speech.

"Name's Ryg. I'm from Thla," said the man, sticking out his hand. Kalu stared at it, bewildered.

"You got a name, son?" asked Ryg.

"Kalu," he had replied.

"Well, Kalu, I've made a right pig o' things. I didn't know anyone came out here. Yer chiefs won't bargain with me anymore if they find out I've spoken with a Tongued One. So…let's keep this a secret, eh?"

Kalu nodded.

"You like fishing too?" asked Ryg. "I'd have known, all your kind do, but then they don't let ye know there's a wide world out there so much. No edu-catin'!"

Ryg paused for a moment, considering the young man before him.

"Well, let's see what we can do about that."

That day, the world was opened up before Kalu, a world beyond fish and palms, superstition and sacrifice. As the Thlai sailor spoke, Kalu saw the world stretched before him in a wild panoply of colour. He saw Soa, dead branches glistening with clear white ice, a land of white snow and silence, men of ice-blue eyes and soft white fur. He saw the Barrens, the proud, powerful women, their skin red-tinted, giants to most, and their strange small winged men, their mysterious spices, their tents, and their gold. An endless flat landscape of sand like a beach that went on forever, and their odd barking language.

He saw Snt, land of eternal change, all seasons whenever one desired, their dark laboratories with phials and glasses brimming with bubbling secrets. The new magic – science – and their language of only consonants and numbers, zeros and ones, strange grid-like patterns that looked like incantations but were keys to the world and how it worked. Their black skin, their serious faces, their dismissal of anything magical or superstitious as passé.

Quiet, lonely Cloda, with its elusive folk, the thick green of deciduous trees and rivers winding secretly through their forests. The land of Chaak, of many lanterns, where all spoke only in whispers, and even then in riddle or rhyme. The stately beauty of the lanterns floating on the peaceful rivers between their well-ordered paper houses. There, organisation was its own kind of magic.

And Loka'i! Glittering, glamorous Loka'i, with food and drink and men like no other place on earth. Kalu's mouth watered at the tales of the bountiful feasts and the excitement of being at the world's centre. He learned of the terrifying Wyltai and their dark ships with the unicorn bowsprits taken from monsters of the deep, of Thla's hardy seafaringfolk. Hois, the half-fish people, the most dangerous port of call. Strange Ona, the island of women and war. The images made him dizzy.

They spent the day talking, but Kalu felt he had nothing to offer and was ashamed at his meagre knowledge and rude upbringing. When he mentioned this, Ryg laughed into his beard again.

"On Thla, men can look as ye do, or as I do, or can be taller, shorter, fatter, or thinner than either of us. It ain't yer fault ye didn't know, Kalu. It ain't. They keep ye like this to preserve the old ways, and that's necessary too. Like the way you fish – we haven't fished that way for centuries."

Kalu hung his head, his face flushed, feeling outdated and foolish.

"Naw, don't take it like that, lad! What I'm saying is, you have secrets we'd all like to get our hands on. You're the only folk that can catch ocean fish anymore. *Kact* is all we have. The Sea King can't control 'em because they're freshwater. Nobody knows how you do it. You have any idea the price your ocean-fish fetch?"

Kalu shook his head.

"Well, no use tellin' ye, I s'pose, as it'd make as little sense to ye as it would to a fish. Let's just say your chieftains ought to be bowing to you. It's you fishermen keep this place alive, up 'n' runnin', as it were."

Kalu stared at him. It was too much to comprehend all at once. He gleaned some important information from what Ryg was saying though: there was something he could offer Ryg after everything he had been given.

"I could teach you to fish," Kalu said shyly.

Ryg beamed.

"Now, wouldn't that be somethin'," he said.

So that day and many days to follow, Kalu taught Ryg everything he knew. Eventually Ryg had to leave, but Kalu had changed. He had far-sight now, and the interests of his island no longer held his attention. The women left him alone though before Ryg's appearance he had been considered the best catch in his village. The medicine men visited him, giving him various kinds of drink and food in hope of a cure, but nothing seemed to change him. He knew he could tell no one about Ryg or he would surely die. He longed to leave on Ryg's old ship and see the exotic ports of call that now swam past him in his dreams.

When Ryg returned, he brought *kact* with him. Kalu was overjoyed that he now would have knowledge, real knowledge, of the world beyond the beaches and thatched huts. He was amazed…*kact* tasted better than any kind of ocean-fish he had caught. He begged Ryg to take him along when he left, but the old sailor refused. He said he could not lose the trade he had gained, or the trust of Kalu's chieftains. Kalu was left behind in a home that no longer interested him among people who would never understand.

Ryg

Thla, the Land of Phantom Light, was a cold island. Most sailors and sea-captains hailed from it. Thla was more than a port city; seafaring was a way of life across the island. The entire population was dedicated to ships and sailing. Contrary to popular belief, Thla did have a summer, but it was often difficult to tell, as it was foggy and raining when it was not snowing. Though the land was green for most of the year, the air remained chilled and misty. Everyone lived a harsh life on the sea. Their hearts were on the ocean, and Thlai children ran free, raised and fed by whatever part of the community was in port. For any Thlai child, the desire to stay home and have a family was rare, making them outcasts among their people. Most children were the result of some dalliance either in port or away. Regardless of their background, the children were all hard-looking and rough-faced because of their upbringing and harsh lives on the water.

The Thlai were fantastic fighters and drinkers, but they had no army or navy, preferring instead to use their ships for commerce and travel. They were expert shipwrights. The Thlai were fair of skin for the most part, but any beauty they had was generally erased by years of hard living and drinking. There were pubs for children on Thla, to introduce them to the culture they had to embrace if they wished to survive. Phantom lights of many colours hung in the night sky. All the ships of Loka'i were Thlai-built; what beauty they lacked in their people, they made up for in shipbuilding. Their greatest commodity was their alcohol, both in production and purchase, but no one outside of Thla would drink it because it was the equivalent of drinking lamp oil.

The Thlai lived in leaning, weathered clapboard houses. All the beaches were pebble, the sky low and uniformly grey. The sunlight was weak but welcome when it chanced to appear. Their beliefs were rich and varied, more in various fairies and ghosts than any specific god. The haunted mist was the closest they came to belief in an all-powerful being, for the mist was said to take the lives of the dishonourable.

Ryg's ship made its way to Lami, nicknamed the Barrens, in good time, on fair seas. The old man had always appreciated the place. With its loose laws and danger, it was what Thla might be like if it had been a desert. Rumours and legends started here, if the storytelling going on throughout the Market on any given day could be believed. Arguments often descended into violence. Anyone looking for a fight could easily find it in the Barrens. Most who tried tended to find themselves at the wrong end of a long knife.

The women of Lami were red in colour, like cherry wood, with white braids of hair. The women were large and muscular and their men were small, pale white, and winged. Nothing grew in the Barrens save a few cacti, which provided life-giving sustenance as well as nightmares, depending on the dosage. The architecture of Lami was famous. Their open floor plans and stonemasonry were beautiful, and Loka'i's pleasure palace was based on Lamian design. The Lami were great dancers and played a tinny kind of music. Most of their songs were laments and warnings about romantic involvement. It was said that it was impossible for a Lamian to fall in love.

Their entire economy was based on the black market trade, without which they would not survive.

Ryg walked through the marketplace of silks and spices. He loved the smell of ginger and curry, of peppers and perfumes, of food sizzling on the grills and exhaling plumes of smoke. Ryg's opinion was that if Loka'i could bottle the scent of the Lami market as a cologne, it would be one of their greatest acquisitions. He came to a stall watched over by one of the tiny, fairylike men.

"Boss is out," the man said, loading the word with derision. "She'll be back soon. Hello, Ryg, how've you been?"

"Good as good's gonna get," Ryg said, "and yerself?"

"Likewise, my man," the man replied. "I have this new assortment of spices."

Ryg looked at the selection on display, picking up one of the small jars and sniffing it. He made a noise of disgust.

"Euh, does anyone use this anymore?" he asked, "it smells of rotted treacle."

"The Chaakai use it in their cheeses," said the man.

"I doubt those cheeses have ever seen Loka'i," Ryg muttered.

"Certainly not," the man said, "but to each his own."

"I won't do trade in deathspice either," Ryg said. "Why do you have that?

98

Isn't it illegal?"

"Very," the man said, "but you find me anyone who'll stop us selling it. It's quite exhilarating in small doses, I hear."

"Still leads to death," said Ryg.

"So does living," the man retorted. "Anyway, you sure? Deathspice fetches a good price, especially if you can get those primates down south hooked on it."

Ryg stared at him, thinking of Kalu and whether to argue against the man's prejudice, then shook his head.

"Somehow I get the impression that you and integrity don't get along," Ryg said.

"Integrity don't pay the bills," the man said.

A tall, handsome woman approached the booth.

"Here's your tea," she said, setting down a tiny cup in front of the man. Upon seeing the sailor, she cried out in surprise.

"Ryg! Good to see you again. How are you?"

"Fine's fine, Elka," he said, "yerself?"

"Tolerably well," said Elka. "What can we interest you in today?"

"Well, I'm thinking of whitespice, ginger, allspice, and saffron. The traditionals also, just for myself."

"Traditional packets have curry, cumin, black pepper, and salt. Cayenne powder's extra if you want that too."

"Certainly," he said. "I'll take all of it."

She packed everything in a bag with admirable speed and Ryg handed over payment.

"Good doing business with you, Ryg," she said.

"Always nice to see you too. Thanks," said Ryg, who disappeared into the crowd.

"He's nice," the small man said to Elka. "Think he knows we gouge him?"

"Sure he does," Elka replied, "but a good business relationship's worth a lot more to him than fighting over it, and if overcharging's the worst we do to him, he can't complain too much. Besides, where else would he go? You can't really trust anyone around here."

The man sagely nodded at this. It was a universal truth.

The only island that could outdo Loka'i in gourmet food was the island of Naia.

In fact, Naia could have been the cultural capital itself, but its decided lack of sunlight on one side and assurance of grisly death on the other, along with its unsavoury inhabitants, meant that there was almost no immigration. Nevertheless, it was a popular honeymoon spot, and many a romantic voyage culminated with a dinner among the Nightsiders of Naia. A delicious meal on the island of never-ending night, combined with the palpable danger provided by the Naienes themselves, made any holiday all the more exotic and thrilling.

Aiea sat with Kane and A'o at the famed restaurant Black, where the chefs and waiters made food they could no longer eat and their pale patrons pushed *foie gras* and chocolate truffles around with their forks without lifting any of the food to their purple lips.

"This is very, very strange," whispered Aiea.

"I think it's fascinating," said A'o.

"But what do they do this for? They haven't been able to eat food for centuries!" whispered Aiea.

"They spent every day of their human lives eating," said Kane, "it's hard to break the habit. Besides, they probably wished for the money to eat in a restaurant like this one when they were alive."

"Interesting," mused Aiea, "first their poverty prevents them from enjoying it, and now their Naiene nature. Still, they're unsettling. They sit with each other and don't speak. I can't see the appeal."

"Wait until you try the soup," said a voice, "and I think you'll know."

They turned to see a thin man, pale and smiling, hair as black as the white of his face, looking at them with expressive ebony eyes.

"Forgive me," he said. "I am Yr, your guide here on Naia Nightside. Charmed to make your acquaintance, Connoisseur."

The strange man bowed deeply. His beauty far surpassed that of any man in the harem, but it was beauty too perfect, lines too fine. An inhuman perfection that left the three of them completely cold.

"Good evening, Yr," said Aiea, as he sat down in a slow, dreamlike movement. She began to notice the other patrons of the restaurant moving in the same way.

Yr smiled slightly and nodded at her.

"You seem to find us curious," he said. "You're staring."

Aiea, embarrassed, shook her head.

"I apologise," she said. "I've just never been to Naia before and everyone seems to move in such a slow, precise way."

Yr seemed to laugh, hidden behind his hand, and Aiea thought she saw the gleam of horrendous teeth, but she could not be sure.

"Goodness," he said, "do we appear that way to you?"

"Yes," said Aiea, and suddenly saw that he was holding the fork she had thought was in her own hand.

"We move in what we call *dreamtime* for the majority," he said, "the chefs in the kitchen making the food would look to you like they were moving in a sort of slow dance. But every one of us can move as fast as you've just seen, or at the speed I am now communicating with you. We usually only live in dreamtime among our own, now that the feuds have ended."

"Feuds?" asked Kane, as the first course arrived and a slow-moving waiter lifted the lids from their plates.

"Oh, yes," said Yr. "I was a part of the movement that put an end them. For centuries, the Naienes were as vicious and dangerous as the Lightsiders. Then we realised that our lives, or lack thereof, could be lived in relative wealth if we changed our ways."

"By selling your blood, you mean," said A'o, and there was a catch in his voice that Aiea did not understand.

Yr nodded.

"Yes, and our food," he said. "People from all over Amala come to experience our cuisine."

"What about the Naienes that did not want to change?" asked Aiea.

"Well, of course, we had ways of convincing them," said Yr, with another flash of monstrous teeth masquerading as a soft smile.

There was a moment of silence after this.

"Aren't you going to eat your soup?" he asked brightly.

Aiea broke his gaze to focus on the creamy broth sitting in a silver bowl on the table. A delicious smell curled up in steam from the soup. She dipped a spoon into the bowl and brought it to her mouth. The taste of sweet pepper cream slid down her throat, a soft liquid heat. After she had swallowed, she opened her mouth again instantly.

"What sort of drug are you putting in this food?!" she demanded.

"No drugs," chuckled Yr, "this is simply the result of our love for the culinary arts. Our chefs have all the time in the world – they cook in dreamtime, which is a sort of rest for us. We are dead, after all; resting is our favourite thing to do. The best cooking is all about patience and timing."

"We have world-renowned chefs in Loka'i," said Aiea, "and I've grown up on the finest foods known to Amala. There's something you're not telling me."

Yr smiled, this time with all his teeth.

"Very well," he said, "I suppose even we cannot put anything past the Connoisseur. The secret ingredient is our blood."

Kane was fascinated; A'o looked slightly ill.

"Your blood?" cried Aiea, "will we become Naiene?!"

"Dear me, no," said Yr, "we choose who we turn – a practice we no longer partake in due to the peace treaty, of course. No, the blood is merely a flavouring agent, like rosemary or cumin."

Aiea caught A'o's expression as Yr spoke. He was clearly unhappy about something but he remained silent.

"Neither of those spices produce this sort of taste or feeling," said Aiea, "a feeling like you are truly alive and enjoying it, like you could live forever. It is amazing."

"Well, there are secrets that Loka'i has not yet discovered," said Yr, dabbing at his lips with a napkin.

"I am counting on it," said Aiea, "or I would be out of a job."

"Indeed," replied Yr, and the main course was set, steaming, on the table.

He turned to Aiea.

"Why do you not take men from Naia?" he asked, his slim white hand encircling his wine glass like fog, "we are by far the most beautiful."

"For the same reason Loka'i does not buy food from Snt," she replied, "It is modified taste and beauty, and therefore worthless."

Yr simply smiled, still a gentleman unchanging.

"Why do you continue to behave as though you are living?" asked Aiea.

Yr sighed and looked at a glass of wine he would never taste. "Wouldn't you miss it?" he asked. "Lucky are those who are born this way."

Aiea stared at him. He removed the white cloth napkin from his lap and placed it atop the black latticework coffee table.

"If you will excuse me," he said. "I must find myself some dinner."

Aiea bobbed her head at him and gazed at his full wine glass as he sauntered away.

Aiea also had to visit the Lightsiders as a part of her training.

They were the opposite of the Nightsiders on Naia. Lightsiders on Naia lived only three days. They had wings like birds and mouths filled with jagged teeth. The dark would kill them as swiftly as the light would kill the Nightsiders.

Aiea walked from the darkness into the bright daylight, as if she had walked outdoors from underneath a canopy. The glaring sunlight hurt her eyes.

A'o and Kane looked up to see the winged men circling above, casting shadows on the ground.

"Be careful here, Aiea," Kane advised, "the Lightsiders are not as refined as the others we have met."

With a mighty beating of wings, one of the men landed heavily on the ground in front of them. He shook his feathers out and folded them against his back, settling like a bird. He looked up at Aiea, cooing, his head turning this way and that, watching her.

"What are they, Kane?" she whispered. She noticed he did not bother hiding his teeth, as Yr had.

"I am sitting right here, madam," said the thing, "do me the courtesy to address me directly."

Kane hid a smile and A'o looked at him, abashed.

"I apologise, sir," said Aiea, "I thought you were..."

"An animal?" he asked, and she nodded. His beatific smile seemed out of place.

"It's understandable. After all, your kind thinks us barbaric," he said, "but our nature is our nature, don't you think?"

Aiea nodded, unsure what he meant.

"Oh, forgive me, Connoisseur," he said, "my name is Dr. Eloyian. Charmed, I'm sure."

"Doctor?" A'o spoke, "but you only live for three days! Oh, I'm sorry – "

"Quite all right, my lad," said Dr. Eloyian. "Also understandable. Makes one learn as much as possible as quickly as possible, eh? I was a young man yesterday. I am elderly today, I shall die this night. When birth and death come so closely together, one wishes to focus all of one's energy on making a mark, as it were – learning what one can while one can. I believe those with longer lives phrase it as: what would you do with your life if you knew you were dying?"

"Are all of you like this?" asked Aiea.

"Mostly, yes. Of course, some fritter their youth away, only to have regrets later – or perhaps to have none. You see, three days for us is as short as it is for you – but infinitely more pressing."

While he spoke, he was aging before their very eyes. New wrinkles had appeared and his hair had begun to grey.

"Please, don't waste your life speaking to us," said A'o.

"This is no waste," said Dr. Eloyian, "this is fieldwork. Research. I did my dissertation on the Connoisseur of Loka'i. Welcome to the Lightside of Naia."

With that, he took to wing and vanished, leaving the three of them staring at each other, confused.

"Where did he go?" asked A'o.

"I think I know," said Kane.

"Well?" asked Aiea.

"The Lightsiders of Naia depend on foolhardy travellers, attracted by the beautiful sunny beaches," said Kane. "That is their food source."

"They eat visitors?" asked Aiea. Kane nodded gravely.

"That's horrible," said A'o.

"Just be happy we are who we are, and he has decided against eating *us*," said Kane. "Doctor or not, he won't care if he gets hungry enough. They enjoy appearing as refined as the Nightsiders, but they are not."

"I just can't imagine—" Aiea began.

"And that's why it works so well," said Kane. "These people are predators. Never forget that."

"But they drink their visitors' blood, like the Nightsiders do?" asked Aʾo.

"No," said Kane, "They eat them, flesh and bone both. The Nightsiders would probably have destroyed their race for being gratuitous – lacking in style – long ago, if it weren't for the border."

Dr. Eloyian came winging back then and landed in front of them. He was chewing on a bone and blood streaked his chest. He did not appear to notice this, or the nauseated looks of his newfound companions.

"As I was saying back when we first met, it is such a pleasure to meet you, Aiea," he said, "I am likewise flattered to meet your friends. I've read of you since I was a small boy."

"Read of us in what?" whispered Aʾo, but Kane shushed him.

"The Lightsiders are a noble race," he informed them, "a swashbuckling race! We fend off the mermen and Wyltai, dying in the arms of our women. Rather romantic, really."

Aiea shot a quizzical look at Aʾo, and her retainer nodded in agreement. The Lightsiders truly were a noble race and other cultures owed them as much as they owed the warriors of Ona. Their short lifespans made them live to the fullest.

"I once loved a woman, a Longlife woman," Dr. Eloyian said. "Always a sad fate. They don't age and die as we do. I believe she's nineteen years old, and as you can see, I am now elderly."

"Where are your women?" asked Aiea.

He sighed. His hair was white now.

"An unfortunate accident," he said, "our society has no need for women."

"How do you create more…of you?" asked Aʾo.

"Same way as the Nightsiders," said Dr Eloyian.

"Nightsiders don't bite anymore," protested Aiea.

"Is that what they told you?" he murmured. "Interesting. But no, Lightsiders are birthed from the remainder of our meals."

"So you were once…human?" asked Kane.

"No. Not as Nightsiders were, in any case. We are created as new beings from the leftovers of our meals."

"Yet there are female victims," said Kane, "so where are they? And there are female Nightsiders too."

"A mystery for the ages," said the old man and winked. "Now as I've been so obliging with information, would you mind supplying me with some? I simply must finish my book on you before it is too late."

Aiea started.

"Oh, I'm so sorry!" she cried, "how very selfish of us. Of course, please – ask anything."

Dr. Eloyian gave an ingratiating smile. His sharp teeth shone in the sunlight.

"We are gifted at death with a last request," said Dr. Eloyian, "to eat a person we highly respect. Connoisseur, I would be honoured."

Aiea blanched, backing toward the curtain of darkness dividing the island.

"Or one of your retainers!" offered the doctor, advancing on them. "Please, it is the only way I can learn!"

Other Lightsiders were circling low in the sky.

"I understand the importance of your work, and could spare you," he was saying, "but either of them would also be a satisfactory last meal."

The other Lightsiders were landing now, with low thumps as they hit the ground. They bared their long, sharp teeth. Aiea and her men backed away, until they stood against the curtain of night.

Suddenly a multitude of pale arms reached from the darkness, smoke rising from skin, and pulled the three of them away from the daylight. The Lightsiders shrieked in dismay and frustration. Aiea saw Dr. Eloyian's wizened old face crumple and tears fall from his eyes. He said, "Now I shall never know," his final dream unrealised. He expired, turning to dust upon the ground as the other Lightsiders hurled insults and railed against the darkness.

Yr looked at Aiea with an accusatory gaze.

"You should not have ventured there," he said, and the group of Naienes that had saved them nodded, "they are not as respectful as we are. The watchfires of your people once kept them at bay, during wartime. How quickly we forget."

"One of them insinuated that you still bite people," said Kane. A few of them looked at the ground. A'o shuddered.

Yr sighed.

"Ah, well, for some reason there are always willing victims," said Yr, "those hungering after the real experience, as it were. Tourists, mostly. I give you my word of honour that we are respectful, and those that wish to be turned are the only ones we take."

"You call that respect?" asked A'o, "I lost a good friend to one of you once. He should not have been taken, but he was. Perhaps you are refined, but there must be others who are not."

"There will always be rogues," said Yr, "in every society. These we hunt down and imprison or kill, depending upon the severity of the offence."

"And you are *certain* that those you turn are willing?" asked Aiea.

"Of course," said Yr, "there are enough of them to go around, after all. There are sensation-seekers, which you of all people should understand. Yet again, there are those who simply fear old age or death. It seems they would rather spend an eternity in darkness than face that."

"I don't see why," said Kane, who loved the sun.

"Come forth, Myta," said Yr.

A beautiful woman with long, curling hair stepped forward with a shy smile.

"I had a wasting disease neither magic nor science would cure," she said. "I preferred this to years of suffering agony. It was a difficult choice, but one I do not regret in the slightest."

"Naia offers a quick death in the sunlight or eternal life in death in the darkness," said Yr, "a land of opposites that are, indeed, the same. For nothing ever goes away. We are always reborn."

Aiea was silent, thinking of the life and death she'd seen, and the promise she and Irya had made.

"You yourselves are bringers of death," said a voice in the crowd, "and so you must at least understand the taking and giving of it."

Iana walked out of the crowd. A'o's heart faltered as his former lover approached him. His old friend was beautiful – more beautiful than A'o by far – and colder.

"Iana," said A'o, his voice breaking. "I see you have attained your goal."

Iana smiled sadly.

"I see you have attained yours as well," he said, "you were right, for whatever that may be worth. However, once the choice is made, there is no way back."

Aiea looked at the two of them, surprised.

"You know this Naiene, A'o?"

"He's from Chaak," said A'o, "we attended the Academy together. One of the Naienes turned him prior to our first voyage to Loka'i."

A'o touched his scar, and Aiea understood.

"This is Iana," she said, and A'o nodded.

"He was not turned," said Yr, "it was I who bit him, as a warning. His jealousy caused him to complete the task by drinking Naiene blood. It was a grievous mistake, and one I will not repeat."

A'o felt the old guilt resurface, his only regret. There was silence as he looked for emotion in his old friend, but could not discover any. A'o reached out, but Iana was empty – a beautiful, empty shell.

"Enough philosophy," said Yr, "it positively bores me. Now, Aiea, we are having a ball this evening, to which you are invited. Will you accompany us?"

Aiea thought for a moment about the wisdom of this. Having escaped death once she did not wish to willingly put herself in danger again.

"We accept," said A'o, and when he saw the look Aiea gave him, said, "I'm sorry, Aiea, but we are here to learn."

He walked forward and took Iana's arm. His old friend responded with a faded smile.

"Lead the way," Aiea said, resigned.

Chandeliers lit the high golden ceilings. The brightness of the ballroom surprised them. The people were quiet, reserved, refined, drinking blood from crystal goblets. Iana disengaged himself from A'o's arm and glided in the direction of the dance floor. A'o looked after him, a bit hurt and confused.

"Worry not, young man. He is younger than I am, and still becoming accustomed to the night. It will be some time before his former personality returns," Yr said. "These festivities remind us of the daylight we no longer experience, and in my case, a daylight I no longer remember, old as I am. Welcome."

The Naienes danced in a slow and refined manner for a society of killers, and Aiea saw that there were, in fact, living people other than herself and her retainers present. They seemed to be enjoying themselves.

Suddenly she recalled the reason she was there.

"I cannot see what treasures we might find among these people," Aiea murmured to Aʻo.

"Aside from eternal life?" he asked.

"Yes, of course," she said, "you seem altogether too interested in this, Aʻo."

He flashed her a brilliant smile, which worried her after his clear unease from earlier in the day.

"I am starting to wonder whether Iana was entirely wrong in his choice. My life has been spent in the pursuit and cultivation of beauty, a beauty that can only last a few decades at the most," he said. "Think of it, Aiea! A night gallery of men for Lokaʻi. Beautiful trophies in the tropical moonlight, most exotic! We've never had one before."

"Are you offering yourself for that purpose?" she murmured.

"Why not?" he asked, "it would be a great draw. Besides, the men are invulnerable to attack; they could serve as guardians of the harem. Iana might be a good choice, as he does have Academy training. Plus – eternal beauty and eternal youth. I doubt anyone would turn that down."

"I will think about it," said Aiea, somewhat swayed, "but not you. You are my retainer, and you would be useless to me if you were only available at night."

Aʻo sighed as Kane came over with glasses filled with red liquid.

"Must we always talk about work?" Kane asked. "This is a party. Let's have some fun."

Aiea took a glass and eyed it suspiciously. She decided it was merely wine, not blood, so she took a sip and tried to relax.

"Thank you for coming," Yr was saying, bowing people out of the door into the night. "It was a pleasure."

As Aiea and her retainers left, they felt the chill wind of the eternal night, where only hemlock and birch grew with night-blooming ivy. The absence of sunlight was taking its toll. They were all introspective and quiet as they made their way to their room.

The Naienes' obsession with making their surroundings approximate daylight apparently did not extend to their living quarters. Everything was black, white, or silver. Aiea supposed that colour was of little interest to them after a while.

She lay in her bed, watching A'o stare out the window at the wide, white moon, and she wondered if he was right about bringing a Naiene into the fold. She knew he missed Iana terribly, and his sudden conversion to his friend's way of thinking was easily explained; if Iana could not become mortal again, A'o could join him in another way. However, while the Naienes were beautiful, their cold emptiness did not suit the harem of Loka'i. Her conviction had been shaken by what A'o had said about guardians. She thought of the mer-people, and the isolation of Loka'i in a time of war. It was likely that one of the Naienes had known war – or even remembered the Ulu'u as they once had been.

She fell asleep then, and did not dream.

"Will you join the harem?" asked Aiea.

Yr's back was to her as he cooked on the stove. The morning was as dark as the night before it.

"Are you going to judge me?" asked Yr, not turning around. "I don't think I will be so easily killed as your other marks, should I be judged *iao*, my friend."

The sound of bacon sizzling on the pan filled the silence.

"No," said Aiea.

Yr did turn around at this, and regarded her with a new expression, a combination of respect and hope.

"You are different," he said. "Sometimes tradition should be left in the past."

She stood her ground.

"Will you come with us?" she asked. "I need someone who remembers war."

Yr stared at her.

"And how do you know that I do?" he asked.

She stepped closer to him.

"You're Ulu'u, aren't you?" she asked. "You're from the original tribe."

"How did you know that?" he persisted.

"You said that you were so old you couldn't remember the daylight," said Aiea, "but you remember the fires, and the war."

Yr, frozen, nodded slowly.

"Yes," he said. "I am from Loka'i, before the island changed."

He looked at her, and through her, far away.

"I remember."

Aiea put a hand on his arm.

"Then come with us," she said. "Come home."

They boarded the ship the following morning, Aiea saying goodbye to Yr as he went down into the hold and away from the daylight that would fast be approaching. Many of the Naienes had come to see them off or, possibly, to say farewell to Yr in their own way. The waves crashed against the side of the ship, foaming white in the darkness. The sailors were uneasy; they were eager to get underway and out of the endless night.

Aiea stood on deck and saw that some of the Naienes stood in the surf. They watched, pale and disinterested, their ghost faces slanted sideways and slack-jawed, like unhinged doors to empty rooms. She could not help the shudder that passed through her frame as she watched them; once human, their humanity lost.

As the land faded from view and the darkness merged slowly into the sunlight of the coming dawn, Aiea breathed a sigh of relief and welcomed the light.

Emydd

The voyage to Ona took several days.

Generally this was an arduous journey, but the Connoisseur and her retainers had every luxury the ship was able to provide. It amused the rough Thlai captain to no end. Ryg had seen terrible storms, been shipwrecked twice, and now he had to play handmaiden to the most spoiled people he had ever met. The Thlai took a dim view of Loka'i and its harem, possibly because no Thlai man would ever be considered beautiful enough to qualify. They were a sturdy, hardy folk, but their loves and talents did not exist beyond the world of sea travel. Still, for a stalwart heart and a loyal soul, one need look no further than the Thlai. They would make the perfect life-long mate.

Aiea was nearly dying of boredom when Ona finally appeared through a window on the ship, a grim and rocky coastline in the low silver-grey of the clouds. She and her men began the painstaking process of dressing in their ceremonial garb, which took more than an hour. By the time they were finished, the other passengers had already disembarked onto the quay.

Aiea stepped off the ship onto the island. She was weary from her journey and she looked forward to a bath and bed, rough though the accommodations on Ona were. Ona was a war-torn nation, and the rooms available were practical and austere.

Aiea's retainers followed a few paces behind her as she walked the dusty streets. Cold as Ona's winters were said to be, they had arrived in the midst of a summer drought and the land was a barren desert.

Aiea saw him as she disembarked, the long blade of a market woman held over his head. She paid no attention at first; a Connoisseur does not interfere with the customs of foreign lands. Then, in a brilliant flash, his eyes and face were lit by the reflection of the blade. He was breathtaking; none in the harem might have called themselves his equal. She had to stop the woman.

Or perhaps she was already hearing the strains of the Song, even then. Stressful situations caused the Song to hum and vibrate, a deep and echoing chord.

He had seen her first, Aiea would later discover. He had seen her step off the ship and thought her a queen.

"Hold!" Aiea cried to the market woman, who grinned and dropped the blade. The dark young man lying in the dust looked up at both of them.

"How much for him?" Aiea asked. She was prepared to pay anything. Such a jewel could not be lost.

The market woman spat into the dust.

"I'll pay *you* to take him off my hands," said the woman, shaking her head. "He is not my slave; he is a stranger here. Perhaps he is a runaway. Just now, he was stealing from me."

The woman rubbed her chin.

"However," she said, considering, "he is obviously of value to you. Maybe he is your slave. But you are no Onai. So you are a collector. The Connoisseur, if I'm not mistaken. He is fair of face, were I that way inclined. The price of his life is a kiss."

Aiea thought this over. The market woman guffawed and shook her head again. To deny her was to slight the culture of Ona and diplomacy was crucial in Aiea's situation. The young man looked on, incredulous.

In its way, it was the least expensive trade she ever accepted. Aiea leaned over and pecked the woman's cheek.

The Connoisseur turned to the young man, holding out her hand. He gazed up at his saviour and placed his hand in hers as the market woman spluttered angrily.

Aiea turned to her.

"You did not specify the kind of kiss," the Connoisseur said, "the deal is done. I expect you to honour the bargain or you will bring shame to Ona."

The market woman's face had turned a bright, angry red, but she did not stand in the way.

"Come, young man," Aiea said, "and walk with me."

Kane and A'o followed after making sure the market woman would not pursue them. They walked the pathways of the city.

"Thank you," murmured the young man, in a deep, quiet voice.

"I would not be so hasty in your gratitude," the Connoisseur said, "for you are now to be tested for the harem of Loka'i."

His befuddled look amazed Aiea.

"Have you never heard of the Ulu'u? Joy in the Battle? Sumptuous Loka'i?"

His blank look was unbelievable. He had never heard of the most famous island in Amala.

"Do you know what I am?" Aiea then asked, indicating her mode of dress, "or why the market woman knew to try and sell you to me?"

Again, a confused shake of the head. The beads and feathers in his hair moved and clacked together.

"Your Majesty," he began, looking at the ground, "I am sorry I have never heard of your land. I am certain it is beautiful."

Aiea laughed. Kane and A'o hid smiles.

"You think me royalty?" she asked. The young man nodded.

"Have you a name?" asked A'o.

"Emydd," he said. "In my language, it means *holy*."

A'o and Aiea exchanged glances. He shook his head slightly. He had never heard a name like it before either, not in any of the history he had studied.

"Where do you come from, and how came you here?" asked Kane.

"I come from nowhere," he said. "My people are the Wyltai, the wanderers of the world."

Now Kane looked troubled, for the Wyltai were greatly feared.

"In my youth, my tribe was slaughtered. Only a few of us escaped, I among them. That was many years ago. I have wandered alone ever since. I have never been to Ona before."

Kane touched Aiea's arm.

"The tests should begin, Connoisseur," he said.

They were in a side street; there was some time before their meeting with the High Councilwoman. Aiea led them into a small cafe, where several women were eating, drinking, and smoking Onai firespice. She sat Emydd down before her and motioned to A'o and Kane to stand at her side.

"I am the Connoisseur. It is my duty to find young men worthy of my tribe, the famed Ulu'u of Loka'i. These are my retainers. Kane, who tests the mathematics and sciences, and A'o, who tests the arts and history. They are both prodigies and worthy of their positions."

Kane and A'o elaborately bowed to each other, to Emydd, and to Aiea.

Emydd looked on, amused by the ceremony.

A'o began. He bowed deeply again.

"Honourable Emydd, we begin simply."

Emydd shifted in his seat, looking uncomfortable.

The questions began. Then he was asked to draw. Although he laboured, he was unable to create anything satisfactory. He danced well, but nothing incredible. He wrote, and again, nothing much. Then A'o asked him to sing.

"No," he said. He was resolute.

A'o raised an eyebrow.

"Honourable Emydd, I know the tests are exhausting, but we must know. You cannot join the harem of the Ulu'u if you have no talents."

He merely shook his head and would not budge.

"Move aside, brother," said Kane. "I will test him; perhaps he is brilliant in other ways."

Kane sat in A'o's seat.

"What is the Anadi Theorem?"

Blank look. Kane shot him an incredulous glance.

"What elements make up the sea?" Kane tried again.

Emydd shook his head. He did not know.

"Wendon's Rule? The root of the world? The Tahn Principle?"

Kane threw his hands up in despair.

"I am willing to judge him *iao*, Connoisseur," said A'o.

"What does this mean?" asked Emydd.

Aiea gave him a sorrowful look. She was disappointed. His beauty had shown such promise, and to lose him…the world had not seen his like. However, it had happened before: a handsome face with nothing behind it.

"*Iao* means 'beauty-without-mind'," Aiea explained.

Insulted, Emydd crossed his arms and glared at A'o.

The Connoisseur sighed.

"Kane, are you prepared to pronounce this candidate *iao*?" she asked.

Kane stared at Emydd, then shook his head slowly.

"Not yet," he said. "There is something about him beyond beauty."

A'o was surprised and gave Kane a questioning look. This had not happened before. In their short time together, A'o and Kane were always in immediate agreement. A'o gestured that they would discuss the matter privately. This left Emydd alone with Aiea. He looked irritated and upset.

"Calm yourself," she told him, "they must decide."

"If I sing," he said suddenly, hesitant, "will I be in your harem, or the harem of the Ulu'u?"

"The harem is the property of the Ulu'u," Aiea told him, "but I am its sole caretaker."

"Then I will sing," he said, "but only for you."

"Why?" she asked.

"Because I would like to belong to you," he said, and smiled.

Charming. If the decision had been up to her, he may have succeeded in dodging *iao* with his charm alone. She found herself leaning toward him, almost unconsciously, losing herself in him, until she came to with a start. She felt, for the first time, a sincere desire for the candidate to have the requirements for the harem. Although the judgment of *iao* no longer meant death, Aiea did not want to lose this one.

"Why does it disturb you to sing, when you would do other things as requested?" Aiea asked.

"I do not like to be told what to do, Connoisseur," he said, "no matter what it is. However—"

He gazed out at the marketplace.

"—things *happen* when I sing."

She raised her eyebrow.

"My name is Aiea," she said, surprising herself, "Sing."

He nodded; he tried to begin a few times without success. He was nervous, agitated, upset...

and then he sang.

Later it would be said that the world had folded upon itself, stars fell from the sky as diamonds into brilliant bowls, that joy was laid bare from the heavens to the earth and all things were connected, and could feel the connection. The heart flowed and wandered like a ship at sea, undulating with the waves.

He stopped singing, and looked guilty as phantom chimes echoed in the still air. It must have been a full five minutes before Aiea's heart started to beat again; she could not speak. As she returned to herself, she realised that her cheeks were wet with tears.

"Is it enough?" he asked, concerned, thinking his talent perhaps less than that of the others in the harem.

Aiea grinned, and Kane and A'o came running.

"Who was singing?" cried Kane. "The Song! The Song of Life! He is the Lost One, Aiea!"

She stared at Emydd. His face was the first and only she would have called *exotic*. No other man looked as he did. His skin was an ashy colour, like charcoal, a dusky grey highlighting his features. His eyes were wide and a rich, deep brown, circled with black after the tradition of the Wylt. His hair was black, but with undertones of blue. He had full lips, a broad nose, and straight white teeth.

There were many words to describe both beauty and a handsome man. There were many more to describe the viewer's reaction upon seeing something intensely beautiful, whether human or in nature.

There were no words invented, yet, to describe Emydd, just as the Ulu'u had painted the pictures of the royal family without faces. There are simply things beyond art and poetry, just as the supernatural is still beyond science.

A'o knew this in his history, Kane felt this in his poetry, the truth of it sounded in Aiea's soul.

Then Emydd smiled, and she was lost.

Wold

Hois was a land highly suspected by other islands, because the people of Hois were the result of an ancient union between humans and merfolk. They did not have tails, but their skin was tinged green. They had gill slits on their necks and could breathe underwater. Drawn to the sea and its secrets, they made salt baths and waterfalls in the jungle of their island. The Hoisdean were comely enough; their eyes were huge and multicoloured, their noses small and well-shaped, their lips large and their faces well formed. They were slender and of medium height, the bodies of the men only defined by the edges of their skeletons, with a distinct lack of muscle. The women had long wild hair, like seaweed, and bodies to match their men.

The sun was low in the sky as the ship docked in Hois. Wold stepped off the gangplank with a deep sense of serenity. There was truly nothing like a Hoisdean sunset. Too bad the war kept visitors away. Too bad for the visitors, that was. The absence of tourists on his beloved island suited Wold just fine.

The sun was setting low over a calm sea. The masts of the large ships moored in front of the bar made an excellent counterpoint to the incredible colours spread out across the ocean.

Wold sat at the pub, sipping on his cold beer and enjoying the music. The warm breezes ruffled his hair and he sighed in contentment. The band was here every night, playing the same set, but everyone loved it. Things happened slowly on Hois, including musical composition. The entire population spent a great deal of time in and on the water, and Wold had never wanted to live anywhere else.

The spirit of the place was very laid-back; most people fished every day and felt no pressing need to do anything in particular. The island was hedonistic – everyone there was a social alcoholic and felt no shame about it. They could not remember what they had done from one day to the next, as the nights were spent in drunkenness, but then, no one cared. It was an easy life, and a strange one, full of colourful characters and amusing stories, when the Hoisdean were able to remember them. Loka'i considered itself paradise, but, in the eyes of the Hoisdean, it had nothing on Hois.

Wold sat up as a beautiful vessel moved into view. He stared at its perfect lines, the long black three-masted ship, and the way she moved like a dream.

He raised his drink and toasted the ship.

"Only a few more, and you'll be mine," he promised, and took a long draught. "Sure as there's sky on the water."

Another man sat down at his table, setting down a drink.

"Evening, Wold," he said.

"Evening, Ive," Wold replied.

"That her?" asked Ive.

"Sure is. The *Obsidian*."

"Ain't she a beaut."

They sat in silence, watching the *Obsidian* ply the water.

"You got something for me?" asked Ive, after a time.

"Sure do," said Wold, and passed him six vials filled with black liquid, wrapped in a large napkin. Ive took the vials and they disappeared into his pocket.

"Sort of immoral, ain't it?" asked Ive, after a moment.

"What's that?" asked Wold.

"This business," said Ive.

Wold laughed.

"You're talking about morality and you're Hoisdean?" Wold said.

"There's morality and there's morality," said Ive.

"Yes, well, I'm helping the war effort," said Wold.

"Which side?" asked Ive.

"Both sides," replied Wold, and they laughed.

Ive slid the napkin back to Wold, and Wold lifted the edge, counting the wrinkled bills inside by sight.

"This all in order?" asked Wold.

"Should be," Ive replied. "Would I try anything? You know where I live."

Wold grunted.

"That's true," he said, "and it's not as if you have anywhere to go."

"Aye," said Ive, finishing his beer. "Nowhere to run on an island. Well, I've got to go. Take care of yourself."

He stood to leave and Wold caught his arm.

"Twice more and I'm out of it," Wold said softly, "you understand?"

Ive sighed and looked out again at the ship. When the other man turned back to him, Wold had done the same disappearing act with the bills as Ive had with the vials.

"I've known since the start," said Ive, "you were only in it for the ship. The others may not be so forgiving."

Wold nodded, looking out to sea.

"That's my business," he said. "You have a good night now."

Ive looked at him for a moment, as if he wanted to say something more, and then nodded.

"You too," said Ive, and he walked away down the docks.

Wold sighed and stared at the *Obsidian* as the sky darkened and filled with stars. Out of the corner of his eye, he saw a beautiful Hoisdean woman looking at him. Her wide eyes and green-tinted skin were captivating, and she was sitting alone. He smiled at her and raised his beer, indicating the empty chair beside him. His smile widened when she stood up and began to make her way over to his table.

The next morning dawned bright and early, as most mornings did on Hois. Wold's head ached from overindulgence the night before, but he figured a good breakfast would set things straight again.

His overnight visitor had gone before he'd awoken. That was fine with him; it saved him an explanation of what he had to do today. Things were pretty laid back in Hois, but occasionally a young, inexperienced Hoisdean maid would get too attached, and Wold couldn't have that at this point in his life. As it was, he had only vague recollections of the night before, of smooth skin and silk. No matter, breakfast was the most important thing at the moment. A big, heavy meal would do him good.

After breakfast, Wold went out on his skiff, ostensibly to do some fishing. The sea was a clear blue window to the creatures below. The Hoisdean harvested sponge and coral, along with other immobile sea life that could not heed the Sea King's command to keep away from the land-dwellers. The Hoisdean primarily supplied the beauty industry of other islands with pumice stones, exfoliants, sponges, and other odds and ends. They did a rather brisk trade.

Wold slid his pole into the clear water, propelling his skiff into a secluded bay. When he arrived, he tapped a certain rhythm on the ocean floor.

A head surfaced in the water, so like his own, and so different. The same wide face, the greenish tint, but Wold and his kind looked far more human than the thing that addressed him now.

"You have come for more, I see," it said, hissing through needle teeth. It moved its tail in the water and approached the skiff like a lazy shark.

"Yes," said Wold, who was always nervous around merpeople, "but only a couple more times."

The thing grinned like a crowded pincushion.

"You sure about that?" it asked. "Not getting attached to the money?"

"No," said Wold, "I just want my boat."

"Not going to do you much good if we win the war, eh?" asked the merman.

Wold sighed in annoyance.

"Yes, I realise that," he said. "Here's your payment. Do you have it?"

Wold dropped the coins one by one into the sea. The merman put its face into the water for a long moment, counting. It surfaced with another unnerving grin.

"Well done," said the merman, and reached out a webbed hand to drop the vials into Wold's outstretched palm.

"Thank—" Wold began, but he was already alone in the bay. He sighed, and then hid the vials in a secret compartment in his cooler. He shook his head, and began to scan the water for sponge.

From the bright blue clear surface, the merman descended into the depths. The water gradually turned navy, then indigo, until utter darkness surrounded him. He swam alone through the blind, heavy silence.

Something began to glitter in the distance, cloudy at first, then the high seamount that was the kingdom of the merpeople rose in imperious and staggering splendour from the ocean floor far below.

An endless and imposing city carved from ancient coral long ago shimmered and glowed in the deep, dwarfing everything around it. The merpeople prided themselves on how modern their city was. The causeways were lit by luminescent fish, and shark sentries guarded the streets. It was a sprawling, gigantic undersea metropolis, and the merman himself couldn't help but feel intimidated every time he approached.

He entered the city by the east gate and proceeded toward the castle on the west side. The guards stood aside to let him pass, and he swam through the empty palace. For years, there had been few reasons for celebration, and the rooms reflected the austerity of wartime. So many merpeople had been lost, and like Ona, the undersea kingdom had not yet recovered.

As the merman, Yondu, entered the throne room, head bowed, he saw a mermaid enter at the same time. Good, he thought. I am not late. He breathed a sigh of relief.

"Yondu, Koyu," said the King. "What news do you bring me?"

The King was as imposing as the city he called his. He had long, blond hair in ringlet curls and clear blue eyes in a stern face. He looked only about thirty, but was much, much older. A retinue of guards stood near his throne, resolute and silent.

"All has been quiet in the south, as far as I have been able to see," said Yondu. His appearance was striking, his dark hair cropped close, and his face told a story in jagged scars. Yondu was a war veteran.

"They have become complacent," he said. "They have forgotten. All islands apart from Ona believe the war is over. It's almost mythology."

"Good," said the Sea King, "this indicates the value of patience. Koyu?"

"They continue to train their warriors in the north, as Yondu says," she said, "though what good they think that will do I have no idea. They can't go on the offensive, but their defence is strong."

"That is to be expected," he said. "Good work. You are dismissed."

Koyu left the palace and meandered down the streets, looking in shop windows. She was a career soldier, but hadn't seen much fighting yet; she was far younger than Yondu and the war was nearly mythology to her as well.

Koyu talked to a few of the people she passed by, and picked up some items from a nearby shop. She turned a few corners and then swam into an opening in a high wall of coral.

This was her home. Various types of seaweed bunched decoratively together grew in corners, and different outcrops of coral held a number of beautiful shells. She found what she was looking for in a pile of jewels and assorted treasures, and pulled out a book of sorts. She looked it over, her lips moving as she turned the pages. Then she smiled, hid the book again, and was gone with a flick of her purple tail.

Shen-Au-Schan

Ona was a harsh and unforgiving island.

The winters were bitter cold, the houses built to preserve the lives of the island's inhabitants over the ten months of extreme weather. Practicality was chosen over art or architectural beauty every time.

Today, Shen-au-Schan, the commander of the Onai army and navy, was training new recruits. Aiea was followed by A'o and Kane, while Emydd trailed behind them. Since Aiea had to wait in order to speak with the commander, they stood back to watch her in action.

"You are here because you are thought to be the best!" the commander shouted, "Today you will find out if it's true! Choose a sparring partner."

As the women paired off, the commander caught sight of Aiea. She flashed a brilliant and rakish smile at the Connoisseur, and Aiea saw that –in one glance– Shen had taken Aiea's full measure. The Connoisseur was unaccustomed to the sight of so many women. They intimidated her and, having mostly known only the company of men, she was unsure how to behave.

The commander made her way over. Tall, thin, and muscular, the woman wore her fatigues well. Her short, spiky blonde hair matched her brilliant blue eyes, set off by the silver earring of cascading diamonds she wore in her right ear. She had a baby face that did not seem to match her military bearing, and Aiea noted the wicked-looking dagger she wore at her hip.

"New Connoisseur, I take it?" she said, grinning. "Welcome to Ona. I am Shen-au-Schan, but you can call me Shen."

"I'm the Connoisseur," Aiea said nervously.

Shen laughed, indicating the women fighting.

"I am a Connoisseur myself, you might say," she said. "It's a tough job. So. You say you've found the king?"

Aiea could hear the scepticism in Shen's voice.

"Emydd," Aiea called, and the young man stepped out from behind A'o and Kane.

Shen took a step back. His beauty was, like a sunset or a stained-glass window, awe-inspiring.

Shen cleared her throat, as she realised she was staring.

"I think we'll need to see the High Councilwoman."

Aiea nodded, and Shen motioned for her to follow.

"Angry, you keep the girls in line," she shouted. A beautiful girl with a face like a child's doll and curly auburn hair nodded at her commander.

"Losers, stand down!" Angry shouted. "Winners, come forward."

The young woman grinned like a wolf.

High Councilwoman

The Citadel of Ona stood on the edge of a precipice overlooking the sea, waves crashing against the cliffs. Its design was ancient and did not match the delicate beauty of the palaces in the south. Aiea felt a chill go through her as she looked up at the darkened towers.

The Connoisseur entered into the cool dark of the castle as the shadows waned to sunset. A'o, Kane, and Emydd walked behind her, silent, into the cavernous emptiness of the throne room. The place did not encourage talking or laughter; it was sombre, a catacomb of royalty. In the echoing emptiness of the room, a robed figure awaited them. It was impossible to make out the features of High Councilwoman, the steward of Ona, as she had sacrificed her name and hid her face upon acceptance of the position. All that could be said about her was that she cut a tall, imposing figure in the silent throne room.

"Greeting, Connoisseur," said High Councilwoman, bowing. Aiea bowed more deeply in return, to show respect.

"Greeting, High Councilwoman," the Connoisseur replied. "May women court thee for forty years."

This compliment made her smile.

"Ah, I have missed the eloquence of the Connoisseur!" said High Councilwoman. "Have you come to make Ona your home?"

Aiea grinned.

"No, High Councilwoman, I prefer Loka'i," she said.

"Perhaps one day, one of you will come to your senses," smiled High Councilwoman. "I heard one of your new boys made a commotion in the market square today."

Emydd stood with his head bowed, blushing.

"This is Emydd, High Councilwoman," Aiea said. "I think he is the Lost One."

The High Councilwoman laughed, but became serious when she saw Aiea's expression.

"Are you certain?" she whispered.

"Quite," Aiea replied.

Emydd stared at the floor.

"Emydd," High Councilwoman said, "Let me see your face."

Emydd's eyes met hers, and her gasp was audible in the empty throne room. For many people, Emydd's beauty was startling. For High Councilwoman, it was different. She was meant to keep the throne for the royal family. Her entire life had been spent as the steward of Ona, and also of the entirety of Amala. She had spent the years of her childhood memorising the countless portraits of the royals, and knew every face, every crease and wrinkle, as well as her own reflection. She knew, the moment their eyes met, that Emydd would end her lonely rule.

But old habits die hard.

High Councilwoman shook her head.

"Ona will not be ruled by a man, no matter how handsome," she said.

A tall, lithe woman stepped from the shadows. A long silver earring of cascading diamond shapes glinted at her left ear. Shen gave High Councilwoman a stern look.

"With all due respect, High Councilwoman, none of us would be here were it not for men," she said. "We have equal part in creation. Is our goal not equality and righteousness?"

"He is the rightful king of us all," Aiea whispered. "The golden days of peace! Think of it!"

Kane's eyes flashed, but he said nothing.

"Yes, and how much war and suffering must we endure to place him on his throne?" hissed High Councilwoman. "The Sea King is responsible for the death of thousands, and our resources are already depleted. Who will be Emydd's guard?"

"We will," said Shen. "He is ours – and therefore he is our responsibility."

High Councilwoman looked out the window to the harbour below. She watched the waves with the trepidation of one who knew that war would come, once again, to her island.

She sighed.

"I will help," she said. "You have Ona's assistance. Emydd, I salute you as king…but I will not bow."

Emydd had been watching this exchange.

"Understood, High Councilwoman," Emydd smiled. "Those of Ona will never have to bow to me."

The massed army and navy of Ona stood on the castle grounds awaiting the day's announcements.

Shen walked to the edge of the balcony and saluted. The women of the military responded in kind.

"Today I have great tidings," said Shen. "The last of the Alyetans has returned."

There was a stunned silence, then whispers through the ranks.

"His name is Emydd," she said, and gestured.

Emydd walked forward from the shadows, into the light of the balcony. The women looked up at him, unimpressed. Apparently his handsome features did not work on everyone.

"I greet my people with respect," he said shyly. "I have only now discovered my royal heritage, so I understand the difficulty you all may have in believing it. I can hardly believe it myself."

"The royal family is a fairytale," one brave soldier shouted. "How do we know you are who you claim to be?"

Emydd glanced at Shen, who nodded.

"Be careful," she murmured, and he smiled.

As he sang, the soldiers only knew the great pride in battle, the loss of the fallen, the life only they could know, blood and death, loyalty and honour, the drums and the drinking and the silence of the empty battlefield.

Emydd finished singing and every soldier's face was streaked with tears. As one, they knelt before him, all the massed army, and cried as one voice:

"Your Majesty!"

Shen smiled, tears in her eyes, for the song had affected her too.

"They will serve you, Emydd," she said, "and willingly."

Emydd smiled back and blushed. He would no longer be alone. His heart was too full for him to speak.

The narrow warships of Ona could hold only ten at a time. Shen's best warriors accompanied them onto the sea. Strong and brave women, they were Shen's lieutenants as well as her lovers. Ona believed the best warriors were those that had the most reason to fight.

The water was calm and dark, the sky overcast. Shen stood against the gunwale of the small ship. Her women were at work trying to find a breath of wind in the stillness.

"The Sea King has weapons and abilities that none of us possess," she said. "Our seas are barren, for he calls back the fish, or calls forth the waves. We must be ever vigilant."

A bubbling sound came from the stern. Shen eyed the Connoisseur and lifted her spear. The army commander went to the side and looked over.

The moon eyes of a mermaid looked back. She was beautiful in her way, her body supple and her eyes shining with the secrets of the deep. Otherworldly and feminine beyond mortal understanding, her eyes pleaded with the warrior who looked down on the water.

Shen raised her weapon.

The mermaid lifted a languorous hand in protest.

Please, no, the words came to them, a whisper across the water.

"You are one of the Sea King's brood, are you not?" asked Shen.

No, replied the strange whispering, *I am merfolk…but not his child.*

"What right do you have to ask me to stay my hand?" asked Shen. "What mischief is this?"

None, replied the whisper, *I have come to help.*

"Help?" laughed Shen. "How can you help?"

Shen motioned that the other women should gather around her. They did so, spears at the ready.

You said you don't know how to fight the Sea King, said the whispering, the mermaid's moon eyes bright with tears, *but I do.*

"And why would you betray your people?" Shen asked.

The maid looked stricken to the heart.

I love one of your kind, said the whispers, miserable. *I would not have him perish.*

Shen stood up so suddenly she nearly upset the vessel. She exchanged glances with the other women. Merfolk and humans did not have relations with each other. It was forbidden on both sides.

"Who is your love?" she asked.

He lives on an island far south of here, said the whisper. *Soka. His name is Kalu. He is life and breath to me.*

"Do you know the place, Connoisseur?" whispered Shen.

Aiea nodded. One of the men of the harem hailed from there, it was farther south than even Loka'i.

"How can we know if we can trust her?" asked Angry, whose nickname was apt. She was always ready for a fight. She would get in a fight with herself if there was no one else at hand.

Emydd knelt against the gunwale of the ship. He opened his mouth and sang a strange, sweet melody. The mermaid's body vibrated and changed, her flesh opened and folded back, to show her small fishlike heart there, beating and glowing gold.

Emydd stopped and the wound in the mermaid's chest healed.

"You can trust her," he said. "She speaks the truth."

Everyone on the ship stared at him.

"What?" he asked.

"You can divine truth with your song?" Aiea asked.

"Yes," he said, "that was one of the things that happened when I was younger. I found it was safer not to sing."

"What else can you do?" asked Shen.

He smiled a secret smile and no further questions were asked.

"What are you called, mermaid?" Shen demanded.

Koyu, said the maid, and she told them her story.

Koyu

Today, as with the months previous, Kalu was pursuing the one thing that could interest him now: finding a fish that tasted better than *kact*. The rituals observed, he cast his line in the water. The sight of the sea, the smell of salt tang in the air, the spread of water that kissed the horizon…it had once pleased him. Now he feared its never-ending, heartless blue would blind him. The ocean seemed a great barrier, mocking him with distance.

He sat on a rock above the water, knowing the fish would have come to hide in the shadows away from the afternoon sun. He was startled to see a woman's head break the surface.

Kalu dropped his spear in amazement. Fear clouded his eyes. He looked around in panic, but he was entirely alone. The woman swam closer, and reached out a wet hand to touch his leg. He jumped away from her, raising his spear at the sight of one of the merfolk, sworn enemies of the land.

"I will shout for my people! I am not alone!" cried Kalu.

I am alone, came the words on the wind like a breath.

Kalu stared at the woman. He paused.

"Alone?" he asked. "Why?"

She shook her head, her seaweed-tangled dark hair curling in the water, her skin green and cold. The strange wind-as-voice whispered across the waves again.

They would not let me see the surface, she explained, *so I ran away.*

Kalu grinned.

"I too ran away once," he said, "but I only ended up back where I started. It is an island, you see."

The woman smiled back at him.

Tell me of your country, she said.

"Me?" he exclaimed. "You are a mermaid, tell me of yours!"

We can exchange, said the woman. *I am called Koyu. I am a commoner among my people.*

"I am Kalu," he said. "I am a poor fisherman on this island. It is called Soka."

He grinned proudly.

"However, I am the best fisherman on the island, and I will catch you a beautiful prize! You will never have tasted better," boasted Kalu, gesturing with his spear.

How can you kill fish? Koyu asked in horror, her eyes filled with pain.

Kalu dropped his spear, realising his error.

"Oh…I am sorry. It's just that we…our people…that's how we must live," he said.

Tears trickled down her cheeks.

"Perhaps I can become a hunter instead," he said quickly.

Koyu smiled at him.

Kalu stood then and strode away down the beach. He returned with a bit of cheese and bread.

"For when I can't catch any fish," he explained, and handed them to her. She looked askance at the food, but put it in her mouth. She beamed at him, and offered her hand. He reached out and placed his own in hers.

"I am pleased to meet you, Koyu," he said.

Many weeks passed, and they visited each other every day. Kalu's family was worried that the magic of their island was no longer working, as their son was not bringing in the catch he once did. They were further concerned when he claimed that fish turned his stomach and began eating only vegetables and fruit. They suspected illness and wanted to send for a doctor, but he refused. Every day, he rushed out of the hut early in the morning, eager to return to the beach and to Koyu.

One day, Koyu decided it was time to share her world with him. They had both been frustrated that they lived in opposite elements and could meet only at the edges. Although Koyu could not walk on land, she did have a way for them to be together.

"Will you come with me, Kalu?" she asked, "for I would like to show you my home."

Kalu was worried, but he nodded. She and her beauty overwhelmed him.

Koyu breathed into Kalu's mouth and beckoned for him to follow. He plunged into the sea, trusting her, and held his breath as long as he could. Kalu pulled him along at an incredible pace. He held his breath until he thought his lungs might explode, and when he could hold it no longer he exhaled peacefully, drawing water into his lungs. To his surprise, he could breathe quite easily. Then terror swept into his heart as his eyes adjusted to the depth and darkness. He resolved to trust Koyu, however, and followed without showing the fear building within him.

Presently they came to a ledge with a sheer drop off and there in the brilliant blue light was the city of the Sea King.

Grander than any city he could have imagined, the great coral edifice rose to a staggering height from the ocean floor. Schools of fish flashed like rainbow lightning around the high-rises and towers of the city. Koyu slowed and pressed a finger to her lips for silence.

They entered the lower realm of the great metropolis. Koyu took him down several winding corridors and then swam through a hidden opening in the city wall.

Kalu found himself floating in a small and strange apartment. The light played around the room, and Koyu approached him.

"This is my home," she said shyly. "I wanted you to see it, as I have seen yours."

"This is incredible," he said, "but Koyu, I don't live on the beach."

She looked at him with such a serious expression that he became concerned.

"What is it?" he asked.

"Kalu, do you know about the war?" she asked. He nodded.

"Yes, Ryg told me," he said.

Koyu sighed in irritation.

"Not the stupid legend," she said, "the war. It's still happening. Right now. If they catch you here with me –"

"I will defend you," he said, "I do not have my spear, but I will fight."

Koyu shook her head at Kalu's innocence and dedication. He would not last very long against the trained soldiers in the Sea King's army.

"Kalu," she said, "there may come a time when I cannot return to you. If that happens, there are things you need to know. About the world, and about the king of the land-dwellers."

"Anything for you," he said.

They spoke at length, wrapped around each other on her shelf-bed, fish flicking past the window in the deep twilight of the undersea city.

The flow of conversation slowed to an ebb, and Kalu felt drowsy. He looked over at Koyu. She was smiling at him, using the enchantment of the merpeople for the first time. She put her arms around him and drew him close.

Light filtered through the water, making the small apartment bright. The shafts of light were almost divine, and Kalu had never seen anything as beautiful as Koyu. She did not look as the women of his tribe looked, nor did she look human at all. Her mouth was filled with the sharp needle-teeth of the merpeople, and her face was all cheekbone and eyes. And Kalu was afraid and Kalu was enchanted.

There was something around her, a kind of aura. He reached out to touch it and found that it was slightly cool and of a thicker consistency than water. He also felt immediately calmed, almost in a trance, and he relaxed, completely boneless. When Koyu opened her mouth and bit down hard on his shoulder, drawing blood, wrapping her tail around him, all he could do was moan. The pleasure he felt was so intense that nothing else mattered. Her eyes closed, the venom from her teeth sinking into his blood, binding them together. He cried out as he thrust against nothing, her tail tightening around him like a constricting snake.

She withdrew her teeth from his shoulder, blood mixing with the seawater.

Kalu shuddered, and came; it was so intense he lost consciousness for a moment, or perhaps it was the venom.

When he came to again, he was breathing so hard he thought he would die. Koyu turned him towards her and kissed him with her strange mouth. His breathing slowed and he stared at her, drunk.

"Why..." he said, "Koyu? What..."

He found his tongue sluggish in his mouth. She caressed his hair and his face, her smile one of knives, but sweet anyway.

"This is the last magic of the merpeople," she said. "Our pheromones are powerful. Once, long ago, we mated with humans – the Hoisdean are our descendants. You'll feel all right in an hour or so."

Kalu grinned stupidly up at her.

"I don't understand why they stopped," he said, "Koyu...that was – it was like nothing I have ever known."

Koyu nodded sadly.

"People fear a power they don't understand," she said. "A great deal of trust needs to be involved in this kind of relationship, and humans do not always like things more powerful than they are."

Kalu wrapped his arms around her.

"I trust you," he said, sleepy, "always."

Koyu returned his embrace.

"And I, too," she said, "I trust you, Kalu."

Kalu fell asleep while Koyu's mind was filled with troubling thoughts, about the shark sentries that would one day smell the human blood on the water if they weren't careful, and about the punishment for consorting with the enemy.

Kalu slept on, blissful in his innocence.

Kalu ducked beneath the grassy overhang of the low thatched hut. The Elders were seated around the fire.

He waited for an invitation and sat down before them.

"My Elders," he said, "you may have noticed a change in me recently. I am tired of island life. Meaning no disrespect, I should like to travel and see the world."

The Elders exchanged looks, and one by one, shook their heads.

"Please," Kalu said. "I am unhappy here."

The Elders looked at each other again, and one stood, walking over to the doorway.

He pointed out, then shook his head emphatically as he then pointed to the ground.

"If I leave, I cannot return?" asked Kalu.

The Elders nodded. Kalu sighed. He wished to travel, but he did not think he was ready to bid farewell to his home forever. Besides, Koyu would not know where to find him.

Kalu sighed and looked at the ground.

"I will consider it," he said, "but at this time I cannot imagine not being able to return to this place. I do love my home and my people. I hope you will not think badly of me for my wishes."

The Elder smiled and shook his head, pointing at Kalu and then hugging himself. He was shown out with kindness.

Kalu sighed deeply. At least he knew he was loved.

The last day I saw him, his sailor friend was returning from Thla, Koyu finished, *so I left because I knew he could not be allowed to see me. That was when I came here, intent on helping your cause.*

Shen rolled her eyes.

"A good story," she said, "and yet I think death is still the answer."

"No!" Emydd said and the women on the boat stared at him. He sighed and looked at Koyu.

"Don't get in my way, young man," said Shen. "King or not, I still know these creatures better than you do. You let one go, they bring back a hundred."

"I grew up Wyltai," he reminded her, "and I know the merpeople well enough. Koyu is telling the truth. Besides, she may be able to help us."

A spear flashed through the water, but Koyu was gone. Everyone turned to stare at Angry, who swore at the loss of her weapon.

"Lieutenant! I did not give you an order. Stand down!" Shen shouted. Angry hung her head.

"I'm sorry, Commander, but you know they are liars!" Angry protested.

"Be that as it may, you are on cleaning duty for three weeks," said Shen. "You may have lost us our best chance to defeat the Sea King."

"I wouldn't say that," said Angry, and looked at Emydd.

"Emydd will not be a warrior," said Aiea, "We cannot risk losing him. Perhaps the harem would be the safest place."

"He is the king, and should stay in Ona," said Shen.

Emydd stepped between them.

"I do not wish to belong to the harem," he said. Aiea stared at him.

Shen smoothly broke the tension between them.

"Even so, you must be presented to King Irya," Shen told Emydd. "Let us return to land and allow the Connoisseur to leave with her prize."

Angry took Shen aside.

"If he goes to Loka'i, we will never see him again," she whispered.

"If he is in the harem, then no harm can come to him," Shen whispered back. "Best to keep him out of the way. Save the king, save the islands. It is our best chance to keep him safe."

Angry was about to argue with her commander, but she saw the resolve in Shen's eyes, and had to admit that the plan was a good one. Ona was not safe for one carrying the Song of Life in his bones.

Shen

"Put that down over there," a voice shouted. "Just where do you think you're going with that, soldier? Look alive!"

End stood confused among the bustle of camp. A tall woman with spiky blonde hair caught sight of him, and she was at his side in an instant.

"How'd you get in?" she demanded, "civilians aren't allowed."

"My name is End," he said. "I want to enlist."

The woman stared at him, then shouted with laughter.

"Take a look out there, young man. Tell me what you see," she said.

End looked around the camp and his heart sank.

"I see women," he said.

"Only women," she said. He nodded.

"That's right," she continued, "so you can see that you're already unqualified."

"That's not very fair, is it?" asked End, "I mean, what's wrong with men?"

"Men are useful if they're beautiful," she said, "but mostly we have to save their hides."

"Maybe they could fight if you gave them the chance," End suggested.

The commander sighed.

"Late nights in the canteen I've had philosophical arguments like that," she said, "and I tend to take your side. My name is Shen. I am the army commander here on Ona. And I have to tell you, young man, philosophy's all well and good over a pint, but it's a different story on the ground."

End grabbed her arm and looked into her eyes.

"Please," he said, "I've left my home and I can't return. I'm no good at anything else."

Shen looked at him and rolled her eyes, muttering to herself. She walked over to the window and looked down at the parade ground. Then she turned to him.

"All right," she said. "I must be going soft. I'll give you a try. But at the first sign of any kind of trouble—"

"I promise, I won't disappoint you," said End, grinning from ear to ear.

"Very well," she said. "Angry, come here and show this new recruit the barracks."

A young woman with beautiful red hair and bright topaz eyes approached. When she saw whom Shen was standing with, her mouth dropped open.

"Shut your mouth and take him along," Shen said. "I'll explain later. End, behave yourself."

"I will," he said, "I promise. And…thanks."

"Sure, sure," she said, before walking off down the hallway shaking her head and cursing herself.

Angry, grinning, threw Shen against the wall.

Her commander stared down at her, returning a quirk of a smile, and kissed Angry fiercely. The lieutenant threw her off, and then drew her knife.

She cut into her skin, blood dripping down her arm, and Shen knelt down, looking up at her lover.

"Yes, you may," said Angry, and Shen ran her tongue across the wound. Angry sighed, fisting her hand in Shen's short hair, dragging her up for another kiss.

They tore at each other's clothes, Angry throwing Shen onto the bed and crawling over her, pressing kisses like fire down her body. Bruised and smiling, Shen hauled Angry up by her shirt before pulling it off of her.

"Did I say you could undress me?" asked Angry, eyes hard, voice low. Shen's blue eyes held a combination of excitement and fear.

"No," she said.

"Then you – " she began, when there was a knock on the door.

Angry sat up and glared at the doorway.

"Yes?" asked Shen. "What is it?"

"My apologies for interrupting, commander," said one of the soldiers, "but your services are needed."

Shen and Angry looked at each other.

"Kind of busy," called Shen.

"He said it can't wait," said the soldier's voice through the door. "Said to tell you it's Ive."

Shen sat up. Angry looked at her, confused.

"Be right there," she said, pulling on her boots. She kissed Angry once, briefly.

"Sorry, gotta take care of this," said Shen. "One of the perks of being the boss."

Angry raised an eyebrow, but did not argue. Instead, she grinned.

"Later," Angry promised. "I won't forget."

"Counting on it," said Shen, and walked out of the room, pulling on her shirt on as she went.

"Okay, whaddaya got?" Shen asked the strange man half-hidden in the shadows. She pulled up a chair by the table and sat down in front of several vials.

"It's all there, prime stuff," he said.

Shen rolled out a white cloth and dropped some of the contents of each vial on it, one by one. She watched as the spots blossomed into multicoloured florets, and grinned.

"You've outdone yourself this time, Ive," she said, removing several coins from a leather pouch at her side. "Here is payment. Thank you. Speak to no one outside. If anyone sees you, things will not go well for either of us."

"Understood," he said, bowing and touching a fingertip to his forehead, "always a pleasure, Commander."

He disappeared into the shadows with his coins, and Shen gathered up the vials. They disappeared into her pouch. She took the cloth and set fire to it, making certain nothing was left but ash before she walked out, locking the door behind her.

Aiea

Aiea set foot on Tika for the second time. They were travelling far outside of the capital city where she had met Kane. The outer villages of Tika were just as dedicated to the arts, but their lawlessness made them dangerous, and all the more appealing to the writers and drunkards that inhabited the capital of the island.

"Watch yourself here, Aiea," said Kane, "the people are violent, often in blood feuds with each other."

"Violent?" asked Aiea, as they walked down the street away from the wharf. "Why are there blood feuds?"

"Lover's quarrels, arguments over land rights, mostly. Anything they can think of," said Kane. "People kill each other in the streets in the name of honour. It's all very noble and ridiculous."

The village leader came to meet them, a wizened old greybeard whose hardy exterior and muscle made him look ready to build or sail at any moment.

"Welcome to the outlands of Tika, Connoisseur," he said. "My name is Myrk, and I hope you enjoy your stay. Come, I will show you our city."

They followed the old man as he pointed out derelict but historically important buildings, and tiny cafes where men sat drinking outside, a few dogs sleeping beneath their chairs. Chickens ran back and forth in the streets, while the dogs lazily watched them, raising alternating eyebrows.

"I think you will enjoy this," said Myrk, leading them to where a small crowd was gathered around what appeared to be a stage.

"Number sixty-three!" called a man reading from a paper beside the stage. Another man, his hands bound behind his back, was brought forward for the crowd.

He was handsome, and his bright eyes shone. There was a murmur of approval.

"Tendanya, of the outlands. Height, three and a half. Weight, one twenty. Bid on Tendanya today, a fine specimen! Have an exotic serenade for your meals! A wonderful addition to any home."

A woman at the front of the crowd said, "We must hear him sing."

"Sing," said the man, poking Tendanya with his spear. The man onstage dutifully opened his mouth and sang a short, sad song. The crowd nodded and murmured appreciatively, patting the woman on the shoulder, who beamed.

"Bidding starts at ten," the man called out. "Ten – the lady in front. Fifteen? – to the gentleman in the hat."

"You see?" asked Myrk, "We are as civilised as Loka'i. We have our own harem."

Aiea was filled with horror.

"This is monstrous!" she gasped. "This is slavery!"

"Is Loka'i so different?" asked Myrk, smiling.

Kane and A'o drew Aiea aside before she could say something rude.

"Remember who you are," advised A'o.

"I know who I am!" she said. "There is a time and place for diplomacy, but this is not it."

"Aiea," Kane said, "did they not tell you of the slave auctions?"

Aiea stared at him. Kane sighed.

"Most islands are jealous of Loka'i. They want to be like the Ulu'u, to emulate the richest people in the world. It's like buying an expensive dinner and playing wealthy for an evening. Slave auctions are a part of that fantasy."

"How many islands practice this?" Aiea demanded.

"All of them," he replied, and she looked at him in shock.

"Why are you so surprised?" asked A'o, "We are in the same business."

"But our men are taken care of!" she protested. "They are fed and cared for! Besides, that man was of poor quality."

"Well, they don't have Connoisseurs on the islands," said Kane, "not for lack of trying, though."

"What do you mean?" asked Aiea.

"Myrk," said Kane, "why don't we take Aiea to the store?"

"Store?" asked Aiea.

"Yes…where people buy things they need," said Kane, giving her a puzzled look.

Myrk smiled and led them away from the auction block, where another man had stepped onto the stage.

Aiea wondered if the Connoisseur was trained young to keep her ignorant of everything, so she could not make her own informed choices. Perhaps that was what it meant to be royalty.

They went into the store and Kane led her to a section of teas.

"You see?" he asked.

She read the names of the products – Connoisseur's Choice, Connoisseur's Best, Loka'i Leaf.

"Is...everywhere like this?" she asked.

"The Ulu'u lead the way," said Myrk, "always we are happy to follow. Of course our goods are nothing like yours...but the people see 'connoisseur' and they buy."

"But I've never heard of any of these things," she said, confused.

"It's the name," said A'o, "it's all that matters."

The name...Connoisseur. Not Aiea. Not her name, but her title alone.

"Show her the beauty products," said Kane.

Myrk led them to a different part of the store, where an assortment of products sat on a shelf. Skin creams and soaps, all promising to make the wearer as lovely as the men of the Loka'i harem.

"Have you used any of these things?" she asked her retainers. They both nodded, as if it were the most natural thing in the world.

"Connoisseur, if you are ready, I will take you to the village," Myrk said.

"I'm ready," Aiea replied.

The village was completely deserted except for a few chickens. The wind blew dust through empty doorways, echoing in the silence.

"What happened here?" Aiea asked as they walked through the streets.

"A man fell in love with another man's wife," said Myrk, "there was a terrible war between the families. Most moved away."

"What happened to the men and the woman?" asked A'o.

"All dead," Myrk said. "A lover's feud usually ends that way. Ka is the only one left. Come, through here."

He led them through a doorway. A tall, extremely muscular man with calico skin was sitting on a stool inside a mostly empty room. A large dog sat beside him, and wagged its tail as they entered.

"Welcome," said the man, whose classic good looks were appealing, but nothing extraordinary.

"I am the Connoisseur," Aiea said. "These are my retainers, Kane and A'o. What is your talent?"

"I am a sculptor," he said, and indicated the statues behind him.

They were statues of merpeople, so realistic that Aiea was sure she could see one breathing. The craftsmanship was superb.

"Are you ready to begin the tests?" asked Aiea, and the man indicated that he was.

He passed only tolerably well, but Aiea took a liking to his personality despite his less than stellar performance. She conferred with Kane and A'o.

"He is *iao*," said Kane, "perhaps even lacking beauty."

"He is handsome," said Aiea.

"Yes, but not exceptional," said A'o, "he is a study in mediocrity."

"What about the sculptures?" asked Aiea, "They are amazing!"

"And disturbing," said Kane. "What sort of man makes sculptures of the enemy?"

"Aiea," said A'o, "years ago, at the Academy, I had a roommate, jealous of my beauty and that of the other boys. Iana – you met him on Naia. He'd have done anything to get ahead of us – even started fights with me, such fights as are for men of our stamp. He clawed at me, pulled on my hair, trying to disfigure and disqualify me – and so I have this scar. In the end, of course, he was…expelled. This is the reason that such violent men have no place in the harem."

Aiea thought of the blades the retainers once wore, and set her jaw.

"I am claiming him for Loka'i," she said. "My vote overrides both of yours."

"Aiea, think of what you're doing," said Kane. "I know you want to make your own decisions, but don't go against us just to prove yourself."

"I'm not," she said, though she was unsure of this.

Kane sighed and shook his head. A'o looked at Aiea as though she had lost her mind.

She stepped forward and took Ka by the hand.

"Welcome to the harem of Loka'i," said Aiea. Myrk beamed, and there were tears in Ka's eyes.

"I am honoured," said Ka, "I would like to make you a present of one of my sculptures to thank you for your kindness."

He gestured at a particularly horrifying sculpture of a mermaid and Aiea's smile faltered, but she composed herself.

"Thank you, Ka, I will treasure your gift," she said, always the diplomat.

That night, amid great celebration of the island, Kane came to visit Aiea in her chamber.

"That was a very foolish choice you made today, Aiea," Kane said. Aiea stood from the bed where she had been sitting.

"Why? Because I made a choice of my own, independent of the opinions of others?" she asked. "The old ways must make way for the new."

"What if you're wrong?" asked Kane.

"Then I'm wrong," she said, and shrugged. "What does it matter? His looks may improve with age, and we have gained a prodigious talent. Talent and intelligence are the most important aspects, are they not?"

"Yes, but…" said Kane.

"Enough," she said, "I want to make my own decisions."

"A decision based on the opposition of your knowledge is as much dictated by what you've learned as anything!" he said. "It's still the same, Aiea."

She turned away from him then, and he watched her for a moment before retiring to his own chambers. He wondered if she was right, and he was letting popular opinion influence his decisions as well. She was the Connoisseur; she knew her business better than any of them. He would have to trust her in this, as he must in all other things.

Ka was thrilled to leave the outlands of Tika and the loneliness of life in an empty village.

Myrk adopted his dog, and Ka decided to bring his sculptures along with him, as he hoped to continue his work on Loka'i. Aiea assured him he would be successful in this. The Ulu'u found particular pleasure in collecting merpeople antiques and knickknacks – a pearl comb or a necklace, for instance, to impress their friends. This strange taste for things from the enemy camp was due to the Ulu'u's romantic image of themselves as warriors, though it had been a very long time since they had fought. It made them feel strong and rebellious even in their extreme luxury. The lifelike statues of merpeople were sure to be a popular acquisition.

Irya

After many days of travel on calm seas, they returned to Loka'i.

Aiea brought her new finds to meet the young prince now turned king. Kane did not need approval, as the Connoisseur's retainers were given special privilege, and the king's opinion did not matter. All other acquisitions had to be evaluated by Irya.

The king was beside himself with joy upon seeing Ka's muscular figure in the throne room.

"*Now this…*" Irya gasped, "is *beauty*! You've outdone yourself, Aiea. The huge, muscular men of old – like the ancient warriors of the Ulu'u. *This* is a man!"

Aiea did not point out that Irya himself was of slight figure, and had in fact preferred men similar to himself since he had gained the throne. Ka stood stern and solemn; he did not laugh or smile, as many candidates would have.

"Ah, and taciturn! Strong! I absolutely approve of him, Aiea. The sculptures will be popular among the wealthy; you know how they love anything to do with the Great War. The bidding alone will bring so much money into the royal coffers that Loka'i will live up to its name in luxury. Ka, the gifts you have brought please me greatly. You have considerable talent. The statues will be displayed here in the throne room so that all visitors will see them. Congratulations, Aiea, on a marvellous find. And I'd like to commission a sculpture made in my own image."

A look of worry barely crossed Ka's face, gone as quickly as it came.

"Oh, don't concern yourself," said Irya, "whatever you make will be fine! You are very talented, after all."

Aiea approached Irya then.

"Irya," she whispered, "what on earth has gotten into you?"

Irya shrugged while hurriedly pouring *iwa* wine for himself and Ka. Aiea's jaw dropped. Irya never even poured himself anything. He seemed very excited, nearly dropping things out of nervousness, having been out of practice with handling any object for many years.

"I just appreciate a fine male physique, you know that," he said.

"Yes, but they don't normally make you act as though you've lost your mind," hissed Aiea.

Ka accepted his glass with a nod and a raise toward Irya, who responded in kind, grinning like an idiot.

"*Irya*! What is going on?!" demanded Aiea.

He sighed and put down his wine.

"This single acquisition could make Loka'i three times richer. This a fortunate find indeed."

"I didn't realise it was your intention to glorify the war! What would your father have said?"

Irya rolled his eyes.

"I didn't bring him here," he said, "you did."

He smiled at Ka, lifted his glass, and knocked back its contents in one swallow.

Her second choice was not so fortunate in his reception.

"You wish to bring…a *Naiene*…into the fold?" demanded Irya. Aiea had taken advantage of the late hour to show off her new discovery.

"I've not been here often at night," said Aiea, "the palace is very beautiful."

Irya glared at the sallow-faced man standing beside his Connoisseur.

"Aiea, pay attention," he said, "this is not a game!"

"I'm not playing a game," said Aiea. "We need protection here. We are too exposed."

"The Onai have turned your head," said Irya. "In time they may change your tastes as well."

"As well they should!" cried Aiea. "I was innocent before, Irya. Loka'i has no protection…and neither does the harem! We need a guard – possibly an army!"

Irya leaned forward and whispered.

"But are you aware…he's a *vampire*?!"

The Naiene smiled at this, amused.

"Yes, of course," said Aiea, "and a beautiful, intelligent man. He passes the test."

"Aiea, how could you bring such vermin here?" he demanded, "this is like bringing the plague, or a nest of scorpions!"

"We need him, Irya," she insisted.

Irya sighed.

"Very well," he said, "but I never want to see him again, is that clear?"

"Yes, Your Majesty," she said sardonically.

"Watch your tone with me, Aiea," said Irya, "and if I hear of even one un-provoked attack, or if any more of his kind turn up like centipedes crawling out from under the rocks, he is to be killed and so are they. *Immediately.* Do you understand?"

"Perfectly," she replied, but couldn't help rolling her eyes. "Come along, Yr."

Yr grinned widely at King Irya, who gasped and started up in his chair. Yr simply shook his head and followed Aiea out into the night.

"Thank you for choosing this life," Aiea said to Yr as they strolled in the darkened green and silver of a Loka'i moonlit night. "I realise it is extremely out of the ordinary for your kind."

Yr smiled peacefully. "Yes, isn't it?" he said. "I find it rather quaint and charming. A bit daring too. What a curious mode of living."

"Do you remember the days when Loka'i was feared?" asked Aiea, thinking of Irya's wholehearted embrace of Ka. "Were people really different then?"

"Heavens no," Yr replied. "That's all romantic hogwash. I do remember those days. The world was a bit more barbaric then, but fundamentally, people are still people."

"Good," said Aiea, "I thought so. Then I want you to train them."

"Train the harem? In matters of warfare?" he asked.

"Yes," she said. "You remember. You are a warrior by nature. I need these men to be able to fight."

Yr paused and turned to her, slowly, as if in an underwater dream.

"So you were serious," he said. "Forgive me, Aiea, but I thought your inter-ests were more petty than that. I have known many Connoisseurs, and they were extraordinarily shallow people. I thought your primary interest was to be the first to have one of the Naiene freaks in your menagerie."

Aiea was angry at first, and then she blushed.

"I admit that was part of it," she confessed, "but that is my job, after all. My real reason, however, was to teach the harem to protect itself."

Yr's face was strange and white in the moonlight, a marble statue without life, the moon a mirror reflected in his ebony eyes.

"You believe the merpeople will attack," he said.

"Yes, I do," she replied. "I want to know that my men are safe."

"What has inspired this concern?" he asked. "Most of the land-dwellers think the danger has passed."

"Do you?" she asked. His expression was answer enough.

"Call it an instinct," she said, "it's the same feeling I rely on as a Connoisseur. There are many foods, spices, drinks – and even men – we can't be sure of. Is it *enough*? That is usually the question. That sense of something being extraordinary, of being just off enough to be a good selection, is the same sense I have about the war. A gut feeling, an *unease*. There's nothing logical or scientific behind it. And I may be wrong. But I'd rather be prepared, if I'm right."

Yr's eyes narrowed to ebony slits. "You don't love your king, do you, Aiea?" he asked.

Aiea was startled by this change in subject. She looked down. "No, I do not," she replied, "and I cannot tell him."

Yr sighed, nodded, and angled his head toward the palace, all in the same slow, dreamlike fashion.

"Indeed," he said, "for his heart beats for you like a heavy drum."

Yr slowly turned his gaze back to her, and the black eyes in his white face suddenly caused her an inexplicable feeling of terror.

"Very well," said Yr, breaking the spell. "I shall do as you ask."

He bowed to her lightly and moved off through the garden, a ghost in the tropical night.

Emydd was intimidated by the incredible and obvious wealth of the island, uncomfortable beneath the stares of people who knew him for what he was:

a new possession, a prize.

He stood in chains in the shadowy light of the pleasure palace's throne room.

Irya sat on his throne, clutching a goblet. His knee was bent over one arm of the chair, his legs spread obscenely. He stared at Emydd with open loathing. Aiea was stunned. She wondered what had brought about this sudden change.

Irya came forward, almost nose-to-nose with Emydd. The two men stared at each other. Aiea was surprised to see Irya's nostrils flaring and realised he was jealous. Emydd was more attractive than Irya, and truth be told, Irya had never felt threatened before.

"Aiea, perhaps you have been travelling too long," said Irya, "to prefer beauty over other qualities! Was this man not judged by the retainers as *iao*?"

Aiea bowed. Emydd frowned. He shook his head, and the beads and feathers in his wild hair rattled. Irya noticed this.

"You object to Aiea bowing to me, Wyltai?" demanded Irya. "Or perhaps you object to being declared *iao*? You have much to learn if you are to belong to the harem of Loka'i. As for Aiea, she knows her place."

He stared at the Connoisseur for a moment, and suddenly spoke as if he were aiming a dagger at Emydd.

"Aiea is very…submissive," he said.

Emydd's eyes flashed. He spoke under his breath.

"I do not wish to belong to the harem of Loka'i," he said quietly.

Irya's jaw dropped. He had not expected this.

"Foolish boy," said Irya, "all wish to belong to the harem! It is only your inexperience that makes you think otherwise. Besides, do you not desire our beautiful Connoisseur?"

Emydd stared steadily at Irya.

"Even if I desired Aiea by my side, it would always be her choice," Emydd said. "I would not treat her as a commodity…if I truly loved her."

"What an innocent!" hooted Irya, though he looked stung. "An antiquated idea! Should anyone control their desires? It would be torture!"

"I have no respect for those who cannot control themselves," Emydd replied. "They are not yet adults, only spoiled children who must have everything upon demand. I thought honour and strength of character were of importance in your harem. Apparently these are not important in a king. Have you been judged, Irya? Would you be judged *iao*?"

"*Silence!*" Irya screamed, and Aiea stepped back in surprise. "What is the point of all this talk? Guards, take him out of my sight. Connoisseur, you may remain."

Irya and Aiea were left alone in the throne room. She watched him, wondering how much of what she had seen was an act.

"Yes, Connoisseur, I believe a new decree is in order. Men of strong mind, regardless of appearance—"

"Irya, stop," said Aiea. "You are only doing this because you are jealous of Emydd. I agree with your decision, but—"

"Jealous?" cried Irya. "I am not jealous of that dirty Wyltai!"

Aiea knew he was lying. She walked to him and placed her hand on his arm. He looked down at the floor, unwilling to meet her gaze.

"Irya," she said, gently, "what's wrong?"

He stared at the ground.

"It's him, isn't it," he said in a flat voice.

"What do you mean?" she asked. He looked up at her, and his eyes were wet with tears that had not yet fallen. She dropped her hand, as she recognised a longing there she had not suspected.

"You love him," he whispered.

"Yes," she said, hardly daring to give voice to the truth.

Irya bowed his head, defeated.

"Then go," he said. "Do as you will. And go."

Aiea turned to leave, and with her back to him, she spoke.

"How long?" she asked.

"From the first day," he said quietly. "And to my last."

Aiea nodded briefly, accepting. Then she left the throne room, in search of Emydd. There was nothing she could do.

Emydd stood on a balcony of the pleasure palace, looking out across the sea.

Aiea unlocked the door, crossed the room, and walked up to him. She saw the look of concern etched upon his face.

"What's wrong, Emydd?" she asked. "I know Irya can be insufferable."

"It's not that, Aiea," he said. "Loka'i is indeed beautiful, and I am grateful for the safety your island offers me. Still, I can't help thinking that I belong in Ona, fighting for my crown."

Aiea looked down at the pavilions of the harem. She wanted him to stay where she knew he would be safe. However, she knew the truth of what he was saying. He did not like Shen and the others, so many miles away, fighting on his behalf.

"Then what do you want to do?" she asked.

"I want to go back," he said. "Is there any way? I know that men judged *iao* are beheaded. Is there a reason I haven't been killed yet?"

Aiea stared out at the water.

"Times have changed," she said quietly. "The rules have changed now."

"So you only want me here as another one of your discoveries?" asked Emydd, his eyes bright.

Aiea blushed and turned away.

"I believe that there is a request from Chaak to come and test two young men," Aiea said. "I could send word to Shen and the women to meet us there."

"Won't Irya miss you?" he asked. "He won't let you go, especially with me."

"I travel to find men all the time," she said. "If I tell him I am going to Chaak, he will be none the wiser. I will get a message to him later that I have gone on to Ona. By then, he may be angry, but his arm does not reach as far as that."

"Very well," said Emydd, "send word to Shen that we will meet her in Chaak. I hope she will accept my apology. Aiea…you don't have to come to Ona with me."

"I know," she said, "but for the moment, you are one of my men. I know you don't want to join the harem, but right now you are my responsibility and I must keep you safe."

"What of the others in the harem?" he asked. "If you leave with Kane and Aʻo, there will be no one to watch over them."

"Olai is their caretaker in my absence," she said, his name bringing with it a pang of guilt.

Emydd studied her expression.

"If you are certain," he said, "then I will be ready for departure when everything is in order."

Aiea bowed, and made to leave.

"Aiea…" he said. She turned.

"Thank you," he said. She smiled and nodded.

She walked out of the room with dignity, and he watched as she left the palace, continuing down the path to her pavilion.

Koyu

Koyu smiled to herself as she swam down her street, stopping briefly to buy seaweed to use for dinner that evening. She hummed and sang as she went, off-key, and waved at one of the shark sentries. It swam past her, slow and purposeful, its black eye reflecting the joy in her face. She was transformed.

She swam through her door and stopped still.

The living room was filled with guards. One of them held up the bracelet Kalu had left for her, an item very out of place in a mermaid's apartment.

Especially a soldier's apartment.

"You're going to have to come with us," said one of the guards. The other tore the bracelet apart, and the beads floated to the floor, where they rolled beneath the ledge-bed where she and Kalu, in their innocence, had slept.

The guards had nothing to ask her, for they knew everything; there was nothing more she could tell. They knew that the last of the land-kings had been discovered, and the ultimate end to the war was in their grasp. They cut into her anyway, because she was a traitor, because centuries of war had bred hatred between the merpeople and the land-dwellers, because doing what they were told was all they knew how to do.

Once upon a time, Koyu would have done the same, before she'd lost her way one afternoon and found herself face to face with the blond man with tanned skin and bright blue eyes. She, too, had been in the army all her life. She, too, would have punished this transgression, because she too would not have known any better.

She forgave them, because she knew she'd have done the same, and she understood, even through the blood and pain.

Koyu was a mermaid and a soldier. She did not scream.

When they thought her near death and too weak to be of any further use, they released her. She floated free in the green water, wafted along like seaweed by the secret tides. What remained of her knew only one thing, and that was Kalu. She opened her eyes and her tail moved, languid and slow in the current, until she was able– in all her pain– to push herself for the last time towards Kalu's island.

The sun was as bright as it had always been on Soka. Koyu pushed herself into the shallows and dragged her body onto land, trailing blood. She lay beached in the sun, too far to pull herself to the safety of the water, her gill slits flexing for breath in her graceful neck. Lying there was living hell, a torture perhaps worse than what the Sea King had put her through…but at least this way, Kalu would find her and know what had happened.

A glorious shadow passed the sun, a friendly cloud to make her ending more comfortable and peaceful. Slowly, sounds came to her and she heard her name spoken.

She opened her eyes and saw Kalu's dear, handsome face, filled with pain. She wanted to ask him why he suffered, but her throat was filled with blood. She reached a hand out to Kalu, who gripped it with a terrible intensity. Koyu hoped he saw the love in her eyes that she could not speak.

Kalu leaned over her as the brilliant tropical sun darkened and the wind made him blind, scrambling his sun-bleached hair. He heard Koyu's voice, her last breath, in the wind and all around him:

The Sea King knows. He will destroy you all. Warn the King!

Kalu

The sun slowly returned from its place behind the clouds as Kalu held Koyu's body in his arms. He swore in his mind that he would do as she asked, and wondered which king she had meant. In his mind, he saw the place Ryg had talked most about, the fantastic wealth of the most luxurious island, with its strange chocolates and mysterious delicacies, its bubbling wines and its beauty.

Kalu stood above the body of the mermaid he had loved. He knew only one thing to do, and that was to finish what Koyu had begun.

The war must end.

He would find the king.

Irya woke to howling and pounding. He lifted himself partway up in bed and flung a disdainful gaze at one of his serving boys.

"What is causing that infernal racket?" he asked, flopping back down. "Make it stop."

The boy hurried out and Irya fell back into a half-dream of the sea. He blinked as he came to consciousness in the brightness of the sun.

Standing before him was a thin, handsome man, his white skin sun-darkened, his blond hair falling into his eyes. His neck and wrists were encircled with all manner of beaded jewellery and shark's teeth.

"I thought I told you to make it go away, not bring it here," said Irya, bored.

"I tried, Your Majesty, but he pushed through us and we couldn't stop him," said the boy.

Irya sighed.

"Well, thank goodness no one wants to assassinate me," he said. "I'd be dead ten times over by now. Very well. What is your wish, primate? To look upon the glory of gods in their towers, after escaping the miserable hole you were raised in? Well, go on, look. You're persistent enough."

Irya gestured for his breakfast, which was brought instantly. He tore into it as only a king could.

The tanned young man in the loincloth glared at Irya and said a few words in a guttural, indecipherable dialect Irya did not know. As Irya never wanted to appear uneducated or foolish, he insulted others instead. The servants were watching, after all, and if he showed any sign of compassion or interest, they would be sure to spread the information around the city.

"What does the primate say? Is that even a language?" asked Irya, covering his interest in the newcomer with an insult.

"He says...he has a message for the king," said the serving boy. Irya glared, in appearance annoyed that a servant would have familiarity with a language he himself did not.

"Very well," said Irya, through a mouthful of food, wiping his fingers with a white napkin. "I am the king. What is your message?"

The boy made a few more guttural remarks with increasing intensity. Irya threw up his hands, shook his head, and looked toward the serving boy.

"He asks if you are the true king," said the servant boy, stuttering as he translated. "He – he says he did not think the true king would be so – rude or lazy. Forgive me, Your Majesty, but that is what he said."

Anger lit in Irya's eyes, his recent encounter with Emydd still stinging in his mind.

"Of course I am the true king!" he shouted, overturning his breakfast. "Remove this man from my sight!"

The servant boy began to lead the blond man from the room. The man shook his head and struggled against him. The other servants helped drag the stranger out into the hallway and watched helplessly as he began throwing himself against the heavy closed doors of Irya's chambers.

As he slumped to a sitting position, sniffling, he felt a tap on his shoulder. He looked up at the servant boy, who put a finger to his lips and pointed down a gravel pathway. He then indicated the large roof of a pavilion off to the left. He nodded and smiled encouragingly, and the young man in the tan loincloth stood and walked down the gravel path.

"Connoisseur," said a reverent voice, "an emissary of the Forgotten Lands to see you."

The wind softly billowed the red curtains against the white pillars, and

162

Kalu saw a woman rise and approach him. She looked as though she had been knit of silk and summertime, her bright green eyes blazing like jewels.

"Hmmm…it's so rare to have a man come to us," she said. "Requiring the men to come here would be much easier, don't you think?"

The servant boy made a subservient little cough.

"Begging your pardon, madam, but I don't believe he is here to join the harem."

Aiea's brow wrinkled.

"Oh, that is unfortunate," she said. "He would make a fine candidate. What does he want then?"

The young man suddenly erupted excitedly, speaking rapidly in his own language. Overwhelmed, Aiea looked to the servant boy for help. The boy's eyes slid from Kalu to Aiea as he translated.

"Says his name is Kalu…from the Forgotten Lands, the island of Soka," he said. "He apologises for not recognising you from Koyu's stories at first, but now he knows you are the famous Connoisseur and he is honoured to make your acquaintance."

The tanned young man flashed a white smile and made a little bow.

"Koyu…" gasped Aiea, "Emydd was right – the mermaid was telling the truth!"

Hearing this name seemed to make the man's eyes bright with tears, and invited another flow of guttural speech.

"He says…he is here with a warning. Koyu was captured, and tortured. The merpeople know about Emydd and plan to launch their final offensive. Koyu…asked him to warn the king. It was her last request…she died in his arms."

Aiea stared at him, aghast. After a moment, she collected herself and tapped her own servant boy on the shoulder.

"Run now. Get Emydd, and bring A'o and Kane to me. Ask them to find out where Shen is and bid her meet us on the shores of Chaak in three days' time. Go!"

The boy ran from the pavilion as fast as his feet could carry him.

"Thank you," said Aiea to Kalu and his translator, who bowed modestly. "We sail this very afternoon, no matter what Irya says. This is the fate of the world and much more important than his whim. See that Kalu is well taken care of. I must get ready."

As she stepped out of the pavilion she felt a hand on her shoulder and turned to see Kalu, who looked at her with a new, hard light in his eyes. She gave him an inquiring look and he made a few noises at her.

"He asks to come along," explained the servant boy. "He says if Koyu was brave enough to fight, he should be too – it is what she would have wanted."

Aiea stared at him a moment, then looked at the servant boy.

"If he comes, you must come too," she said, "or none of us will be able to communicate."

"As always and ever, Connoisseur, I am at your service, and your wish is my command," said the servant boy.

"Thank you," she said, and beckoned them both to join her. "Go now – we don't have much time."

The long hall was lit by patches of sunlight. Irya sat on his throne, holding a glass of bloodflower tea up to the light. It was the same colour as the garnets and rubies set in the gold rings on his fingers. Two servant boys fanned him slowly with palm fronds. All were dressed alike, their muscular bodies rubbed and gleaming with oil. The servants wore large, flat, ornamental collars around their necks. Irya's neck was bare like his torso, save for a gold chain that affixed a long red velvet cloak to his back, heralding him as the king.

"Speak," Irya said in a bored tone. His long, straight black hair shone with oil, and he admired the almost feminine beauty of his face in the gold encrusted mirrors that lined the chamber. He did not bother to look at Aiea as she spoke.

"Alone, Your Majesty," she said.

Irya nodded to his guards, who left the throne room. Instantly, his entire manner changed. His expression softened, and a warm light kindled in his eyes.

"What is it, Aiea?" he asked. He stood up and walked over to her, and they went to the balcony together.

"Your Majesty," she said, and her courage began to fail her.

"Yes?"

"Your Majesty, I wish to leave," Aiea said, her head bowed. "There are two boys on Chaak awaiting evaluation."

Irya stared at her.

"And this sudden news has nothing to do with the young Wyltai you brought here?" he asked.

Aiea raised her head and looked at him.

"Was it real?" she asked. "Were you really that jealous?"

Irya's mouth tightened. He sighed, his body slouched as though he had been waiting to take a weight off himself.

"Playing this role has given me some bad habits, Connoisseur," he said, "and much of it was for show, but…at the base of it, there was something."

He paused, listening to the wind rustling the palms. The day was bright and calm and deceptive, like every day on Loka'i. Aiea watched him, curious.

"Not jealousy," he said, "but resignation. You won't love me, or you can't. I see how you look at him, and I think him fortunate. Do as you will, Aiea. You have always been free."

"You are a good man, Irya," she said, and then turned to him. "You did not take me like a thief on our First Night, because you were strong. Strong enough not to take that which was unwillingly given. Strong enough to keep it a secret all these years. You have spared me, my body and breath, both of which were yours by the right of kings. You must understand my decision to be as strong as you, to give myself to one of my choosing, and not take the lives that according to my title are mine to take."

She put a gentle hand beneath Irya's chin and lifted his head, looking into his eyes.

"You are not without honour, Irya. And you will let me go, because you are strong."

Irya held her gaze with his dark eyes. The wind lifted strands of his hair, and his skin glowed in the sunlight.

"I love you, Aiea," he said, and then bowed his head.

She kissed him on the cheek and was gone in a rustle of silk and a breath of perfume.

Miserable, Irya collapsed onto his throne, the sound echoing in the emptiness of the room.

Siro

The sun was hot and bright as the crowds gathered around the glass partitions of the harem. Tourism was a thriving business on Loka'i, and everyone wanted to visit their favourite member of the harem. The men were celebrated all over the world. Articles and photographs were circulated throughout Amala, and collector's items, including portraits and miniatures, information about the lives and interests of the men, could be purchased on most islands. Everyone had their type, and their favourite; each man's personality and particular talents appealed to different people for a wide variety of reasons. Frequently, the visitors brought their own paintings or stories to share with the men, if they were fortunate or rich enough to pay the fee it cost to meet them. People argued about and insulted the favourites of others, speculated about relationships within the harem, and discussed the fine points of each man's qualifications. What might have been a philosophical exercise was tantamount to attacking a person's religion, so fervently did some of the tourists believe in their particular man.

The tourists milled eagerly around the viewing areas, reading signs that described the different men, their talents, and their home island. Occasionally a shout came from the crowd as one of the more popular favourites waved or smiled in the direction of the crowd.

There was beer spilled across some of the pavement, but Siro paid it no mind. The women were shouting and getting into good-natured fights all around him, trading punches and laughing. He pressed up against one of the windows, watching one of the men of the harem painting at an easel. Another man holding books came up to speak with the one painting, and this brought out another rowdy cheer from the women around him.

Siro read on the wall that the man with the books was named Olai, and he was the official librarian of Loka'i. Any of the ancient prophecies or books were under his care and he was responsible for the binding of any new works the harem produced. He wore long robes, unlike the other men in the harem, who were bare-chested and wore loose trousers. Siro admired Olai; while he may not have been as handsome as some of the other men, Siro understood the appeal of hiding in a cavernous hall of books.

Siro had no particular favourite. He was, as he always said, still waiting.

He pushed out of the crowds, buying an ice cream from a street vendor in an attempt to cool down in the punishing heat. As he walked along the boulevard, he saw men leaning over the upper level's wrought-iron balconies, waving at him from above a small storefront.

Siro knew exactly what the store was, and what it was selling. He stood for a moment, eating his ice cream, staring up at the men with indecision.

Then he shrugged. After all, everyone had to experience Loka'i once in their lives.

He stood in the parlour, too shy to speak.

The woman at the desk smiled up at him, her pen poised above a book.

"Do you have a reservation?" she asked.

He tried to speak and failed, and then shook his head.

"Name?" she asked. "It's all right, we get a lot of tourists here."

"Oh," he said, "My name is Siro."

They get a lot of tourists, he thought, dismayed. He wanted this experience to be special, even if he was paying for it, and he knew he would never see the other person again. He wanted it to be important, *he* wanted to be important to someone.

To anyone.

He knew it was foolish to visit a brothel hoping for that kind of connection, but he'd just been to the harem and it had put romantic ideas in his head.

Like many people of Amala, he had saved for many years to afford a single trip to Loka'i, wanting to make sure that the experience would not be marred by financial worry. He'd saved the harem for the last day, and now he wished he'd gone to see them first, and every day after that. The men were breathtaking, and he must have fallen in love a thousand times. They truly were the jewel in the crown of Loka'i. Now here he was, in the waiting room of a brothel, halfway between going ahead with it and bolting.

"Who's your favourite, sweetheart?" asked the woman, and he was frozen on the spot. He didn't really know.

"Who's this?" came a voice behind him.

"His name's Siro," said the woman. "Better be careful around this one, he's like a spooked horse."

"Well, let's see what we can do," said the voice, and Siro recognised the drawl of a man from the western side of the island, God help him.

He turned to look at the man, and his breath caught in his throat. He saw a gentle, confident smile on a man more handsome than any he'd seen in the harem. This man seemed spun from gold. Tanned skin, bright eyes, short hair, muscular but the kind of muscles that come from daily labour rather than exercise, this man was the favourite, in looks at least, that Siro hadn't known he had.

And then, the beautiful man held out his hand.

"You're welcome to come with me, if you like," he said, "but there are other men here that might suit you better."

"No," squeaked Siro, who was immediately embarrassed, "You're – it's fine."

"Have fun, boys," said the woman, waving them off.

Siro willed himself not to start hyperventilating as the man led him to a room and opened the door.

"So, this room's mine," said the man.

The room opened out onto a wide balcony, the air moving slowly through the room as the sun set in brilliant colours, and the entire great city of Loka'i spread out beneath them, all the way to the ocean. Siro forgot to be frightened for a moment, and walked to the edge, enthralled.

"It's beautiful," he said softly.

"Thanks," said the man from behind him, "Name's Jin, by the way, So, how d'you want to do this?"

Siro turned toward him, shy again.

"Can we – is it all right if we just talk? For a while?" he asked.

"Sure thing," said Jin. "Your money, your time. Whatever gets you going."

Siro nodded, and sat down on the edge of the bed.

"You're handsome," he blurted, and then turned red. Jin grinned, scratching the back of his neck.

"Yeah, well," he said.

"Why aren't you in the harem?" asked Siro, growing bolder.

Jin nodded, hopping off the bed to pour himself a glass of *iwa* wine.

"You want some?" he asked. After Siro shook his head, Jin continued, "Well, see, I've got no talent, and I'm not smart. You gotta have one of the two to qualify. Looks ain't going to cut it."

Siro stared at him.

"Oh, I'm sure you're talented," he said.

Jin winked.

"Sure," he said, "in the way that counts."

He approached Siro, who stood up. Jin leaned forward, and Siro's eyelashes fluttered as he stared at the ground. Jin grazed Siro's cheek with his own, his lips soft against the other man's skin. Siro stood like a statue. He could feel himself reddening, and cursed himself inwardly for looking like such a – well, like such a virgin.

"How far does that blush go, I wonder?" murmured Jin, unbuttoning Siro's shirt, his hands warm against the other man's chest. He drew Siro towards himself, kissing and sucking at the juncture of his neck and shoulder. Siro let out a long sigh but still did not move.

"You blush all over," said Jin, mouthing at Siro's collarbone, and walking him backwards towards the bed, "so, what are you? Farm boy, out in the big city? Businessman? Choir boy? Ah, probably not, nobody believes in the royal family these days…"

Standing at the edge of the bed, Siro's eyes went wide.

"*Choir boy?*" asked Jin, startled.

"We – uh. We aren't allowed, to, our – we," Siro trailed off.

"*You're a royalist?!*" said Jin, backing off entirely. Royalists were those who committed their lives to the memory of the lost Alyetans, leaving the secular world presumably forever.

"Yes," said Siro, miserable, "Well, I was. When they found out, about it, about me, I – I was expelled."

Jin sat down on his heels, looking up at Siro.

"I don't know you, Siro," he said, "and you probably don't want to hear this from a whore you hired for the night, but … unless you're doing something very, very evil, believe me, it's not wrong. This," he gestured to the two of them, "is not wrong. You are normal."

Jin pulled Siro down to sit in front of him on the bed.

"I don't know much," he said. "Always was better with my hands than my words. But Siro – if the royals are still around, or looking down on us from somewhere, I don't think this is what would disappoint them. Royalty should never have become a religion."

Siro stared down at his hands. Jin swore, startling him.

"I'm sorry," he said, "I didn't mean to offend you, if that was blasphemous. I just – hey, you just seem like a nice guy, and I've seen my share of guys that aren't. Got a sixth sense about it, I guess. You need that kind of thing in this business."

Siro looked up at Jin, eyes suddenly blazing with a fire that hadn't been there before.

"It was because they found out I thought there was beauty outside the royal family," he said, "I said there wouldn't be a Connoisseur if there wasn't, and that was blasphemous."

Jin shook his head.

"That's all?" he asked. "Hell, I don't know how you survived there so long."

Siro shrugged.

"It was the only life I knew," he said. "I was raised in it. I found out about Loka'i, about the rest of the world, and – well, there's a reason the people of Soka aren't allowed knowledge. They aren't the only ones."

Jin whistled.

"I had no idea," he said, "in this day and age, too! You'd think – well, you'd think a lot of things."

"What about you?" asked Siro, "Why'd you choose this life?"

Jin laughed.

"You could say this life chose me," he replied. "When I heard the Connoisseur was going to come calling, I enrolled in the brothel. It was the only way to save my life. Everybody knows the prostitutes of Loka'i are beautiful. They don't have to be smart, too. And once you're in, you're safe – the Connoisseur won't take a man bound to the brothel. Something to do with conflict of interest."

"Surely you are bound either way," said Siro.

"Except the brothels don't kill you if you don't pass," said Jin.

Siro put his hand on Jin's arm. The other man was not so confident now, his eyes downcast.

"I wish I could do something for you," he said. "We both ended up in lives we didn't really plan. If you don't want to – it's all right."

Jin looked up at him, bright eyes shining, and Siro's heart skipped a beat. *Don't fall in love with a prostitute, you idiot*, his mind scolded him from somewhere very far away.

Jin grinned, confidence returning, and pushed Siro down onto the bed. He climbed on top of the other man, and Siro looked up at him, breathless.

"You wanted this," he whispered, his voice low and dirty, "you wanted to come here, to be taken by one of the whores of Loka'i."

Siro was silent, and gasped when Jin reached down and pressed his hand against the line of Siro's cock, already hard.

"Tell me," said Jin.

"Y – yes," whimpered Siro. Jin started to grind down against him, and Siro couldn't help himself, rutting against the other man, panting. He saw something in Jin's eyes, he thought; some sadness he could read between the lines of his casual confidence.

He suddenly pushed himself up against Jin, turning them over. Jin stared up at Siro, surprised.

"You are breathtaking," Siro stated plainly, "You are the most beautiful man I have ever seen."

"What're you doing, knock it off," said Jin, embarrassed. Siro smiled down at him.

"Now you're blushing," he said, kissing him tenderly, "and I want to take care of you, Jin."

Jin turned his face away, closing his eyes.

"Don't say that," he said.

"Why not?" asked Siro, "My money, my time. You said it yourself. Let me do this for you."

Siro kissed him deeply, and put his hand on Jin, kissing down his body, whispering praise against his skin. Jin would never tell another soul how quickly he finished that night, tears in his eyes, wordlessly staring up at this strange man he had only met hours before. Siro joined him – the only time he'd ever had a simultaneous orgasm with a client – and when they lay together afterward, Siro combed through the sweat in his hair and on his forehead, holding Jin.

"Siro," he mumbled as he neared sleep.

"Yes?" asked the other man.

"D'you think – maybe I could see you again?" he asked. "I mean, not here, not for money. Ah, forget it, it's stupid."

Siro hushed him.

"Of course, Jin," he said. "I would like that. Tomorrow, you can show me the city. Sleep now."

Jin's smile as he dropped off lit a warm fire in Siro's heart, and he kept his promise. Tomorrow, and for the rest of their lives.

Aiea

Chaak was strangely silent at night. The boys of the Academy had jostled each other excitedly when they saw that the Connoisseur had come to their island, but now all was quiet as the Academy slept.

The evening air was balmy and reminded Aiea painfully of home. The thought of what lay ahead frightened her, but she had chosen her course of action. She decided to take an evening walk beneath the stars.

The pathway was made of small stones, but Aiea's bare feet were accustomed to the gravel paths of Loka'i. Her way was illuminated by tea-lights that put her in mind of the fiery torches that lit her way along the pathways back home. She walked, half dreaming, towards the sea, where the stately palms paid homage to the sand.

"Connoisseur Aiea," said a soft voice in the darkness, and she gasped. Emydd emerged in the starlight near the water.

"You startled me," she accused him, stepping onto the sand. Her heart was beating fast.

Emydd looked up at the moon, reflected in his eyes.

"When I was a child, my Wyltai clan would come here and have celebrations on this beach," he said, "but other people have found this place now, and made homes here. There will be no more Wyltai celebrations on this island. They have moved on to places where they are safer."

"This place reminds me of Loka'i," said Aiea.

Emydd stared at her.

"Connoisseur..." he began and, as she looked at him, he felt his courage failing.

"What is it, Emydd? Is something wrong?" she asked.

He took her hand and looked into her eyes.

"I know many young men have told you of your beauty," he said, "but none of them with as much honesty. Aiea, I have desired you since I saw you step off that ship. I thought you royalty then, and despite what you say, I do not believe I was mistaken."

Emydd drew her towards him and kissed her. It was a naïve and amateur kiss. She hesitated a moment, and then melted against him. When he stood away, his smile was that of a man who could hardly believe where he was standing.

Emydd reached for Aiea again, his hands trembling. Her soft smile encouraged him, and he surged forward to kiss her. All around them, the crashing of the waves seemed to fill him. The touch of her skin and the sound of the sea became his entire universe.

She gently removed his shirt, kissing him, and he made a tiny keening noise in the back of his throat as he leaned against her, breathing hard.

"Do you want to do this?" she whispered. Emydd looked at her, uncertain.

"We don't have to," she reassured him.

"No, it's not that," he said, "I just don't know what I'm doing, I don't want to disappoint you."

Aiea smiled.

"Then I will teach you," she said, "If you are uncomfortable at all, tell me to stop."

Emydd nodded, still nervous. She touched his face, drawing her fingertips down his chest and stomach.

"You are more to me than the harem, than the spices I have found on my journeys," she said, "you are exquisite, Emydd."

She knelt in front of him, and looked up to ask him if he was all right. He nodded, gazing down at her as she touched her lips to the soft skin beneath his navel, and then opened his trousers, gently taking him into her mouth. His mouth dropped open in a silent cry, his hands on her shoulders, clenching involuntarily. Her eyes sought his, and as he looked down at her he felt as though he was at the edge of a precipice, his soul, his heart, and the sound of the waves filling his mind.

He touched her shoulder, and she understood, moving away from him as he lowered himself onto her, above her, around her, the sand against the flat of his palms. His heart was beating a wild tattoo in his chest, and he entered her, breathless. Her eyes closed, and opened again, the moon reflected there, and as he moved in her he felt he knew the sky and stars. Her hips thrust upwards, met his with insistence, and she cried out as her nails dug into his back. He halted, a sound he never thought he could make falling from his lips, as he found his release inside her. Quivering, he stared down at Aiea, his universe.

Her slow smile calmed his wild heart, and he smiled back. He lay down beside her, his head on her shoulder, falling asleep with the thought *I love you* ebbing across the sea of his mind.

A'o, on the hillside, had been standing guard as was his responsibility as retainer. He sighed and turned onto the path to his hut. His heart had broken once before, and he doubted he could feel such a deep sorrow again, but what he had just witnessed still hurt. He went to lie on his pallet and to fall asleep, to dream of a young man he had once loved beyond all reason.

Emydd awoke to the sound of the crashing sea, and panicked, terrified that the night before had been only a beautiful dream. He heard a sigh behind him and smiled with relief, his entire body suffused with the joy only new lovers can know.

He sat watching Aiea as she slept, the curve of her face and her soft neck. She opened her eyes sleepily, taking in his form. Neither of them had bothered to dress again, and had drifted to sleep on the tropical warmth of the sand.

"Good morning," she said, and smiled.

A mighty cheer arose from the direction of the huts. Shen and Angry, still in travelling clothes, were grinning like mad and making rude gestures. The silent citizens of Chaak stood with gaping mouths, and the boys from the Academy were hugging each other as though they had just witnessed a historical event.

"We just got in," Shen said, "good to know we weren't missed!"

Emydd turned many shades of red but kept his hand firmly in Aiea's.

"All right, you two," Shen said, "come on. We've got work to do."

Ryg

Three weeks after he had left Soka, Lyonid's ship made landfall in Thla. The island was enveloped in a thick fog and a chill set in his bones as he stepped ashore. He was starving, penniless, and now thoroughly sick of *kact*. He never wanted to see another *kact* for the rest of his life.

He walked the busy streets, nodding to those he knew. The people of Thla were hard-faced and serious. Any one of them could punch Lyonid's face into the back of his skull with one hand while drinking liquor from the other and not spill a drop. The city and countryside were grey and brown, drab colours that were only given a period of relief in the summer. Then, a brief explosion of colour would turn Thla into a paradise of warmth and well wishes, hardened faces softened by a summer glow and new romance in the air.

Not so now. Thla was every bit as discouraging and unfriendly as Lyonid remembered. After his visit to the enchanted southern isles, he was all the more miserable. His inability to trade in the Forgotten Lands had deprived him of the money he'd intended to use carousing in the south, and had turned what should have been a wonderful experience into a bitter one. He was no diplomat, and had not yet learned how to communicate how trading with him would benefit the islanders, having only his own wealth in mind. Jealousy of those who lived in warmer climes notwithstanding, Lyonid needed to eat. He sighed and lowered his head. He knew this meant he had to ask for a favour.

He found the Green Hill Inn as the swinging sign became visible through the fog. He swallowed his pride and pushed through the door.

The inn was crowded and filled with the familiar smoky smell of Onai firespice. Sailors shouted at each other and women laughed raucously, every conversation more foul than the one before.

"Young Lyon!" a voice called, and Lyonid turned to see Ryg, the burly and bright-eyed sailor with a rude joke always at the ready. Ryg waved him over and Lyonid sat down with him at a booth near the fire. Lyonid took off his coat, thankful to feel his bones begin to thaw.

"So, how was your first voyage?" asked Ryg, his eyes twinkling.

"Ah, well, you know," muttered Lyonid, looking down at the table.

"Lost everything, eh?" Ryg asked, and laughed. "Me too! I spent weeks coming in off a failed trade down in Chaak my first time out – what strange people! I think I ate wood chips when I got hungry enough. Speaking of which…"

Ryg raised his hand and waved at the serving woman.

"Come on over here, Lona, get the boy some chowder!" he shouted.

"All right, all right, keep your pants on," the woman retorted, but she went into the back.

Ryg turned to Lyonid.

"Anyway, don't let it get you down," he said. "We all start off like that."

Two steaming bowls of chowder were set before them, and Lyonid inhaled his before Ryg was halfway finished. With the hot chowder in his stomach, along with the heat of Thlai liquor in his system, he started to feel better.

"Thank you, Ryg," said Lyonid. "I was starving. If there's any way to pay you back—"

"Forget it," Ryg said, "all sailors help each other. You remember that, when you get older. Now, let's enjoy the night and welcome you home!"

Ryg rubbed his eyes and blinked into the slate-grey sea the following morning. Celebrating with Lyonid had been great fun, but, at his age, late nights were no longer easy to come down from. Especially since he had to sail to Lami, usually referred to as The Barrens, this morning. That was not a good place to go when one was recovering from the night before.

Shen

Shen and Aiea were alone in the Connoisseur's dedicated hut on Chaak. Emydd had gone with Angry and the other women to stock up on supplies for the voyage ahead.

"Good to see you again," Shen said, "and thanks for giving us the head's up. It was fortunate that Emydd was with you when Kalu came to Loka'i."

"Yes," said Aiea, "Loka'i is the centre of the world. It would make sense that the king might live there. I'm surprised Kalu was even aware of the island."

"Still," said Shen. "I'm not sure why you accompanied him. You would have been safer on Loka'i. Emydd could have returned alone."

Aiea looked out to sea.

"I love him," she said simply.

"And you will have to leave him again," Shen replied.

"I know," said Aiea, "but for a while, I can live like other people."

"Be careful that your selfishness does not make you forget your responsibilities," Shen said.

Aiea was surprised and hurt. She glared at Shen's face, half-shadowed from the sunlight.

"Selfish?!" she cried. "I've spent years of my life doing things for others! I'd like something for myself for once!"

"As would I," said Shen, and as she turned Aiea was startled to see the great tracking scars across Shen's neck and down her arms, "but we both have our positions in life, and we have our responsibilities. Like it or not, that's who we are – and the harem is your responsibility, much like Ona and the safety of the land-dwellers are mine."

Aiea was shamed before the warrior woman, who gave her a crooked grin.

"Think about it," said Shen, "now is the time we must act, all of us. We will withdraw onto the land and advise others to do the same. Most of the war has been won by making sea travel impossible. We don't know how they were capable of murdering the royal family and that means they may have had spies on land sympathetic to their cause. Ona must be protected at any cost."

"And Emydd?" asked Aiea.

"He will be with us in the field," she said.

"Won't he be in danger?" Aiea asked.

"Not as much as he would be if he were alone in the castle with no one to protect him," Shen said. "That is where every member of his family fell to the sword. I want him where I can see him."

Aiea nodded, her heart filled with fear.

"I have never fought anyone in my life," she said.

"Well, now is the time to learn," Shen said, slapping her shoulder as Angry returned to tell them the ship was prepared to set sail.

The Sea King

Emydd sat with Aiea against the gunwale as the warship crested the waves. They were on their way to Ona, where the army would protect him. Kalu stood at the bow with the servant boy brought with them from Loka'i. He was determined not to let Koyu's sacrifice be in vain. Emydd and Aiea stared at each other and smiled, new love between them.

Shen turned from her post to see Aiea suddenly sitting alone. The young king was nowhere to be seen.

"Where—" Aiea began, when green arms wrapped around her. She was overboard before Shen could react.

"Aiea!" she cried, and threw herself to the side of the ship in time to see the Connoisseur disappearing into the murky depths, her mouth open in a silent scream.

As she was dragged deeper under water, Aiea saw spears slice through the surface. Shen stood with the other women, and was shouting something at her she could not hear. Aiea was filled with terror at the thought of drowning, and took a deep breath in her panic. She was amazed to find that she could breathe.

She twisted around and looked at her abductor, startled when she saw the creature pulling her along. Green and strange with wide yellow eyes and needle teeth, the merman's face was etched with scars. He was like a monster in a fairytale. Ahead of them, Aiea could dimly make out Emydd also being towed by another merman into the darkness of the deep.

Presently, an incredible undersea city rose before her eyes. Had she not been so frightened, Aiea would have been impressed.

Crowds of merpeople turned and stared at them as they were dragged over a main thoroughfare of the city, as if they were being paraded to show the superiority of the undersea race.

Aiea glanced up to see a towering building before them and realised where the mermen intended to go.

The castle—and the king.

She began to struggle in earnest, but the merman only tightened his grip.

They entered the throne room, and Aiea was surprised to see a handsome young man with long blond ringlets seated on the throne. He appeared human, unlike the mermen that had carried them there.

The Sea King's throne was a tall green monstrosity carved ages ago. It was a jade masterpiece, fallen by shipwreck or thievery into the deep, the chair's interlocking stone branches formed the arms and back of the throne.

He looked at the two land-dwellers he had had imprisoned with interest. The young man was the last of his kind. The Sea King was planning to kill him, but he would torture him first. He was jealous and fearful – the Alyetans always allowed him the sea, but he knew Emydd now had reason to call up the land from the waters, and destroy the Sea King's realm forever. Fortunately, the young man did not know the extent of his own power yet, nor how to wield the Song of Life as a weapon.

The Sea King stood and regarded them as they floated there. Emydd and Aiea exchanged a terrified glance.

"So, it is true, then. There is another in the royal line," said the Sea King.

He approached Emydd and looked him in the eye. The young king held his gaze.

"Alyetans are lovely, are they not?" murmured the Sea King, to Aiea, "and difficult to kill. Of course, an Alyetan can kill another of his kind, but they destroyed themselves after putting your father to the sword."

Emydd stared at him in shock.

"Ah, you never knew your family, did you? A pity. It does explain why I did not know of your existence. Kholi, the last of the Alyetan scholars, murdered your father and most of your Wyltai clan. I have spies everywhere in the sea, and the savagery of that day was well known by all. We had not seen its like before. The Alyetans were looking for you, I suppose, but of course I had no idea at the time."

The Sea King moved away then, appearing to consider. Emydd felt long-ago cracks in his heart begin to bleed, remembering as he watched his people sail away, without him, on that beach so long ago.

"Yes, the Alyetans did me a great favour," said the Sea King. "Imagine! They killed their own king. After all this time and effort spent hunting down the royal family, their own people end up doing my work for me! Had I known they would respond that way, I'd have just left the royal family among their own people. I wonder what made them do it? Maybe there's something wrong with those born to wear the crown."

Emydd struggled violently against his bonds, furious. The Sea King looked at him closely.

"Your people have excelled at doing my work for me," he said. "The land fell and I had no idea why. It seems that your people eradicated themselves. You are the last of the Alyetans."

The Sea King smiled.

"Ah, the Connoisseur," he said, "who thinks her own world best. I can see why you wanted this one for your harem – excellent choice!"

As he approached her, Emydd thrashed in his bonds. Aiea looked up as the Sea King raised his spear and threw it at her, turning away before it reached its mark. He knew his aim had been true.

He turned to see Yondu, the same soldier who had brought Aiea down to the Sea King's palace, with the spear lodged within his stomach, Emydd's hand in his. Yondu's wide eyes spoke of disgust and hate.

"You were our protector," he said. "I no longer owe allegiance to you. What you did to Koyu…"

"Traitor," snarled the Sea King, "You are no better than she was."

The chains fell from Aiea and Yondu took her by the hand. The three of them were out of the palace and in the murky depths in an instant. Yondu heard the Sea King call for his guards, and wondered why the king hadn't moved to stop him from rescuing them.

"Land-dwellers!" he gasped, and saw Aiea and Emydd struggling to hold their breath as the Sea King's magic left them. He knew the humans would drown before he could ever reach the surface.

"Listen to me!" cried Yondu, "we cannot rise too quickly! You must breathe out slowly. We cannot travel any faster than your breath rises!"

The Sea King's voice spoke clearly in his head.

Once they die, you will be captured, Yondu, he said, *I will not suffer traitors.*

"*No!*" cried Yondu, wrenching his mind away. "I no longer belong to you!"

He cried out in pain as a spear from a pursuing merman buried itself in his side. He glanced behind them. The Sea King had been swift in retaliation.

185

Yondu looked desperately from Emydd to Aiea, who had come to the end of their breath. How could he save them? Several fathoms still remained, and he did not have the power of speech above the water.

Yondu decided it did not matter, and put on a burst of speed. Aiea and Emydd's heads broke the surface and they gasped for air. He must lead the Sea King's men away from them. Here, at least, they had a chance. He ducked underwater and swam off.

Aiea stared at Emydd in worry. They trod the water in still silence.

"Oi! Here!" they heard a shout across the water. They could see the flag of Shen's warship in the distance.

Shen helped the two of them aboard.

"Thank goodness you two are alive," Shen said. "We thought you might be dead—"

Emydd wrapped his arms around Aiea, and turned to look at Shen with an expression she had never seen on his face.

"The war will come to Ona," said Emydd, his voice flat and toneless, "We have to go back to the Citadel."

Aiea

Aiea was miserable living a soldier's life on Ona. She dreamed of Loka'i every night, the scented breeze and the ripe fruits ready for picking. She dreamed of swimming in the cerulean sea, and found herself near tears upon waking in the frost of dawn. As the weather began to change, moving from autumn to winter, her mood worsened, and when the first flecks of snow came spinning from the dull grey sky she fell into an agony of despair. She slept on a rough cot in her tent, which kept out the wind but not the cold. She could barely uncurl herself from the ball of heat her body produced underneath her light blanket when Shen woke her for morning patrol. Seeing the army commander leap lightly from her bed and walk around outdoors without winter wraps made Aiea feel soft and ashamed. If she ventured to comment on the cold, Shen would give her a puzzled look, or laugh uproariously and tell her it was nowhere near cold yet.

As the season progressed, Ona became monochrome, and the thin, silvery sunlight barely peeked through the clouds. Aiea missed the vivid colours of her homeland, its warmth and gentle sea, more than she could have imagined. She worried about the men of the harem as well, and felt foolish and irresponsible for leaving them behind. At this point in the year, however, sea travel was unspeakably dangerous. Besides, Aiea felt she could not leave Emydd. She was torn between her home and her lover, and knew Emydd would not be protected on Loka'i. Even though they were called Ulu'u, Joy in the Battle, it had been centuries since any of her people had lifted a weapon in anything other than sport. So Aiea stayed, for his sake, and because she feared that he might try to follow her and, in that way, doom them all.

After a night of strange dreams, Aiea woke with a start in Shen's tent. The military commander still slept, as did Emydd, Kane, and A'o. They had been assigned patrol duties in exchange for the food and bedding provided. Although Aiea had told Shen that Loka'i would pay for anything, including the most sumptuous accommodation that Ona had to offer, Shen had laughed and shaken her head. The commander told Aiea that she wanted them to be ready for war, and soft, regal surroundings would do nothing for this purpose. So Aiea and her retainers were miserable, experiencing want for the first time in their lives. On the other hand, Emydd looked no worse for wear. He was accustomed to hard living. Kane and A'o, however, missed the warmth of Loka'i just as Aiea did, and they looked wretched on their cots. They had taken to sharing a bed, A'o curled up against Kane's larger form, simply to share the warmth of each other. The two handsome men hid their faces beneath the blankets, shivering against the cold. The silver of Shen's earring shone against her stately neck, as she breathed easily in her sleep.

Aiea walked out into the first breath of dawn, desperately wishing for a cup of bloodflower tea. She longed for her pavilion and for the rich foods of Loka'i instead of the heavy bread and hard white cheese of Ona. Shen told her it was the food they ate when on campaign, and after three months of no change in her diet, Aiea was tired of it.

Movement down the hill caught her attention. Suddenly, Aiea realised what had woken her – the sound of splashing. She stared down at the sea in shock and fear. *Not on my patrol. Please.*

But her prayer was in vain.

The Sea King's army was marching.

Aiea ran to the tent and woke Shen. The commander rushed outside, rubbing her eyes, and saw the army approaching.

"I never knew they could walk on land," Shen breathed, then shouted, "To arms! To arms!"

The tropical evening air was still, lacking the breeze that traditionally wafted the scent of jasmine into open windows. Loka'i slept, save for the drunken revelry of the late-night parties where attendees had not yet decided to call it a night.

In the houses of the rich, the moonlight fell on the statues of mermen. In the deep silence, they began to move.

The celebration was going splendidly. Wai, a duke of Loka'i, had this party every year. The best of Loka'i were always invited to his mansion for the Joy in the Battle festival. Everyone wore their colours and danced the old dances, sang the old songs, and were proud of the warlike tribe they had once been. Tla, the Soan, played at a keyboard enclosed in a glass case, with a glass of *iwa* wine in front of him, smiling at the several handsome young ladies who had taken a liking to him.

Wai was very fat and proud of it. He smiled a great deal and his bald head turned a bright red when he laughed, infused as he was with wine. He was very popular in a way that only a rich man who delights in giving away money and throwing opulent parties can be. Each of his fat fingers wore a gold ring encrusted with jewels. Everyone was royalty tonight on Loka'i.

He dug into the meat dish, appreciating every succulent morsel and sucking the juices from his fingers, a true gourmand eating in warrior style.

"Splendid party!" cried Ensa, a man who did not speak to Wai except at this yearly celebration. The fat host waggled his fingers and grinned widely. Tonight, everyone was his kinsman. Tonight, there would be no petty jealousies or animosity. The candles burned brightly and everyone was dancing or eating, drinking bloodflower tea or *iwa* wine, shouting their ancient war cries and congratulating Wai on the festivities. The fat man, who was always happy, was never happier than on this night of the year.

A strange face appeared in the window behind him. Wai saw the frightened faces of his guests, and he thought there might be something wrong with the music or the sweetmeats. He was trying to remember if any of the food prepared had been less delicious than the rest when his throat was slit from behind by a merman's blade and his head fell forward into the meat dish.

In the harem, the Naiene stood ready.

"Ka has betrayed us," Olai reported to Yr, who turned around.

"I thought he might," said Yr, "but come, now is no time for regrets."

As Olai went out to rouse the men, Yr cursed and shook his head. He went to Ka's pavilion and saw that the statues were missing. He remembered the gift Ka had made to Aiea and blessed what Naiene gods there were that she was elsewhere. He hated to think of her asleep while her 'sculpture' awoke and took her life. It would put everyone in mind of how the former Connoisseur had been lost. He only hoped that the men would be able to stem the tide.

As Yr walked from his pavilion, he saw fires erupting from all parts of the great city. He realised then the extent of the betrayal. The merpeople had attacked from the inside, playing on the Ulu'u's desire to pretend they were stronger than the enemy. Now they were shown how weak they had truly become. The last stand would be there, in the harem. This Yr knew in his very bones. He had prepared the men as best he could.

He knew how it would end.

Yr pulled himself to the roof of the Connoisseur's pavilion and blew the herald trumpet, crying in one voice with Olai: *To arms! To arms!*

The fires that lit up Loka'i reminded Yr of the place it had been, centuries back, when the Ulu'u were terrifying warriors in the mud and the heat, their savage howling making the island as off-limits to visitors as Cloda.

This night, he had to work with the weak. Standing atop a pavilion, he screamed "*Now!*" and a new barrage of stones assaulted the merfolk. Yr's strange white face was lit by the fires, the orange reflecting in his ebony eyes as his hair whipped around his face in the wind. He knew they would not survive, but the men felt it was their responsibility to fight for their Connoisseur and their home.

The throne room of the pleasure palace was in chaos.

The retinue of guards had fallen swiftly. They had no training in combat and were more ornaments than warriors. Even so, they sacrificed their lives as the merpeople advanced to the throne itself. This last secret, that the merpeople were capable of walking on land if the Sea King's magic so decreed it, had been kept hidden. Even Koyu had not known; only an elite squad sworn to secrecy were given the skill of inanimate magic as well as the power to survive on land.

Irya crouched behind his throne as the battle raged around him. *And so it ends, in fire and death,* he thought, *and we believed that we could change the world. Just wait a little longer, Aiea; only wait until the older generation has passed away. Did I fear losing this life of idleness, despite my brave words all those years ago? She expected this violence, and I did not.*

I am sorry, my Connoisseur.

A spear came down, ready for his heart. He bowed his head, beautiful in his last moments, his hair falling in a shining silk curtain before his noble features. *I have failed you, my people,* he thought, and accepted death as a fitting punishment.

The blow never came.

Irya opened his eyes to see the black eyes of the Naiene he so hated, dark hair falling around a pale face. Yr put a cold hand in Irya's and smiled as colour flooded his skin, and he turned suddenly human in death. Irya was shocked to see a face like his own, warm autumn skin and eyes of a beautiful colour he had never seen. He realised that Yr was, like him, Ulu'u –but *real* Ulu'u, Joy in the Battle, the best of them.

The last of them.

Irya lay down beside Yr, keeping his hand clasped in his own, and whispered *forgive me* as he waited for the end.

Shen

The battle met in death and screaming. Shen's eyes were wild as she destroyed the merpeople in explosions of foam and blood. Her spear was thick with gore and water.

A reddish mist arose from the battlefield and the stench of death filled the air. The smell alone may have overcome them, when Angry saw the Sea King far back from the field. Emydd, her own king, stood in the thick of the fight.

The Sea King held back, disgusted.

"These humans are so messy," he said.

"Coward!" Angry shrieked. "You call yourself a king. You are not as brave as Emydd!"

The Sea King smiled.

A rogue wave towered behind where he stood on the land and surged toward Angry. She tried to dodge but the water engulfed her.

A'o plunged into the water after her and was caught in a terrible current. Kane sprinted for the Sea King, but the mermen who stood guard before their leader parried his attack.

Aiea glared at the Sea King. She could not let A'o drown or Kane perish. They were her responsibility.

"Aiea, no!" Shen shouted.

The Connoisseur ran forward and threw herself toward the water. She stopped short.

The blade of a grinning merman had run her through. She coughed, confused, and Emydd saw her, pinned.

Kalu's spear was swift and true as he destroyed the merman who had attacked Aiea, dispatching several others that came at him from all sides. Shen's mouth dropped open in surprise. Kalu looked proudly at her, declaring, "I am a fisherman!"

Suddenly, another young man emerged from the ranks and waded into the water, anchoring his feet on the ground by digging his toes underneath the rocks in order to brace himself against the tide. End wrapped Angry and A'o in his arms and hauled them out of the water. He knelt down to give breath to them once again as the water crashed to the ground and dissipated.

Shen stared at both End and Kalu, impressed despite herself.

"End, I should have listened to you," she murmured, and then whirled to block another blade.

Emydd stared at Aiea's prone form, and a strange vibrating noise issued from his throat. Anger and grief, hatred and sorrow. One by one, the merpeople fell.

The Sea King turned in his chariot, clutched at his heart and gasped, "So he has found love...and despair."

"No!" cried Shen, "Emydd, you can't kill him, he rules the sea! It will die—"

It was too late. Emydd's song echoed through the company, and he gathered Aiea, broken and bleeding, into his arms. He sobbed in the middle of the field of battle, the place of the Sea King's death, and the resting place of the brave Onai who had fought for Emydd's crown.

Loka'i was fire and devastation. The once-warrior tribe had known nothing of war, and perished easily. The men of the celebrated harem died well; they fought, for the Connoisseur that was absent, for the pleasure palace, and all that was now memory. The rich gardens, the beautiful feasts, the palatial homes had become the glorified tombs of the dead. As Emydd's song encircled the world, the merpeople vanished into foam.

Shen wandered among the fallen, looking for survivors. She muttered about traitors, as the Song killed those who were not on Emydd's side, but also those of their own who had a secret allegiance to the Sea King.

Gently, she touched Emydd's shoulder. He looked up at her, grief in his dark brown eyes.

"Emydd," she said softly, "if you could do this...if you could do this with the Song, why not tell us? Many lives would have been spared."

Emydd sniffled, choking back a sob.

"I didn't know I could, Shen," he said. "I wish I had. I'm sorry."

"I know you would have done anything to prevent Aiea from getting hurt," said Shen. "I believe you."

"Thank you," whispered Emydd.

"The Sea King is dead," breathed Shen, standing above the desiccated corpse, then she shouted. "The Sea King is dead! The war is over!"

A mighty shout went up from the exhausted Onai army. Emydd sat clutching Aiea. He no longer cared for war, or his promised crown.

Aiea blinked up at Emydd in confusion. His face was a mess and he seemed very upset about something. She struggled to put her arms around him and comfort him, but found herself unable to do so. She spoke instead.

"Emydd, don't cry," she said, and was surprised to hear that her voice was barely a whisper. "Let me comfort you."

Emydd wiped his face and stared down into Aiea's eyes, uncomprehending.

"Aiea?" he asked wretchedly, "you're not dead?"

Shen's brilliant grin interrupted the reunion. She slapped Emydd on the back.

"Congratulations," she said, "the Song can heal as well as kill. You saved her life."

Aiea felt her strength returning, the sickness draining from her, and she helped Emydd to his feet. She kissed him, the horror forgotten, and he smiled at her. As Aiea turned to Shen, his expression darkened as he realised he could never guarantee her safety, or his people's. The poison had already begun to seep into his mind, the memory of all that had happened eating away at his soul. As one grown wild and strange, with only a façade of civilisation, he knew only one response to his fear of being overthrown, of being unable to protect Aiea.

Revenge.

The sun set in brilliant tones behind the castle as the remainder of the Onai army raced through the fields. They were all shouting and laughing as one voice and they barrelled down the hill to find High Councilwoman standing at the gate in black mourning cloth, her mouth open in amazement.

"The Sea King has fallen!" Shen shouted above the tumult. "We are free!"

High Councilwoman smiled at Emydd, his hand clasped in Aiea's, the young king beaming, radiant as a star.

"The palace is yours now," she said, bowing. "You are the king, Emydd Wylt."

Emydd raised her from her subservient position.

"High Councilwoman," he said. "I once swore an oath that no Onai would bow to me when I was king. I will uphold that vow."

High Councilwoman grinned at the Wyltai man, and removed her headdress, long brown hair falling around her face. Everyone present gasped.

"My name is once again Liana," she announced. "I return the throne to its rightful owner. May you govern well all of your days."

Angry spoke then.

"I feel this is cause for celebration," she said gravely, and then smiled for the first time that anyone had ever seen. The effect, in the light of the setting sun, made her more beautiful than anyone could have imagined. She had a round, heart-shaped face and light brown eyes, and the sunlight illuminated the red in the brown curls that fell over her shoulders. She was lovely, and war seemed to have made no impression upon her beauty.

Shen saw her there, and swept Angry up in her arms, kissing her hard. She let the other woman––who looked fairly dizzy and pleased––go and gestured widely at the gathered company.

"A party!" Shen cried. "Roll out the casks of *iwa* wine and let us dance!"

The ballroom in the dome was filled with people, and food such as Aiea had not seen since she began her travels. The luxurious meat dishes, the piles of cheese, the dark and light sweetmeats and the endless supply of wine made her almost feel as though she were home again. As Emydd drew her around the dance floor to the jubilant music, her smile felt like her own and not the ghost of what it had once been. As the orange hue of the sunset was replaced by the glow of thousands of candles, Aiea knew perfect happiness, a happiness only found from going through great privation and pain and winning through to the other side.

The following day, Emydd sat on the throne.

Emydd

The Citadel stood at the edge of a very high cliff that jutted out into the sea on a small peninsula of land. From there, the geography of Ona changed, and the land sloped down to several beaches and Onai Harbour. The harbour was to the left of the castle and visible from many windows as well as the parapets.

The Citadel was an imposing and beautiful sight to behold. It was also the perfect place to hold off an attack. Scaling the cliff was too difficult and it was easy to bottleneck enemies via the bridge that ran over a ravine to the isolated promontory. The towers had spiral staircases so that a person coming down the stairs would have full range of motion, but the wall would be in the way of the soldier coming up.

It was a curious place with many moods. Light in colour save for the black dome atop it, by day the Citadel radiated a muted joy. At the end of the day, the sun set behind it on the water in a dazzling display of fire and colour. By night, each cornice was lit by candles and strange shadows played upon the walls and windows, giving it a look that was foreboding and ominous. As the night fell and the candles were lit, the funereal aspect of the palace entered the hearts of the people, and a sombre aspect fell upon the edifice, reminding them of the dungeons and torture chambers tunnelled throughout the entire cliff. The dungeon was a maze below the castle lost in darkness. It had been out of use for so long no one alive knew the way. The people of Ona believed that only ghosts travelled the deserted darkness, but the castle at dusk, lit with thousands of candles, stood as a reminder of the horrors once propagated beneath its silent walls.

"There are those who will not allow Emydd to keep his throne," said Liana, her face grave. The days of peace had brought them to the consideration of Emydd's ascension.

"Who?" asked Aiea. "He holds the Song of Life! He is the last of his people."

"So it is even more important that he produce heirs to continue his race," said Liana. "If he dies without children, everyone dies. The lands vanish beneath the water. The Sea King wins, even in death."

"Oh," said Aiea quietly, knowing that, with all the wealth in Amala at her fingertips, this was the one thing she could not offer him. Still, she did not regret the choice to become Connoisseur, and would not have reversed it, even now.

"A suitable mate must be found, then," said A'o, "but from where? Are we sure one of Alyetan blood can mate with any extant race?"

"A woman of the Wyltai may suffice," said Kane. "Legend has it they are descended from the Alyetans. Generally, as a scientist, I do not put much stock in legends, but as they seem to be coming true before our very eyes, I may have to change my opinion."

He smiled at Emydd, who blushed, uncomfortable being the centre of attention.

All this time, Aiea remained quiet, struggling with the emotions that fought within her. She knew the proper thing to do was to let Emydd marry and produce heirs. She had her duties, after all, and he had his. He was the rightful king over all people. So she kept silent, pretending she did not see Emydd looking at her with hope.

In the throne room, Emydd sat upon the seat that Liana had graciously vacated as beautiful women from every island presented themselves before him. He saw the hunger in their faces, lusting for the power that would be conferred upon them by such a union. He smiled in relief when Aiea entered. He was exhausted from his expected evaluation of the women brought before him.

"I am leaving," she said. Emydd started.

"Why?" he asked.

"There are men I need to evaluate on other islands," she said. "My ship waits in the harbour."

Emydd held out his hand.

"Why not you, Aiea?" he asked.

Aiea bowed her head.

"You are our king," she said softly. "I am not worthy."

"Since I am king, I will decide who is worthy," he said. "These other women..."

He shook his head.

"I cannot provide you an heir, Emydd," said Aiea. "I am barren."

Emydd looked down at the floor.

"Connoisseurs do not have children," she continued. "It is my duty to provide for the harem."

"No," whispered Emydd. "I don't care, Aiea. If I must be with a woman, I want it to be you."

"You knew I was leaving," said Aiea, her voice faltering. "You knew I had my responsibilities—

"I love you, Aiea," he said. "I don't want you to go. I couldn't bear it."

"You must, Emydd," she smiled.

"Aiea—" he began.

"My ship awaits," Aiea said, backing out of the throne room. "Goodbye, Your Majesty. I am glad you are restored to your throne. May you live a long life and find happiness."

Emydd stared at her, his eyes filled with tears. She could no longer bear to look at him, his features more lovely in sorrow. She also thought she saw anger? Or some other, darker thought flicker across his countenance, before it vanished and only that gorgeous sadness remained, almost holy in its ethereal beauty.

"I love you," she whispered, and ran swiftly down the stairs of the castle.

Aiea stood before Kane and A'o.

"Today I release you from my service," she said, smiling.

The men looked at her, and at each other, dismayed.

"Have we displeased you, Aiea?" asked A'o.

"No," she said, "you fought admirably, and have served me well. I feel you deserve your freedom – from the tyranny of beauty, and from the Connoisseur. That is, if you wish it."

A'o was hesitant.

"I know no other life, Aiea," he said, frightened. "Please do not send me away."

"If that is your wish, you are welcome to stay by my side," she told him. "What say you, Kane?"

Kane looked at his Connoisseur with tears in his eyes.

"I have enjoyed serving you," he said, "but I would like to return to the life I had before, on Tika. I had no desire to join the harem, but it was decreed, and I had no choice."

He took Aiea's hands in his own.

"I am glad you found me, Aiea," he said.

The Connoisseur embraced him.

"Go then, Kane," she said.

Kane looked at A'o, his friend, and drew him into a strong embrace.

"A'o," he said, "you are beautiful and brave, please take care of Aiea. I will miss you, and you will always have a home wherever I am."

A'o smiled shyly.

"Thank you, Kane," he said. "It has been an honour to serve with you."

"You are welcome on Loka'i at any time, Kane," said Aiea. "However, it may do you some good to experience life without expectations."

"Consider yourself served by me to the end of my days, my Connoisseur," he replied, bowed and kissed her cheek. Then he hugged her.

"Thank you," he whispered into her ear, "for I never thought I would get the chance to make a choice."

Aiea

Aiea boarded a vessel along with A'o, who took their belongings down into the hold. She silently bid Emydd farewell. She could see him standing atop the palace, and her heart cried out for him.

I have a responsibility to the harem, Aiea thought.

You love him, replied her heart.

I am too busy to throw my life away on this kind of foolishness, Aiea thought.

You love him, insisted her heart.

Aiea bade Shen farewell as she left the ship. The Connoisseur's soul felt torn from her body as the sails of the vessel filled with wind.

The ship set sail from Ona six months after its arrival. Having seen blood and war, Aiea was much changed. Accustomed as she was to the simple cots on Shen's battlefield, she no longer found joy or comfort in her sumptuous quarters on the ship. Her body was aching, as was her heart. What children they had been! What children she must return to now! Aiea knew her days as a Connoisseur were numbered. She wondered if any before her had left the service. The only example she could think of was that of her predecessor, and she had taken the permanent way out.

Shouts broke out on deck. Aiea hurried up the stairs.

Chords of lament hung in the air, and the seas were becalmed under a dark grey sky. The world stood still.

"All hands on deck!" shouted the captain. "That crazy bastard! Not now! Not like this!"

He caught Aiea staring at him.

"Begging your pardon, miss, but he's about to bring the whole world crashing down on us," said the captain, and rushed off.

Aiea was shocked to see huge waves rolling towards them, something large and dark looming behind them.

"He's calling up the land!" gasped a sailor.

"Not this way, you fool!" the captain screamed into the heavens. "You'll be the death of us, and her too!"

The sailors cast murderous glances at Aiea, tears streaming down their cheeks from the effects of the Song. The waves were upon them, *one, two,* and *three,* before the gunwales had a chance to clear the water, and they had already consigned themselves to the fate of those sailors unfortunate enough to encounter one of the most violent phemonena at sea. They gripped the ropes to keep from pitching over the side, waiting for the inevitable *crack* that would herald the sinking of the vessel. The winds fell in the grey light, and died as quickly as they had come.

Aiea climbed to her feet and looked around.

The land had returned.

Emydd had kept them safe somehow, but from the Far Lands to Nona, a continent was born again. He had called forth the old lands in his sadness. The sailors whipped off their caps and knelt in prayer, for the ship was cradled on a calm sea, and surrounding them were the Wide Lands of legend.

Elka

The sun was low in the desert, and the wind blew sand in swirls from the dunes. A tall woman stood watching the sand, her cherrywood skin gone dark in the evening. Her name was Elka, and her business of running spices was failing. She looked now to the west and to the sea.

A man of her tribe came to her with a gourd. His skin was pearlescent white and he shimmered. His delicate wings were veined like a dragonfly's, and he was unclothed after the manner of his people. He was very small, as all the men were, and about a quarter of Elka's size. He and Elka lived together in the dunes, against custom. Until recently, they had run a stall in the famed Barrens Market, but since the end of the war, business had dried up and the Market was just a colourful memory.

The man's name was Kyia, and he loved Elka as he was able. They had been together many years, as their decision to live together had banished them from any other society forever. With the death of the Sea King, their money had run out, and life in the dunes was difficult.

"The evening light colours you well," murmured Kyia, grazing his lips on her skin. Elka sighed and put her hand on the small of his back, below his wings, as she sat down beside him.

"Kyia, we will not have gold enough to survive the Dead Season," said Elka. "We will perish in the dunes, and not be mourned, or remembered."

Kyia straightened his back.

"Let us not speak of endings," he said. "The night is beautiful, and we have food enough."

"A trader brought news today," said Elka. "The Lost One has returned. He fought for his throne and for the land."

Kyia looked at his wife.

"Then we are not lost!" she said. "We may join with him, and find our fortunes."

"How can we?" asked Kyia. "We, who have no friends, no ship, and no money? What have we to offer him?"

Elka stared out again in the deepening gloom. She shielded her eyes and stared hard.

"Do you see the ghost?" she cried to Kyia. He squinted into the purple darkness as the stars were coming out. A flutter of white could barely be discerned. As they watched, the spectre drew closer and materialised into the shape of a man, swathed entirely in white. As he neared their small campfire, they saw that every part of him save his eyes was covered in purest white cloth, which was folded, bunched, and arrayed in the most splendid fashion. What little they could see of his skin was bronzed, and his eyes blacked around. He bowed elaborately. Elka was put in mind of ancient legends best left undisturbed, and she trembled.

"Spirit of the dunes," ventured Elka, "what have we done to disturb your peace?"

The blacked eyes smiled.

"I am no spirit," said the phantom, "but an outcast like yourselves."

Elka nodded.

"It is to you I must appeal now," said Emydd. "I have a proposition for you."

Irya

The rest of the voyage to Loka'i was both strange and familiar. There were so many new vistas to behold, and the civilisations that once were islands were now the cultural links holding the new lands together. There were mountains, drying in the warmth of the day, standing between Soka and Loka'i; vast green fields separating Ona and Thla, but the land was one again. The sea still crashed against certain parts of the islands; Lokai's harbour and the harem beach remained intact. Aiea recognised the towering grandeur of her island from afar, and caught the scent of flowers on the breeze.

As the ship drew closer, she went to the side and stared. All was not well. There was a strange silence in Battle Harbour. Her heart beat in fear of what she might find. No one waited to greet them on the docks. The palm trees swayed in the wind.

A'o came on deck to stand beside her. The expression on his face, too, was easy to read. Loka'i had never been silent.

"Will you go to the outer villages?" she asked.

He nodded and swallowed.

"I will do as you ask, Connoisseur," he said, and lightly jumped from the plank to the dock, his bare feet making little noise as he ran and vanished into the forest, taking the pathway that led to the roads for the outer villages.

Aiea's first responsibility was to the harem.

The ship left Aiea on the dock, the crew thankful to be on their way once again. She walked alone on the planks of wood, her footsteps echoing against the silence, broken only by the hiss of waves on the white sands of the beach. Aiea continued onward with deep foreboding. This was the first time no one had come to greet the Connoisseur upon her return to the island.

The streets were empty. The once-bustling capital was silent. She looked up at the empty windows of the primary brothel on the main thoroughfare, and at the mansions on the hill that were dark. She found no bodies, no blood, just emptiness. She walked the gravel path through the jungle, and recoiled in horror as the path gave way to the great lawns of the harem.

The pavilions had all been destroyed. Not even a pillar remained standing and rubble was spread across the entire lawn.

One pavilion remained standing: her own. The floor was almost destroyed, and there were cracks in the pillars, but it still stood. She saw, in her mind's eye, her men dying to protect her pavilion and her memory.

Unable to breathe, she stepped onto the cool red tiles, and went to her knees. Among the ash and rubble, she laid her cheek against the cool stone floor.

The day was sunny and beautiful, with a soft breeze off the sea.

She lay in the fragments of the place where she had once slept, watching the petals of the skyflowers dance by on the wind and listening to the silence. Everything had changed, and she saw Emydd's dark eyes in her mind, filled with love.

Loka'i and its beauty, its earthly pleasures, would be consigned to the realm of the dreams of the past. She had become a relic, a memory, and she watched the skyflower petals float one by one along the ruin of the once-beautiful stone floor and down to the sea.

The pleasure palace. It was her responsibility now. She thought of Irya; he would have died defending his home, the last stand would have happened there. She willed herself to her feet.

She climbed the familiar path, thinking of times when she had walked this way for grand parties, or at Irya's request. She remembered the leaves filled with lights, leading her to some evening festivity at the palace. The wind rustled the leaves now, dark in the silence.

The palace was nearly in ruins, but somehow the elegant throne room had remained intact. The floor was covered with dust and rubble.

There was a sudden sound in the quiet. She glanced sharply at the shadows behind the throne, and saw dark haunted eyes.

Irya.

She went to him in the silence. He put his arms around her and cried like a child, no longer the imposing king of the cultural capital of the world.

As his tears subsided, he looked at her.

"Will you have me now?" he whispered, and the desperation in his voice broke Aiea's heart. She should have been there.

"Yes," she murmured, and Irya sank into her arms.

After encouraging Irya to eat a little, she took him outside into the sun.

He walked with her in the sacred groves, his mind only there in the present, only wanting to be near her.

"Irya," she said in the stillness, "what happened to the men?"

He looked at her. She reached out and took his hand, smiling softly, encouraging him.

"They fought well," he said quietly, "they fought with a noble mind. Yr died protecting me. You were right about him."

"I am sorry, Irya," she told him. "I should have been here."

"Don't say that, Aiea," he said, "for I would have lost you too. After everything...I can't bear to imagine it."

Aiea was silent for a while, just being with him, being there for him. Still, she would know.

"Where are they?" she asked.

"They?" he replied.

"Everyone," she said.

He paused, staring out to sea.

"They were lost," he said. "They died to protect this land...to protect me."

He was silent for a long time. Aiea waited patiently.

"You were gone so long," he said, "and they suddenly vanished, the merpeople, I mean. I have become a king without a country."

He put his hand to a white skyflower and looked into its blossom. The blue sky covered the two of them, the clouds matching the petals, the forest quiet in its brilliant green.

"I could think of nothing to honour them," he said, "and I had none to rule. And so I did what I had always washed my hands of."

Aiea looked at him, a question in her eyes.

"I buried them."

She stared at him, uncomprehending.

"Everyone?" she whispered.

"Every one."

They stood together in silence.

"It took a very long time," he said. "Houses I burned to the ground, buildings too. I cleaned what I could, and…"

His head fell to his chest.

"Oh, my arrogance!" he cried, his voice breaking. "My people were so loyal, and to an unworthy king! My father would be horrified. I asked the dead for forgiveness. I keep asking, but no ghost has come to pardon me."

He turned to her.

"One night, long ago, we made a promise," he said, "and I was so earnest, my heart full of plans for change. After all these years of acting the part, I had started to become it; in waiting for the elders to die out, I grew accustomed to the luxury. And they died for me, thinking I was only this, never knowing their king, the man he was…the man he had intended to be. It has cost me much, and no one, apart from you, has ever known the heart and soul of me."

He bowed his head, and Aiea put a hand on his shoulder. He looked up at her, his eyes filled with tears, and she was surprised to see humility and supplication there.

"Can you forgive me, Aiea?" he asked, tears streaking his handsome face. "Can you ever forgive me?"

Aiea stood aghast at the young king, cut down by a horror they never could have foreseen.

"Irya, you have always been a good man," she said. "Of course I forgive you."

She leaned in and touched her lips to his, a gesture of comfort. He looked at her, a mix of confusion and light in his eyes. He collapsed in her arms, exhausted, and was silent.

Aiea gently took Irya's hand, and started to lead him from the throne room until she realised that she had no idea where his chambers were. She turned to him, asking with her eyes. He must have understood, because he wordlessly led her down a hallway and turned a door's ornate handle.

Aiea was stunned. There was nothing in the room save a small bed, and a side table upon which was a cup and a small miniature of herself, the type sold in the tackier tourist stalls on the main thoroughfare of the city. The austerity of his chamber, echoing in its emptiness, told her that Irya had tried, at least, to live as one of his own subjects would, and the opulence of the pleasure palace ended at the doorway.

"I often slept in one of the larger guestrooms," he murmured, "but this is my home, where the servants never ventured. I made certain of that."

Aiea walked with him to the bed, and sat down. They looked at each other, both survivors, with no experience to compare with this kind of loss and devastation. Aiea kissed Irya again, in her own mind providing the comfort that was expected of the Connoisseur; in reality, they found solace in each other. A lifelong wish of Irya's, finally granted in that small bed, he surrendered himself completely. In every touch they drowned out the grief and sorrow, the loss of everything they had ever known, and the knowledge that Loka'i, as they had always known it, had come to an end during their lifetime. There was no lust, only comfort, and the certainty that they were the last of their kind, watching an era fade from the world, and desperately saying *I was here, I knew the passing of an age.*

Afterwards, they lay together, staring at the ceiling, hands entwined, saying nothing.

And so, we changed the world, they both thought, but neither said.

Shen

When the first Hoisdean were marched up the hill towards the castle, Shen stormed into the throne room.

"What is the meaning of this, Emydd?" Shen demanded. "The war is over. Why are you taking prisoners?"

Emydd stared at her, impassive.

"They are half-merpeople, Shen," he said. "My family perished from inaction. I have learned from their mistakes."

"Your fear will be the death of you," Shen said. "All you do is sit here with your memories, skulking in the shadows. And you deliberately defied me and sent my women to capture innocent people!"

"Shen," he said quietly, "they wish to make war upon us."

Shen stared at him.

"What do you mean?" she demanded. He indicated a parchment lying on a table near the throne.

Shen lifted it and read, her mouth dropping open in shock.

"What is this?" cried Shen, staring at the words on the parchment in disbelief.

"Apparently the Hoisdean want war," he said. "You yourself said there were those who would not want me to regain the throne."

"Then…" Shen said, disbelief in her eyes, "…all the races of the sea are suspect. The Wyltai – your own people! The port island of Thla—"

"I am Alyetan, not Wyltai," said Emydd sadly. "The Wyltai are not my people. Neither the Wyltai, the Hoisdean, or the Thlai are universally loved – it makes sense that they would war against me, as they all probably had dealings with the merfolk."

"Then Ona itself is suspect," said Shen.

Emydd nodded.

"Yes," said Shen, "though the Song will protect you, Emydd, you cannot have eyes all over the world. We have always been your family's protectors and now we cannot fail at any cost. We will have Onai warriors stationed in every port from here to the Barrens!"

The military commander clicked her heels together and saluted her king. Emydd put his head in his hand as she marched through the Great Hall and down the stairs.

Shen was horrified that the war continued. If Emydd fell now, how much worse would it be than if he had fallen to the Sea King? The poor thing, she thought, shaking her head; beset on all sides. The Hoisdean, of course! They had far more reason to have sided with the Sea King, it made perfect sense that they would hate Emydd and want to see him dead. When would he know peace?

She knew that Aiea's leaving had broken his heart, and he had not been able to understand her dedication to a harem of men she owned rather than loved. He had read her heart and he knew she loved him, and he could not understand her choice.

Shen stared grimly across the water. The prisoners they had taken told her only of a man who had paid them fascinating amounts of gold and promised them great wealth if the war began again. The world's economy no longer worked for many islands; the fish had returned, so the talents of Soka had become a mere tourist curiosity. There was no longer a call for *kact*, because although it was without a doubt the best tasting fish on earth, people were tired of it. When the ocean-fish returned and people could do their own fishing, no one wished to pay the high price the Soans were accustomed to receiving. Deathspice and other high sellers in war were also no longer necessary. Amala was in the twilight between war and peace that would forge a new economy. Therefore many people, accustomed to things as they were and unwilling to change, would have preferred the war to continue so they could gain wealth from the bloodshed.

Ryg

The waves washed the shores of Thla, green and cold. A few of the shacks along the shoreline had already begun to light the fat in shallow bowls. It was a tradition for those out at sea, so they knew they had returned home – a welcome sight.

Ryg sat in the chill night, cracking the knuckles of his big hands as he sat down with a mug of mulled *iwa* wine. He stared wearily at the lamp, the creases of age and weather visible above his thick brown beard. He wore a knobbly cream-coloured sweater over his corded muscles.

This part of Thla was always silent – a respectable silence, a cold seaside austerity. For wild carousing, Ryg could always go to the capital, but he had never wanted to live there. So many of his fellow sailors lived there for the conveniences and the women. Ryg had to admit that they were probably right, but he preferred peace and quiet. He could put up with the difficulties inherent in living so far away from the docks.

The door burst open and Ryg leaped to his feet.

"What is the meaning of this?" the old sailor demanded, before he recognised the man in the doorway. "Lyonid? What are you doing here?"

"Ona has declared war," Lyonid responded.

Ryg looked puzzled.

"Against the Sea King?" asked Ryg. "I thought the young king destroyed him."

"Not against the sea-people," Lyonid replied, "they are gone. They have declared war against us."

"Us?" Ryg was confused. "Why?"

"Ona claims that we have been openly aggressive towards the new kingship. No one seems to know why."

"But that's absurd!" shouted Ryg, "the Thlai could not care less."

"It matters not," he sighed. "Nevertheless…Ona is marching. They are here, Ryg. A favour returned for a meal you once bought me – information gleaned from my travels. And now that you know…run, while you still can."

Shen

Shen had no pity for those she tortured, she loved Emydd so much. She could not understand their cries of protest that they were innocent, that they were willing to serve Emydd and always had been (though of course now, they were not so certain). Shen would have none of it; she must know who was behind this plot against the king. She was infuriated. Her life had been one great battle, glory and blood, and she had no idea how to protect Emydd against a new and ephemeral evil.

Liana had reacted strangely to the news and become withdrawn, pacing along the dark floor beneath an enormous palace window, moving in and out of the square of light like a metronome. When Shen had questioned her, she was surprised to see tears in the former High Councilwoman's eyes. Liana bit her lips and shook her head, and would say nothing no matter how often Shen questioned her.

Emydd took to haunting the dungeons, presiding over the torture and sometimes taking part himself. He also stood in the tiny widow's walk atop the castle, staring at the sea for many hours. He demanded that women, food, wine, anything his heart desired be purchased and brought to him under threat of death, but it seemed his heart was not in any of it. He grew listless and extremely withdrawn, and wandered the palace like a ghost while the girls he bought lolled about, bored.

Soon, the snow began to fall again, and piles of untouched, expensive fruits and cheeses froze in little mountains behind the castle.

Shen took hold of the old man as he was hauled into the dungeon. He lifted his head.

"You? You, Daughter-Son-of-Laughter? I knew ye great in battle, but never did I see cowardice in ye."

Shen stared at him in horror and shame.

"Fidelity keeps my hand from you for that insolence," Shen said.

"Ha!" said Ryg, "and it should be honour. Ye never had to leave us, Shen-au-schan. We loved ye well, and many a strapping girl grows up on Thla."

"These are my people now," said Shen.

"Aye, and they were warriors once, instead of fools!" cried the old sailor.

"What did you say, old man?" Angry put in. Shen pushed her back.

"Our soldiers are good women," said Shen.

"Aye, they were once," said the Thlai captain. "*Ye were* once. I remember many a riotous night with the women of Ona, battle and joy, drunk on *iwa* wine and dreams. Now ye disgrace yerselves."

Shen stared at the ground furiously.

"What! Ye'd put me to the torture too!" cried Ryg. "C'mere, wretch! I've got somethin' to say to ye."

The women began to roughly drag him down the corridor.

"Stop," she said, something giving her pause.

She approached the old Thlai captain, whose mouth was bleeding from where he had been struck.

"I see you still wear the earring of rank from the days you lived by honour," said Ryg.

Shen touched the cascade of diamonds at her ear, doubt creeping in.

"Tell me, brother," she asked, "who is behind this war?"

The captain laughed; his eyes glittered, and his teeth shone white through the red blood, making him look like an ancient, mad pirate.

"There is no war," he said, "except that which you have made with your own hands."

Shen stared at him.

"Do you know who's behind it?" she asked.

"How can you not, Shen-au-schan?" Ryg asked. "The man you seek through torture will not be named from rack or wheel, because those you torture do not know – because this war was invented, and those who are considered the cause were merely convenient scapegoats."

"And you, who travel? Who know and see all?" Shen inquired. "Do you know?"

"I am surprised you need to ask," he said, "for all this time he has been beside you, and you are blind."

"Who is it?!" cried Shen.

"Do you not yet know, Shen-au-schan?" Ryg asked.

Shen thought of the change in Emydd, of the young king haunting the castle, of his strange behaviour, and could not believe it.

"You lie," she said.

"So you have guessed. Think of all the years that have passed, my sister, and tell me how often I have lied to you," said Ryg.

Shen's mouth dropped open, confusion infused slowly into her eyes.

"Emydd. But...why?" she asked. "Why would he do such a thing?"

The old man shook his head.

"That I do not know, Shen-au-schan," he said sadly. "You must ask him."

"Believe me, I will!" she said, and made to run off when a hand like iron closed around her arm.

"Shen," said Ryg, "it must end here, now. You know the truth. Swear to me you will never raise your hand to torture or kill for this false war again."

Shen held his gaze, and her silver earring winked in the light.

She did not reply, and vanished then, leaving Angry and the rest of the guard, still holding onto the old Thlai captain but with less interest than before.

"Come here, Emydd, and answer me!" screamed Shen, pursuing him in the dungeon darkness. He came to a halt in the yellow light of a torch, his head hung low, panting.

"I will have an answer from you if I have to torture it out of you myself!" Shen shouted. "Did you do this?"

Emydd was silent for a moment, his round, dark eyes staring at the army commander. Shen was surprised to see tears begin to track down his cheeks.

"*Iwa* wine was made from the magic of the merfolk; their pheromones are powerful," she said. He stared at her, puzzled.

"The stories of mermaids enchanting sailors to their doom...it was because of that, not their beauty but their power, which was distilled and used in the production of *iwa*."

Shen sighed, and rubbed her face.

"I only wanted to protect our kind," she said, "but so many had forgotten about the war. We were living on the bread and cheese you saw during our patrols, so little money did we have. So…I began to trade with the Hoisdean, to produce the *iwa* wine, and support the military."

She gave him a meaningful look.

"So I understand secrets," she said, "Do you feel like sharing yours?"

Emydd stared at Shen for a long while, speechless.

"It matters not!" he cried. "If this is true the merpeople have been a menace for centuries, and not only to my family!"

"The merpeople are gone, Emydd," Shen said gently, "you destroyed them on the field of battle. There will be no more *iwa* wine."

"Their kind lives on in the Hoisdean," said Emydd, "they must be eradicated."

Shen took a moment to absorb this.

"So it is true," she said, "*You* started the war again. The Hoisdean were on your side! And the Thlai? I am one of them! The Wyltai? The tribe that took you in as a child?"

"All people of the sea were a part of this!" Emydd shouted. "The sea, and all that is in it!"

Shen stared down the madness in Emydd's eyes, to the pain that had caused it and his inability to heal the rift made there. It was strange he was still beautiful; for some reason she had expected to see ugliness there. She knew then what a treacherous thing beauty was. She realised she could not convince him of anything, and he would not stop until he had destroyed everything he feared.

"I refuse to be a part of this any longer, Emydd," she said. "The army will no longer serve you. They will not obey you in order to make war upon a lie of your own devising."

She turned smartly and began to walk away down the dark hall.

"Go then!" he roared. "You have all betrayed me! I will find a new commander, build a new army!"

Shen smiled grimly. She looked over her shoulder.

"Be my guest," she said, "if you can find anyone willing. From this moment all of Ona stands against you. For as the front line in this war, we are also people of the sea."

"I could destroy you with a word!" Emydd hissed.

"You could," said Shen, "but who would serve you then?"

She walked away, down the hallway, and as she turned up the corridor she saw Emydd silhouetted in the dim, flickering light. She sighed and walked up the staircase, only then realising that she could hear her own heartbeat pounding in her ears. When she walked out of the palace, she broke into a run. It mattered little; if he wished, he could kill her in an instant, no matter where she was hiding. The Song would find her and that would be the end.

The darkness lay thick about them. There was silence around the crackling fire. Shen hung her head in shame.

"Propaganda! I should have known," she lamented. "I believed, because it was written! All those people dead…tortured…ugh!"

Tears lit in her eyes as Liana and Angry tried to comfort her.

"None of us knew, Shen," said Liana, "although I suspected. We all acted on good faith, not realising Emydd was far past that point. We can only pick up the pieces now."

With a sudden shout, Shen hurled her dagger. It stuck in the trunk of a tree.

"I am the army commander!" she cried. "Twenty years of service! I should have known, should have behaved with honour! I *know* better."

She sighed and threw herself into her chair.

"But I was afraid. Afraid! And blind. I cannot believe it."

They were silent for a while, then Angry approached. She stood behind Shen and placed her hands on her commander's shoulders.

"We were all afraid," Angry whispered. "All of us."

"That's no excuse," said Shen miserably. "A true warrior does not respond to fear."

"Warriors are also human," said Angry gently. "You are human, too."

"The real problem is, we cannot apologise for this," said Shen. "In our usual warfare, forgiveness may have been possible. Emydd will go on torturing and killing, and no one alive can stop him. It is as you've said, Liana."

Liana's eyes came to life, as a sudden fire was kindled there.

"And I was right," she said, "but someone who is dead could stop him."

"What use is that?" Shen said. "They're dead, all of Alyeta, and we cannot resurrect them or duplicate the power of the Song of Life."

"I don't mean the Alyetans," said Liana. "The Sea King, Shen. The Sea King! He killed them all."

Shen's eyes blazed with realisation. She stood in one fluid motion.

"How?" Shen asked. "How did he do it?"

"I don't know," Liana replied, "but I know how we might find out."

"The Hoisdean prisoners," said Angry, and nodded.

They looked at each other in silent agreement, and started on the journey back to the castle.

Shen was engulfed in darkness as she entered the dungeon, Angry by her side. She approached the first cell containing a Hoisdean maid.

Her face was froglike but somehow beautiful. The ceiling dripped cold water and the hollow silence was cruel. She had been tortured almost beyond recognition, and at the sight of Shen, her head lolled and she moaned.

"Please, no more," she rasped, her gill slits flexing. "I know nothing."

Tears fell from Shen's eyes as she looked upon a ruin that she had caused.

"I know," Shen whispered, "I believe you."

The Hoisdean maid smiled.

"Too late," she said. "I've only a few hours left, by my reckoning."

"No," said Shen, encouraging her, "you will have the finest doctors, the best of Snt will be sent for…"

"Is this what you've come for," asked the Hoisdean maid, "to minister to my wounds?"

Shen smiled, a sickly smile.

"No," Shen said, then lowered her voice to a whisper. "We need to know how the Sea King did it."

"Did what?" the maid coughed, her water-blood bubbling at her lips.

"How did he destroy the Alyetans?" asked Shen.

"Ah," said the maid. "So the torturer turns traitor. Those of Hois never wished Emydd's death."

"I know that now," said Shen, "He has confessed everything. Please. He

220

must be stopped."

The maid nodded slowly, looking at Shen through slitted, bleary eyes.

"I know of your trade with my people, Shen-au-Schan," she said, "the guilt lays upon you as well. Your contact was a man named Wold, my lover for one night – I saw what they traded at the pub that evening, though they endeavoured to hide it. I am surprised Emydd did not put you to the torture as well – but perhaps he did not know."

Shen hung her head.

"But you did right to purchase it," said the maid. "*Iwa*. It was *iwa*, the pheromone of the merpeople. The Alyetans can only be killed by one they love under its influence. There is enough, in the wine, for the task. It was…our greatest secret."

She coughed again, violently. Shen held her cold, wet body until the fit passed.

"Thank you," Shen said. "I appreciate it. And you, and your people, will be released with the best of medical care."

"Do not bother yourself with me," said the maid, "this will be my last day. Even so…if you succeed, it will be the end of us all. All is forgiven, at least by me. I'm only glad I lived long enough to know the end of the suffering."

Shen turned to go, thought better of it, and said, under her breath, "I'm sorry."

The maid smiled and nodded.

"I know," she said.

Shen's heart was heavy, the weight of all she had done upon her. She stood in silence over the body of the Hoisdean maid, and silently mourned her and the state of the world, in the depths of the Onai dungeon.

Aiea

The air was warm and the sky overcast with clouds on the island of Loka'i. Aiea stepped onto the dock as the captain disembarked from the ship.

"I saw your approach," she explained. "I am sorry to say that Loka'i has been lost; you will find no pleasure here, sailor."

The captain offered her his hand, which she shook.

"I know," he said, "leastways, I assumed. I'm here to bring you a message from Shen. I'm her brother, Ryg."

"Shen's brother?" asked Aiea. "Is she all right?"

"Been better," he said, "but she's not why I'm here. It's about the young king. I was told to fetch the Connoisseur. You are needed on Ona."

"Emydd?" Aiea said, her heart aching at the word. "What has happened?"

The captain scratched at his beard.

"Is there somewhere we can talk?" he asked.

In the bright throne room, Aiea stood from her seat, trembling. Irya put his hand in hers.

"There is something I must do first," she told Ryg. The old man nodded, and she motioned to Irya to accompany her outside.

The two of them walked down the path together. Aiea turned to Irya after a while.

"You know what will happen," she said.

Irya looked at the ground.

"Yes," he said, miserable. "You will have to be with him again."

She kissed him gently.

"Only for a short time," she said.

"And you will come back?" he asked. She smiled.

"Yes, I will," she replied. "Will you help me?"

He nodded. She produced a basket, and pulled a white skyflower from a tree. He stood beside her, and they filled the basket with white blossoms, occasionally touching the other's hand for reassurance. They worked together in shared silence and camaraderie, occasionally smiling at each other and finding solace in the other's company.

Aiea knelt in the powder sand, and Irya placed the basket dutifully beside her. She dipped her fingertips in the salt sea, and concentrated on the love once shared between her and Emydd. She sprinkled the water over the flowers, careful to keep love alone in her mind, and cupped the first white flower in her hand. She placed it gently into the water, and they watched as the first white flame spun away across the waves.

Aiea turned to Irya then, and touched his cheek.

"I will return," she said, "that I promise."

"When you do," he said, "can we leave this place? I fear its ghosts, and the pain of its memories."

"Anything you want, Irya," she said. "We will settle in a place far from here."

"And you will be with me?" he asked.

"I will be with you," she said, returning his smile.

"You won't leave again?" he asked, his voice tinged with fear.

She put her hand to his cheek.

"I promise," she said, "but you must let me go for a little while."

Irya looked into her eyes and touched her dark hair.

"Then go," he said, "and remember me."

The perplexity and commotion when the first skyflowers floated into Onai Harbour was bordering on chaos; a few blossoms at first, sparkling with seawater like dew, spinning and dancing. The king sat in his tower window, watching as the harbour filled entirely with flowers, one touching the other, until no vessel could leave port.

In Loka'i, Aiea lifted her hand from the last flower, brilliant droplets falling from her fingertips as the sun illuminated the seawater.

Emydd

The Citadel was fringed with a lacework of snow as Aiea's ship plunged through the green waves. She thought she could see the silhouette of a figure atop the highest dome, and was alarmed to see the palace, once a place alive with a myriad of emotions, appear as dead and silent as the cliffs. Aiea gripped the neck of the bottle of *iwa* wine and prayed that she would make Emydd comfortable enough that he wouldn't use the Song to read her heart. There were things in it she did not want him to know.

She was no longer innocent. She had seen war, and grief, and cold…so that her island home was hollow to her. She wondered briefly if she would ever find herself in a place where she would be happy again. She pushed the thought from her mind. Such loss was the price of knowledge.

The harbour was still filled with skyflowers, some of which had wilted. The blossoms parted before her ship. They would crumple, wither, and sink if she were to fail in her mission. No ships had been able to leave Ona for the last month. The entire island was surrounded by spinning skyflowers for a mile out to sea in all directions. Emydd had been told that her message was one of love and that Aiea wanted to return to him. No one informed him why the ships were unable to leave the harbour. He wanted desperately to believe it was love that brought her back. He still believed himself to be in the right, but love, once pure, had begun to rot in his soul. It had driven him mad and made him careless. He had stood in the observatory day and night for the last month, watching the changing seas, impervious to the elements.

He went down to the palace doors to greet Aiea. It was all he could do to hold back from throwing himself down the snowy hill and into her arms. As he watched her approach, more majestic than a queen, he knew nothing more than her beauty. He was senseless before her, and all his efforts to keep the intense emotion from his expression failed.

Aiea looked upon the beloved face of Emydd with regret. In that moment she couldn't believe the stories she had been told, of the horrors he had propagated across the world. She saw his face, his eager brown eyes, and the charming naiveté glowing in them. With sharp surprise she realised it was this naiveté that made him a tyrant. He did not comprehend what he had done. This made him more dangerous than any knowing man who had ever held the sceptre of a king.

She forced herself to smile. A tumult of emotions assaulted her. She had to stay calm.

"Hello, Emydd," she said. "I've missed you."

Emydd only stuttered, staring at her. He could not find the words. He suddenly swept her up and kissed her, tears streaming down his cheeks. He could think of nothing but the woman in his arms. All his previous horror and paranoia was forgotten. The attendants he had been using as sexual companions glared at Aiea with jealousy, but said nothing. Now, they drew near him with territorial menace as he released Aiea from the kiss. Her heart was beating rapidly and she again had to force herself to remember why she had come. She realised as she stared at him that he was only a very spoiled child with the body of a man, but none of the spirit. She resolved to be on her guard and not become distracted by outside appearances. This was merely a badly behaved child before her and regardless of how she felt about him, he had to be destroyed.

"I have prepared dinner for us," Emydd said, "the most succulent food that Ona can provide. My attendants prepared it."

Aiea looked at the attendants and their sharp, glittering eyes.

Don't eat the food, she thought to herself.

"Aiea?" Emydd asked anxiously, "Is something wrong?"

More than you will ever know, Aiea thought.

She tore herself from this idea with effort. She looked at him with a lopsided smile, and lifted the bottle in her hand.

"I brought wine," she said, and felt as though she might never breathe again.

She followed Emydd up the grand winding stone staircase as he talked. The attendants followed, silent and terrifying. Aiea tried to focus on what Emydd was saying.

"I am relieved to have you back," he said. "Thank goodness you have arrived safely, what with the war and all…"

Aiea thought, *What war, Emydd? The Sea King died by your hand. Shen was right. You are fighting ghosts and using living things as cannon fodder. You jump at your own shadow…and you don't believe you're doing anything wrong!*

"We dine here tonight," Emydd said, throwing open the doors to the ball-room.

This room, where they once danced in the blaze of the sunset, the joyous and innocent fools that they were! The wine that flowed like rivers, the delicious food; A'o, Kane and Emydd standing out like exotic treasures as the only men in the room...and Shen in her finest military uniform, appraising the other women in their beautiful raiment, grinning mad with pride!

The room was unlit now save for the radiance of the moon and stars, filling the room with silver light.

"You will not be needed," Emydd snapped at his attendants.

"But sire—" one of them began, staring at Aiea with unmasked hatred.

"Silence!" Emydd shouted. "We are to dine alone!"

He slammed the door in the faces of the women and turned to Aiea with a smile.

"They are good girls, but sometimes overprotective of their master," Emydd said.

Aiea stared at him. She thought, *It doesn't even matter to you that you have been with those girls? You think I'll just come running back into your arms at your say-so? Your infidelities matter nothing to you, and yet, if you even thought for a moment that I had enjoyed any of my harem you would have flown into a jealous rage and destroyed me!*

She thought of the men she had lost, the men who had fought and died for the harem, and that Emydd had not even asked after them, or about Loka'i.

She felt her jaw tighten. She wanted to punch him in the mouth.

"Aiea?" Emydd said. "You look angry. Is something wrong?"

She immediately realised that she was treading on dangerous ground. He spoke lightly, but she could see the madness in his eyes.

She smiled again. Each time it was getting harder. *You must get through this*, she told herself, *you are the only way!*

"I am sorry, Emydd," she said softly. "I was thinking of how long it has been since we saw each other. How terrible for you to have to wait for me!"

"Yes, I did wait a long time to see you again," he agreed, "no matter. I blame the seas, and the incompetence of the sailors. You are here now. I hope you will be happy as one of my attendants."

Anger boiled in her, threatened to consume her. *He wants me to join those women! No better than a consort! He would not ask me to be his queen for fear of his authority being undermined! And the Connoisseur! How dare he?*

Really, Aiea? And what, exactly, were the men of the harem to you?

And with that revelation, she was no longer the Connoisseur.

Emydd smiled affectionately at Aiea. She grinned back across the enormous table at him. In her mind, her thoughts were a tumult of confusion.

"I've missed you, Aiea," he said. "I'm glad you've come back."

She still loved him. Her mind examined every feature of his beautiful, exotic face. She thought of that gorgeous night in the palm gardens of Chaak. She thought of his innocence, his complete gift of himself to her, as they made chaos in a land of perfect order.

She reached out and uncorked the bottle of black *iwa* wine.

Emydd grinned.

"Particular plans for the evening?" he asked. Aiea smiled back, but her hands shook as she poured the wine into the pewter goblets.

Shen said this was the only way, Aiea assured herself. *He may be the man you love, but remember he is also dangerous…more dangerous than any human that has ever lived.* Would the loss of the land and all the life on it be a fair trade to stop Emydd? The Sea King had won after all.

Emydd raised his glass to Aiea and drank deeply. Aiea did not touch her wine.

"You aren't drinking," he pointed out, his charcoal-tinted skin flushing with the wine, "don't you like the wine?"

The blade was in her hand, she struck before he was aware of what was happening.

The blade turned away from his skin, clattering to the floor.

They stared at each other in horror.

"Aiea – you…?" he stuttered. "You wish me dead?"

"You never loved me," she said flatly.

"Of course I love you," he said, "but – you would do this? Why?"

"You did not love me, Emydd," said Aiea. "Whatever it was, it was not love."

"I am sorry, Aiea," he said, "but I cannot bear traitors."

He opened his mouth and took a breath. Aiea waited for the Song that would end her life, as she sent a silent apology to Irya for not being able to keep her promise.

A strange whistle parted the air, and a spear hovered before Emydd's heart. He looked up.

A wildman stood before him, tears streaming down his face. Recognition dawned in Emydd's eyes, and the spear continued its journey, finding its mark.

"I—" began the young king, then fell to the floor in a crumpled heap.

"*Iao,*" whispered Aiea, just as Emydd breathed his last.

She stared in confusion as the stranger staggered forward and fell to his knees, gathering Emydd's lifeless body in his arms.

"*Wyltai,*" she breathed.

"He was my son," said the Wyltai chieftain, as his huge chest shuddered with a sob, "or as like as makes no difference. *Ach, Emydd chykkik...tka ch'en kolo sing...*"

Aiea stared at his broad back, and the beads and feathers in his hair, and thought of the day she first saw a young man with the same decorations, his eyes reflected in the light of a blade. She knew the wildness and beauty of the wind, close upon the man's skin. She had never seen a Wyltai in the flesh; they scorned Loka'i.

Aiea heard a noise near the window, and she looked up.

"With the Sea King's death, the spell was broken," said a voice from behind a column.

Aiea turned, her face wet with tears, and stood from Emydd's body. She stared at the jet-skinned young man standing before her.

"Science and magic," he said, by way of explanation. "The world will be different now."

"Are you Sntai?" she asked.

"Yes," he said, "but Chieftain Eld is, likewise, almost my father. I am called Po. I was told the secret of the *iwa* wine, knowledge I paid dearly for. The land remains after the Sea King's death, and likewise the death of our king is the end of land dwelling magic. The trees will whisper together no longer."

He looked at Eld, holding Emydd's body. He smiled ruefully, and without humour.

"Science wins the day," Po murmured, almost to himself, "My father would be proud."

She looked at Emydd's lifeless form. So the Song of Life was no more, and along with it, magic. There had been precious little magic left by her time as it was, but the idea of the world without it was incomprehensible. She looked out through one of the wide windows to see the last of her skyflowers sinking beneath the surface of the sea.

The door opened, and Emydd's attendants burst in. Upon seeing him there on the floor, they bowed as one.

"Thank you, kind sir," they said to the Wyltai chieftain, who did not hear them. Aiea looked at them in surprise.

"You are thanking him? He just killed the king!" she said.

One of the women nodded.

"Yes," she said, "he has released us from our bondage. We are free now."

"You certainly didn't behave as though you wished to be free," said Aiea, as they turned to leave. One of them looked back.

"Of course not," she said, "with a man like that – who would dare to show displeasure?"

The women left the ballroom, wrapped in each other.

Eld

The big man held Emydd's still body, tears tracking down his face. He took a deep breath, sitting back. Presently, he looked up at the Connoisseur.

"And who be you?" the Wyltai chief demanded, "Who else in Amala would have dared cut my boy down?"

"I was once the Connoisseur of Loka'i," whispered Aiea. "No more. I am sorry. It had to be done. There was no choice....I loved him, too."

"Aye, you must have," said the Wyltai chief, "for no one could cut down the king if the bond of love were not strong between them."

"It was not," she said weakly. "He did not love me."

"Let us bury him," said the Wyltai chief.

"But Emydd..." she said, torn once again.

"We will give him a proper burial," said Po. Aiea looked hard at him, and the Wyltai chieftain, but their faces were honest and she could see only empathy in Po's eyes.

"Thank you, Po...and...Chieftain Eld," she murmured, "Make sure someone sings, and well, at the interment."

Po nodded. The Wyltai chief bowed his head over Emydd's corpse, oblivious to them once more. Aiea paused.

"It will break you," Po said, as though he could hear her thoughts, "you must not linger here."

Aiea nodded, blinking back tears, and went outside to where Shen and Liana were waiting. She explained what had happened, and Shen agreed to help Po and the Wyltai chief with Emydd's burial.

It was time for Aiea to go home.

Many Years Later

The wind was cold, the world a monochrome of brown and white. The old woman sighed smoke and pulled her red cloak tightly around her. She shook her head, trembling, and hid her gnarled hands from the air that had already cracked her skin red.

The old woman lived mainly in dreams of the past now. She thought of the days when she had always been barefoot, laden with flowers in her hair and around her neck; how she had laughed with innocent joy as she had run down the palace stairs to the gravel path through the rainforest, every part of her warm, alive, and lovely.

Her beautiful eyes looked skyward to the ceiling of steel grey. She could never seem to get warm enough, these days. This place was so strange; how could being outside feel cloying and claustrophobic, as if she had not gone out at all? Imagine…a world that was inside forever, and nothing was open, not the sea or the sky.

The old woman thought of things that were gone: bloodflower tea and *iwa* wine. She had heard there might be a few bottles stored in deep cellars by the rich of Loka'i, but she did not know for certain. Since the demise of the mer-people, there was no more *iwa* to be had. The Hoisdean had tried, but their product was weak and watery. The next generation of Hoisdean had been born without gills and only vestigial fins. Po was right; magic and science would go forward together, but since science explained magic and made it non-magical, many races were dying out, or changing. The people of Cloda were able to mingle with the others then; so much had been destroyed, but so much also achieved. The men of the harem gone, their sacrifice remembered by few still living. Beauty was no longer the way of things. Loka'i had fallen; Irya was just a man, no longer a king. They could not bear the island in ruins, or its memories, and so had abandoned it. Loka'i became a haunted and desolate place. Aiea thought about it often, saw it in her dreams, the island's beauty and wealth, and her own; the sparkling garments and dazzling feasts, the coronations…and the men, the jewels of Loka'i.

Someday, when she felt only a handful of days were left to her, she might go back. She would walk the empty pathways in silence, listen to the wind, remember.

The children already doubted there had ever been merpeople, though there were occasionally strange reports from the Thlai of sightings, which Aiea could not understand. None of the children had ever heard of the Connoisseur, the harem, or Loka'i. *Strange life*, she thought, *how quickly we are forgotten*. She also remembered a time when she thought the Wide Lands and Alyeta were merely a fairytale, and smiled at the memory.

She rubbed her hands together and sighed again. They were old hands, now.

She stared up at the edifice before her.

Onai Citadel was deserted now, and crumbling. Vines had embraced it. None went near the place; it was considered haunted. The story of a mad king, his victims, and the woman who betrayed him echoed through the lands, and though most thought it was just a story, no one would approach the place anymore.

Aiea beheld the structure one last time, remembering the joy in the battle. Now, she thought she understood what that phrase meant. It was not joy in the fighting, but the moments of joy when the fighting stopped for a time. So perhaps the Ulu'u had, in fact, been living the goal of their warrior tribe all along: to extend the moments of joy between the times of war. The Ulu'u had reached their own ultimate goal, but in the end, the joy had merely been an extended respite between battles, the last of which destroyed their tribe forever. Aiea smiled. The Ulu'u had accomplished everything they had set out to do: a beautiful respite of wealth, food, wine, and a noble death in battle. So perhaps it had not all been a waste. Not every tribe could say they had succeeded in their purpose so well.

Aiea's eyes were still a lovely jade green, and as she stared up at the empty battlements of the palace, snowflakes began to fall. She said a few words of love to Emydd's spirit, and of prayer to those who had passed away.

Then she turned her back on the Citadel for the last time in her long life, and began to walk away, toward Irya and home, where a fire was waiting, to look forward to the coming days and the new world that was forming.

What did I do then, Little Ones? I suppose I could have given up, and I thought about it. In the end, however, one must go on…continue as I ever had, in the new world that was as much the creation of my love and Emydd's as a child would have been. The world has changed, but sometimes I can smell the skyflowers on the breeze, and think of a time when my skin was smooth, my hand was taken by one of a dozen handsome young men, and I walked in perfumed forests in an innocent land...or I think of caravans, dusky secrets, and incense, and Emydd's beautiful face looks out on me from the years, and his eyes still ask me Why? For I loved you.

The children left Old Grandmother nodding in the corner as they crept away to play their own furtive, secret games. Today the play was half-hearted, as they saw themselves valiantly battling mermen, tasting *iwa* wine, catching *kact*, or caressing the soft fur of the Soans. Eventually all play stopped, as they dreamed of a perfect paradise, and a woman wrapped in light white garments, white pavilions dressed in crimson curtains that made pennants in the breeze...a man more beautiful than imagination, smiling and taking her hand.

Of such dreams, religions are made, and new heavens.

List of Characters

Loka'i Harem

Aiea – the new Connoisseur.

A'o – one of Aiea's retainers.

Kane – one of Aiea's retainers.

Aio – one of the retainers of the former Connoisseur.

Ilo – one of the retainers of the former Connoisseur.

Tla – a Soan member of the harem, specialising in music.

O'ala – a Loka'i harem candidate.

Loka'i

King Saya – the king of Loka'i, and the official head of the harem.

Prince Irya – King Saya's only son, and prince of Loka'i.

Jokjo – a Loka'i merchant.

Siro – a tourist.

Jin – a prostitute.

Olai – A boy in Aiea's village.

Wai – Duke of Loka'i.

Ensa – a wealthy man of Loka'i's capital city.

Chaak

Iana – a student at the Academy.

Minai – a love interest for Iana and A'o.

Aya – The headmistress of the Academy.

Thla

Ryg – A captain.

Lyonid – A young sailor.

Lona – a waitress.

Wylt

Eld – A Wyltai captain.

Essa – one of Eld's wives.

Emydd of the Wylt – A harem candidate.

Ona

Shen-au-Schan (Shen) – The commander of the army.

Angry – Shen's lieutenant.

High Councilwoman – Steward for the Aleytan royal family.

Tika (the Summerlands)

End – An inhabitant of the Summerlands.

Tendanya – a slave.

Myrk – a village leader in the outlands of Tika.

Ka – A sculptor from the outlands of Tika.

Snt

Po – A young boy.

Ld – Po's father.

Naia

Dr. Eloyian – a Lightsider.

Yr – An inhabitant of Naia Nightside.

Myta – a female Nightside Naiene.

List of Characters

Soa

Hush – a famous sailor.

Allian – a harem candidate.

Soka

Kalu – A young fisherman.

Hois

Wold – A Hoisdean smuggler.

Ive – A Hoisdean trader.

Lami (the Barrens)

Elka – A trader from the Barrens.

Kyia – Elka's husband.

Alyeta (the Far Lands/Lost Lands)

Kholi – A young librarian priest of Alyeta.

Sea Kingdom

The Sea King – Leader of the merpeople.

Koyu – A mermaid.

Yondu – a merman.

Cloda (Island of Ghosts)

Olo – King of Cloda

List of Places

Amala – The entire kingdom of islands.

Loka'i – A tropical, mountainous island, the cultural capital of Amala. The Ulu'u, the people of Lokai, have brown skin and light eyes.

Snt – A tropical island lacking vegetation, Snt is the scientific capital of Amala.

Those native to Sntai are black, but others with a scientific mind also move to the island, so it is open to immigration and therefore multicultural.

Soka – Soka is a tropical, 'lost world' island, in that it is kept in a pristine state as though time has not marched on. It is also called the *Forgotten Lands*.

The Sokai people are white, wear very little clothing, and have bleached out brown or blond hair with naturally tanned skin. They tend towards the slender, muscular build, as people who spend most of their day fishing and doing manual labour.

Soa – A northern island of eternal winter.

The people of Soa are white-skinned, blue-eyed, with long, straight white hair and their bodies are covered in a fine layer of white fur.

Thla – A chill island of mist-covered moors in the north.

The Thlai are a large, strong, sturdy people. They are white and generally haggard-looking.

Ona – A cold northern island, primarily rocky outcrop and scrub brush.

Ona is called 'the island of women' and the inhabitants are of all races. Many of the women in Ona are gay but not all of them, and there are a few male inhabitants, though those are few and far between.

Chaak – An island with four mild seasons, Chaak is the location of the famous Academy, where harem hopefuls receive their training. It is also called the *Island of Lanterns* due to the millions of tiny lights lit each evening to illuminate homes, pathways, and gathering places.

The Chaakai people have copper skin, with long black hair and black eyes.

Tika – Also known as the *Summerlands,* Tika is an island of endless summer.

Tika is home to poets, artists, and singers; people of many different backgrounds make their home there, so there is no particular look associated with the people of the island.

Lami – Known also as the *Barrens,* Lami is a desert island, where nothing much grows. The markets are famous throughout Amala.

The women of the Barrens are large and muscular with dark cherrywood skin, and the men are small and fairylike with wings, pale skin and white hair.

Alyeta – A fragrant isle, called the *Far Lands* or *Lost Lands* by the rest of Amala, has a temperate climate. Most of Amala thinks that Alyeta is a myth.

The Alyetans are bronze-skinned, are considered the most physically beautiful of all the races, and they wear kohl around their eyes, particularly the men.

Nona – The southernmost island, a land of snow and ice, almost barren of life.

The Nonai live in caves beneath the snow, and all are covered in fur of different colours. They can roll into balls and use this for speed along the surface of the snow, but when standing are human-shaped aside from the fur. They can be any colour that animal fur would be, including calico.

Cloda – A midway point island between the north and south, it is also called the *Island of Ghosts*. Since the entire island is covered in a permanent fog, it is difficult to tell what it looks like. The forests are thick and the weather is mild year-round.

A variety of different types of people live in exile on Cloda.

The Sea Kingdom – An underwater metropolis is the central point of government, but the Sea King rules the entirety of the ocean.

All types of merpeople live in the city of the sea. The merpeople can be any colour, many of which do not occur naturally in humans, skin and tail both, and they have needle teeth, wide eyes, and sharp cheekbones. They are surprisingly both lovely and frightening to look upon.

Naia – An island with one half in permanent daylight and the other in permanent night.

The inhabitants are the undead, on one side, and winged feral men on the other.

Hois – A subtropical island of beach bars and hedonism.

The Hoisdean are the result of unions between humans and merpeople – human shaped, but with colours seen in tropical fish. They have the same high, protruding cheekbones, needle teeth, and wide eyes of the merpeople, but are human in all other respects.

Wylt – An uninhabited beach island, primarily sand and pine trees. The Wyltai call it their home and anchor their ships in the region.

The Wylt resemble Alyetans in appearance, but are stronger and more weathered due to their lives spent at sea.

O'a – The name of Aiea's childhood village.

Wide Lands – The legend that Amala was once a continent rather than an island archipelago is referred to as the *Wide Lands* in legends and folklore.

The Connoisseur
Reading Group Discussion Questions

1. Aiea has to say goodbye to her mother, her village, and her ability to have children in order to become the Connoisseur. What do you think the book is saying about sacrifice and the idea of identity?

2. Aiea stands out at a young age because of her love for Olai. How does the act and feeling of love function in the story?

3. From the ornate palaces to the gorgeous men in the harem, beauty seems to be closely linked to ideas of ownership and power. Who has more power? Those who are beautiful or those who collect beauty?

4. Does having the focus on male beauty change how women act or are perceived in the story?

5. There are several different examples of kings and of leadership in the story. Who is most in tune with the needs of their people? Why is that the case?

6. Heritage and culture are used to demarcate the different ways of life in Amala. Which island's way of life do you like the best? Did any cultures scare you?

7. The people on Naia are beautiful but no Connoisseur has ever brought one back to the harem before Aiea. What is the correlation between beauty, life, and mortality? Does the knowledge that beauty can fade change how people encounter it? What does Aiea's changing of this position communicate?

8. Who is your favorite character and why? What character undergoes the most hardship?

9. Po is conflicted with his interest in magic and his father and community's worship of science. Both are powerful, but which prevails in the story?

10. At different moments in the book, knowledge comes at a very high price. Po loses his father and Aiea loses a naiveté and innocence about the world. She reflects towards the end of the book that "such loss is the price of knowledge." Do you think that is true? How does such staggering loss affect how you view knowledge?

11. There are several moments of recognition in the story where one character recognizes a similarity between themselves and a character they have disliked or fought against, such as during the fight between Kholi and Eld.

Do these moments bring understanding or empathy, or do they estrange the characters further?

12. The story echoes more traditional stories such as *The Odyssey* and *Gulliver's Travels*. How does having a female main character influence what you noticed about each island and culture? Did Aiea have to make more sacrifices as a woman than the more classical male adventurers? Were there any benefits to being such a woman in the story?

www.ingramcontent.com/pod-product-compliance
Lightning Source LLC
Chambersburg PA
CBHW030126180626
46812CB00002B/575